SEDUCING CAT

ISBN: 9781094685182

Manufactured in the United States of America

SEDUCING CAT

a novel by

Korinthia A. Klein

DEDICATION

This book is dedicated to my husband, who understands what the word "fiction" means, and knows he has nothing to worry about.

CHAPTER ONE

The naked people were a surprise. As the young couple ran across the stage, Cat noted that a woman's naked body tended to elicit scrutiny but a man's, laughter; even if the man's body in question was gorgeous, and this one was. Had there been a notice about nudity in the handbill for this production at the Avenue Repertory Theater? She didn't remember one, but it had been fun to be startled. It was her first time seeing *The Play About the Baby* by Edward Albee and it was strange. Cat was fascinated, but after the young actors were done chasing each other giddily in the altogether and had donned some basic pajamas, she wondered if her husband Nick was uncomfortable, or even following any of it very well. She was glad they'd left their 14-year-old daughter at home.

As the actors took their final bows Cat got to her feet. Nick did too, but to begin putting on his coat, not as part of an ovation. Cat had a million thoughts circling around in her head, and to work through them she needed to put them into words. She started talking in Nick's general direction afterward about the subtle use of the lighting and how clever some of the blocking had been considering the shape of the stage. About halfway on the long walk to their car she realized Nick hadn't said a word.

"So, I've just been babbling on and on since the theater! What did you think?" she asked with interest.

"It was good," Nick said.

"Just good?"

"Well, it was nice to go out. Going out with you is always fun."

"We could have walked around the block and accomplished that!" Cat laughed. "I want to know, I mean, didn't you like it?"

Nick managed to frown and smile at the same time. "There were a lot of funny parts, especially in the first act. I wasn't expecting that, so that was good."

"Sure it was funny, but it was way more than that, even in the first act." She stopped walking and looked at her husband. "You didn't like it, did you?"

Nick shook his head a little. "I wouldn't go that far. I did like it, but....It...Cat, it was *weird*."

"Of course it was weird! Weird is challenging."

"I suppose. Give me a chance to think about it for a while, all right?"

Cat had been disappointed but not surprised. Asking Nick to the play with her was a bit like his asking Cat to watch NASCAR with him. She seldom got out to events like plays but this one had sounded too interesting in the reviews to pass up. Cat didn't know who else to go with, so Nick had obligingly accompanied her.

"What didn't you get?" she wanted to know.

"I don't know. Any of it, really. Was there a baby or wasn't there? How can anyone not know they had a baby?"

"That's not the point, Nick. Look, the baby represents the idea of innocence. The Man and the Woman represent time and experience. When they come to take the baby away from the Boy and the Girl, it's simply a way of illustrating that time and experience rob us of our innocence."

"But what was all that with the guy's arm and the weird stuff the Woman kept carrying on about? And that whole thing with the Man holding down the Boy? What did any of that have to do with the story?"

"I'm pretty sure that was ho—" but as she looked at Nick's face she decided against finishing the word homoeroticism. "Just...never mind. Next time we'll go to a movie and you can pick it out, okay? I'll even see some shoot 'em up thing where everything explodes and people die two days before retirement and we'll call it even."

3

"Hey, Cat, I'm trying, here! I'm sorry I don't pick up on the same things you do, but don't I get a little credit for making the effort?" He took her hand and gave her a small smile. "Can we at least agree dinner was nice?"

She smiled back. "I guess," she said rolling her eyes in a perfect imitation of their daughter.

Nick laughed and swung her arm gently in the cold February air as they walked the last few steps toward the car. They didn't discuss the play again, but Cat was obsessed.

Cat was 39 and not looking forward to turning 40 in the fall. She found herself reevaluating nearly everything about her life, and the play seemed to touch on all of her hot button issues at once. Some of them she didn't even know if the play was intended to address, but they spoke to her. She wanted to discuss it with someone to work out her thoughts, but that wasn't going to happen. She'd have to work out those ideas in her novels instead.

The first thing she wanted to sort through was the shifting connection between sex and age that the play exploited. That was something she hadn't considered too deeply, but as they walked toward their house in silence except for the crunching of old snow beneath their feet, she began to.

She didn't think of herself as being that different from who she was in college even though those days were long behind her. She'd been cautious then, and had thought she was putting off sex for all the best reasons. There was the risk of pregnancy and disease to start with, and lots of emotional complications to worry about. Cat didn't necessarily believe in the idea of no sex until after marriage, but the idea of sex without love seemed empty and pointless. If someone were going to be so close to her as to actually be inside her body, it should be someone she wanted to feel that intimate with on every level. That sounded right to her, and special and sane. She wanted her parents to be proud of her and all of her right decisions, even the ones they wouldn't know about.

Now when Cat thought about it, her choices about sex (or lack thereof) reeked of fear. Why couldn't she have had sex simply for the pure physical experience of having sex? It didn't seem that big a deal to her now. Maybe it was unrealistic for her to think she ever could have had the temperament to do that, but now it only looked like lots of lost opportunity to her. Nick was gentle and nice and she liked sleeping with him, but he was Nick every time. She knew Nick. She was curious about men who were simply not Nick. If she'd experimented, she would have something to compare the experience to. Surely other bodies felt good in other ways, and she would never know that and it bugged her.

Watching Girl on the stage made Cat reassess the power she herself must have possessed at that age and never fully appreciated. She had known she was acceptable in appearance when she was young. She didn't have any hideous scars or a hump, so that was a plus. But she seldom felt pretty. There were rare, perfect occasions where she would be in the right outfit and her hair did what she wanted for a change, and she would feel radiant for minutes at a time. However, most of her life was spent spotting flaws when she looked in the mirror and wishing she were bigger in one place and smaller in another. Or just better, so she was always looking for a different eyeliner or fussing with hair removal or hoping this new fill-in-the-blank product would be the answer. Now she saw how alluring youth was with no help at all. At one time that had been her and she hadn't noticed. She had possessed great power and had never wielded it.

But was it really power? That was the part that confused her now, because at the time she knew as she walked on campus in a tank top and shorts in the hot spring weather, that she felt more like a target than anything else. Men looked at her and she seldom felt flattered, and when she did feel flattered that became muddled with self-esteem issues. She was insulted by the idea of guys who would sleep with her and care nothing about her. Her mind mattered, and who she was mattered, and the package shouldn't since it was not much in her control.

But the package did matter. She saw Boy on the stage and it physically hurt to know he was out of reach, but how shallow was that? She didn't know him, she simply liked his body. And now she wished someone like him would look at her body the same way. Was she crazy? She'd spent her whole life championing the idea that inner beauty was what counted, and that age was irrelevant since it was your mind and your heart that others should see. If her grandmother were still alive, Cat would call her and apologize for ever spouting such rubbish in front of her. It was easy to be idealistic and generous from a youthful, beautiful podium. Not so easy to hear when the concept of your having sex could be a joke to the rest of the world.

Cat saw *The Play About the Baby* a total of five times, which was nearly half its run. She felt like some kind of addict, and she had the thing almost completely memorized at that point. The absurdist world being portrayed became less bizarre with repetition. When she no longer had to adapt to the odd premise she was free to enjoy the small details, and every time she saw it she discovered something new.

On closing night Cat was reluctant to let the experience go, and decided to congratulate the director. She thought he might appreciate the compliments she had to offer, but mostly she wasn't ready to walk out of the space that had struck such a chord with her.

Cat was not naturally extroverted, but she could fake it if she knew being shy might prevent her from an experience that interested her. She made her way to the space near the area backstage, but didn't want to intrude. The four actors were still milling about, the two women still holding bouquets of flowers they'd been handed at the last curtain call, and there were friends and family excitedly lavishing them with praise and smiles.

"Excuse me," said a stagehand. Cat realized she was blocking access to a nest of cords nearby that apparently needed to be addressed.

"Sorry!" she said as she stepped aside, first the wrong way, then the direction he preferred her to go. "Is the director around?" He pointed her toward an older man with a neatly trimmed beard wearing khakis and a black shirt. He was thanking two older women in expensive jewelry, and Cat decided to hover nearby until he was available.

The more formidable looking of the two women was talking to the director as he nodded repeatedly. "It was so interesting," she said, "in the later scenes how dreadfully unkind the Man and Woman were. Envious I think. It's as if they could barely tolerate that anyone else still got to be young and beautiful. Since they couldn't go back they practically hazed others into their fraternity of pain and despair! Don't you think, Nannette?"

The director turned his patient smile toward the other woman who, when she realized she was expected to speak asked, "So did those two people have to rehearse naked, too? Does that get cold?"

Cat stifled a laugh which caused the director to glance briefly her way before he turned his attention back to the first woman who continued on, markedly ignoring Nannette.

Cat turned in the direction of the actors as she

waited. They looked different off duty, no longer wearing their bodies as other people but as themselves. Although they were finally done and could relax, the various technical people in black were still scurrying around, dealing with the nest of cords and checking switches.

"Brian?" she heard the actress who had played Girl call out. She had changed into a pair of jeans and a tight pink shirt that strangely seemed more revealing than her nudity on stage had been. Cat had read the biographies of the actors what seemed like hundreds of times, and knew Miss Stephanie Banks who had played Girl so well was only 19. This had been her first professional acting job.

"Brian!" Miss Banks said again, this time with the mild triumph of having spotted her quarry. She slipped her arms around the waist of the actor who had played Boy as easily as she had in the play. He was talking to someone and smiling and he absently held up a finger to Girl as a signal to wait. She seemed impatient and gave him a look that was somewhere between adoring and exasperated which he didn't see.

At one point Boy glanced up and caught Cat looking at him. He was extremely good-looking and she'd liked having the opportunity to simply admire his body on stage, but something about his being a real person again—albeit, one wearing nothing but pajama bottoms—made her realize staring at him was now inappropriate. She genuinely appreciated the acting job he had done, but the degree to which

9

he aroused her she found embarrassing, so she gave him a shy smile and glanced quickly away.

According to her memorized program, Cat knew his name was Brian Smith. She wondered if it was a stage name or if anyone could have been given a name that bland. She wondered if Smith replaced something unpronounceable and made life in the public eye easier. Or maybe there really were people named Smith in the world.

The director finally wrapped up his goodbyes to the two ladies and turned his attention toward Cat. She smiled and extended a hand.

"It was wonderful!" she said.

He shook her hand happily. "Thank you so much! I'm glad you enjoyed it."

She continued, "I'm so sorry to see it end. I saw it a few times and each time I came away with something new. There were so many different themes to consider. I must have ideas for at least the next three novels based on this play."

"You're a writer?" he asked with interest.

"Yes, my name is Catherine Devin, I—"

"Catherine Devin! Well my goodness, I had no idea we had a celebrity in our midst! I knew you lived in town and I've always hoped I'd get introduced at a party at some point. I very much enjoyed your last radio interview a few months ago."

Cat was self-conscious but pleased. "Well, thank you. I don't know how many people actually listen to that show, but it's nice to meet someone who does."

"Oh my. Catherine Devin. I'm Tom Olsen, and I'm always looking for ways to use local talent. Your short stories in particular have such marvelous dialogue, and I wonder if you've ever considered adapting any of them into a play?"

"Well, no I don't have any experience at that. I—"

Tom Olsen gave her a sly look and smiled as he said, "But life is all about new experience! How do you know if you don't try?"

Cat laughed. It was an interesting thought, actually. What would that be like? "Really, I don't know that—"

Tom glanced behind her at someone and seemed as if he needed to go, but he dug around in his pocket and found his wallet and fished out a card. "I wish I could talk to you longer right now, but I have to get moving. Take my card, and *please* give me a call when you have time, and give it some thought. I think you'd be an excellent playwright, and it's something we should explore." He pressed the card into her hand, looked her straight in the eye with a smile and said, "I really am glad you enjoyed the show."

Cat studied the card a moment, and then stood there in thought. She liked new projects and new challenges, and this was one that hadn't occurred to her before. It could be interesting. Eventually she realized she was standing in people's way backstage for no reason at all and decided to head for an exit and go back home. By the time she got there Nick was in bed. Liz was still up, but paying attention to texts on her phone.

Cat was in an odd mood. Her night out had made her happy because she loved to think and stretch her mind, and the idea of working on a play in some capacity was intriguing and new. She liked things that were new. But she also felt a strange yearning and an absence. She decided it was a kind of withdrawal. The play was over and those people would never be assembled in that way again, and the experience lived only in her memory and that depressed her. She wanted ice cream.

That was highly unusual for Cat, but it was an unusual night so she chose to indulge herself a little. She went into her spacious kitchen that she'd had remodeled two years before, and got out a bowl and a spoon. She loved the way the kitchen had come out, with an island in the middle where they all liked to eat together while standing around. It made for a good compromise because Cat was a believer in family dinners every night and her daughter resisted it, so something about eating at a counter while standing or using a stool made it seem less strict. It accomplished the same thing for Cat so she didn't care much. She still got decent food into her family and they were all in one place at one time to touch base with, and that was the real point, even if she never got to use her nice place settings or the expensive dining room table.

The kitchen had been the last big project on the

house. They'd moved into it when Liz was five and their first house seemed too small to hold all of that pre-school level energy. Another reason they finally moved when they did was that the original place was too small for a child and a dog, and Nick was not good at living without a dog. The new house was large enough for a kennel if they wanted it. It had undergone a tragic history of remodeling mistakes, most of which involved bad carpet from the 70s and a truly unfortunate wall of textured mirrors in the living room, but Cat had plugged away at it little by little with different designers and contractors over many years, and it was finally at a stage where every room made her happy when she stepped into it, even the basement.

Cat searched in the freezer, and behind the bags of Brussels sprouts and frozen blueberries she found a container of Neapolitan ice cream. It was an arrangement of ice cream that seemed designed specifically for her little family. She didn't care for chocolate, but that was the only flavor Nick ate. Liz liked vanilla because she always added things to her ice cream and said any other flavor got in the way of enjoying good butterscotch sauce or sprinkles or nuts. Cat liked strawberry because there was at least the illusion that something healthy was going on with some kind of fruit involved. However, Cat didn't indulge in her share often, so there were three boxes piled up, two of which contained only walls of untouched strawberry ice cream.

She decided to throw out the two older boxes

and pulled out the fresh one, and set herself up at the island with a small bowl and the ice cream scoop. Cat knew she was probably right over the line into the health nut group, but she was in pretty good shape and wanted to stay that way. It seemed stupid to undo the work of decent exercise with poor food choices. That concept was difficult to impress upon Liz because she was young enough that it was hard to see any ill effect of whatever she put into her body. Cat was sure the junk food her daughter ate with her friends at every opportunity was not good for her, but there was little evidence on her energetic, healthy frame to point to, so Cat took her stand every night over dinner and hoped she was getting enough real nutrition into Liz's body to have an impact somewhere.

She wished she could get Nick to take his health more seriously. Being a vet wasn't exactly the same as being a doctor, but every time he lectured people about how not getting their pet to exercise more was tantamount to neglect, she would give him what he thought of as the "physician heal thyself" look. He wasn't terrible or anything, but she suspected he was at least a good 20 pounds heavier than when she'd met him, and she missed his once lithe frame. He was fine for the longest time, but once he hit 40, his metabolism shifted and his habits didn't. She tried to keep junk out of the house, but she knew he ate lunch at the hamburger place near the veterinary clinic, and there were always cookies and treats at work that he was bad at resisting. It frustrated her a little that he didn't try. She could still fit into her college jeans and she wished he could still fit into his, too.

Of course, the biggest key to the difference in their health was probably exercise, and she had to admit that he really didn't have the kind of time for that that she did. Cat swam every day without fail. When she'd started she used to count laps, but now she didn't care, so long as she got in at least an hour of it. Swimming was the only exercise she really liked. It was like flying, and she appreciated that she could work that hard and come out cleaner for it at the end instead of a sweaty mess.

Her daily routine had started when she was frustrated with the baby weight after having Liz. The baby was nearly a year old and Cat used to try to get her out of the house at least once a day (more for her own sanity than anything meant to benefit Liz), and one day she went to investigate the local YMCA. They had a weight room and a pool, but more than that, they had daycare. If you were a member, for a nominal fee you could have some enthusiastic education major watch your kid while you exercised, and Cat jumped at it. She organized a schedule for herself where she and Liz left the house at the same time every morning, her daughter would play happily, and Cat would swim. By the time she was showered and dressed again, Liz was ready for a nap, so it worked out perfectly.

She felt justified in using her time that way, because as much as she appeared to be a full-time stay-at-home mom to the average observer, she really considered herself a working mother. Writing was simply a hard thing to prove you were putting any effort into. So much of it was in her head and she needed clear time to think and imagine. In the time she spent underwater every day she propelled her body back and forth across the pool while her mind went elsewhere. She dreamed up new people and gave them names and hang-ups and desires and flaws and imagined unusual situations that would challenge her new creations as they stumbled about in the mazes she designed for them. The pool was her think tank, and she only answered to bubbles and splashes and the walls at either end where she lazily did her flip turns.

Cat loved writing. She'd started later than she imagined other writers had, but she didn't know. However, when it hit her that writing was what she wanted to do, she was prolific. Her first novel didn't do well and vanished into obscurity, but the second one did better, and then a short story got picked up by a women's magazine and that started to bring in real income.

Then came the *County Vet* books.

Nick always returned home from work with stories about people and their pets and there was always something new. Right when you thought there wouldn't be anything compelling about one more puppy story, something would come up and it would make them laugh or cry as they shared their dinner together. So Cat asked if he would mind being the inspiration for a new book about a vet. She thought it would be fun to do a modern city version of the *All Creatures Great and Small* series by James Herriot. She'd loved those books as a kid and thought there might be a market for something new in that vein. Nick thought it sounded great and contributed however he could by feeding her stories and double checking her facts about basic procedures and vet terminology.

She renamed her husband "Jack" and gave him an adoring wife named "Susan" with beautiful blond flowing hair. She went with blond for her alter ego to make it different from herself and her own long, dark hair which was usually in a ponytail. She also made Susan tall since Cat was on the small side and had always wished she didn't need help reaching high shelves. The "Jack" character was a more dashing version of her husband, but she was sure Nick flattered himself that she was simply being accurate. The puppies were cute and did funny puppy things, and Jack saved seeing-eye dogs from becoming blind themselves and rescued cats and did kindly things for old ladies who were alone except for their pets and the visits from the handsome vet.

The book was a smash. When Cat got the check from her agent she thought it was a mistake. It was more than she'd made in all her years working after college, which wasn't much, she knew, but still....

Her agent wanted more. Cat hadn't ever considered doing another one. She studied what she'd done and laid out a roadmap so she could duplicate her success. It worked. There was a definite fan base for that formula.

Cat had mixed feelings about it. On the one hand, being paid for doing what she loved was nothing to complain about. It was better than the lottery, because she could even feel she'd earned it. But it wasn't exactly the kind of writing she wanted to do. The first time was more of a lark, to feel more included in what her husband did and to amuse herself a little. The second time was out of curiosity to see if she could repeat herself but still have it be new. Much beyond that she didn't know if she cared enough to write another. She was more interested in darkness than in light, in people dealing with complications within themselves that needed to be worked out before they could feel whole. There was nothing like that in the *County Vet* stories. They were light, and sweet, and improbable with a ring of truth the way you wished it could be. There were carefully calculated tear jerker moments, but they were only there to give the illusion that the lighter stories were more profound than they were. They were fake.

But fake or not, people liked them. She got lots of letters, mostly from dog lovers who seemed overly involved in their dogs' lives in her opinion, and Nick's practice grew. He and his partner had to expand and bring in another doctor to meet the demand. She thought it should be obvious that Nick wasn't really Jack, sweet as he was, and she never used real names or descriptions of actual cases. However, everyone who needed their cat spayed or their dog's nails clipped believed they and their beloved pet could end up in the next book and live out a moment of fame on a best-seller list.

She told her agent she'd need some time off from the *County Vet* books for a while and Michelle, who was normally accommodating in their work together, was dumbstruck.

"But, Cat! They're doing so well! If they are that easy for you to crank out, why wouldn't you just do it?" Michelle wanted to know.

"I know, I know, it's just.... They don't make me happy."

"Well, they make me and a lot of other people happy, and the checks should make you happy, so isn't that enough for you?"

Cat tried to explain that the short story writing she did interested her more, as did some of the more complicated novels.

"So, you're saying those depressing things you'd rather write make you happy?"

"I guess *happy* isn't the right word. Maybe fulfilled is a better one, but they matter more. They feel more real."

"But they're not, Cat. None of it's real. For me, it comes down to the fact that some of the things that come out of your head make people want to open their wallets and other things don't. Don't squander an opportunity that any other writer I know would kill for."

So Cat had written the third *County Vet* book, but this time doing it on the side, while concentrating on the work she really liked during her more productive hours. She was disciplined about her writing and she gave the things that were important to her higher priority in her schedule. Each morning she got up with her husband, fed everyone breakfast, cleaned up after her husband left, went with Liz to the Y, and wrote in her office during nap or quiet time. Once her daughter started full day school, Cat began taking her laptop with her to a coffee shop downtown.

It was the perfect spot as far as she was concerned. The coffee shop was up the street from The Avenue Repertory Theater, and in the middle of the most dynamic part of town. People were always out walking when the weather was nice, and there were galleries and interesting shops and a great independent bookstore within walking distance. The coffee shop itself sold exotic tea and even offered fresh fruit, which she appreciated, and the owner of the coffee shop was pleased to have a famous writer use his location as an office of sorts, even if she took up a pair of loveseats by the window for all of the early afternoon nearly every day.

It gave her the sense that she was in the world more, to write at the coffee shop, although with her laptop in front of her like a shield she was more than a little cut off from it. Still, there were distractions, including the occasional stealth selfie from the next booth by people who figured out who she was, so the important parts of her writing she did at her desk at home where she could think. The less creative nuts and bolts stuff of writing and the *County Vet* books she did at the coffee shop.

As Cat was debating if she should indulge in a second small scoop of ice cream, Liz appeared with Pogo, their skinny little mutt with one crooked ear, trotting behind her. Pogo was a funny little dog who could jump very high and was so thin when Nick brought him home from the shelter that Liz (at age nine) had laughed and called him a Pogo stick. The "Pogo" part stuck, and the dog had remained a fixture of their lives while other foster animals came and went because the dog was in love with Liz.

"Hey, Sweetheart," said Cat.

"Hi Mom. How was the play again?" Liz spotted the ice cream and got herself out a bowl and some sprinkles.

"It was good again. It gave me a lot to think about, which is why I guess I wanted to see it so often while I could."

Liz sat across from her mom and started scooping herself some vanilla. Cat decided another scoop of strawberry wouldn't kill her, and she liked the idea of some real time with her daughter. Liz was a nice and responsible girl for 14, but she was more impatient and aloof with her parents than she'd been even a year or so before, and it made Cat sad. She missed her little girl who was looking more like a woman every day. It scared her sometimes when she realized how little she knew about Liz's life at this point. So much of it was private now, and off limits.

"So, you never told me what it was about, anyway," said Liz.

"I didn't?"

"No, and when I asked Dad that first time you went he said he wasn't sure."

Cat smiled, then took a slow lick from her spoon. "Your dad is a lot of wonderful things, but a play reviewer he is not."

"Yeah, but he's good for help on science homework," said Liz as she picked at the seal on a new jar of hot fudge. "He helped me get that osmosis project finally finished tonight."

"Oh good." Cat thought a moment and then asked, "What did your dad say about the play?"

"Just that there was some funny stuff, but that most of it was strange, and that there was a couple with a baby and a different couple comes to take the baby away."

"That does sum it up, in its own way, I guess," laughed Cat. "I probably should have taken you to see it, but there was a lot of sexual stuff and, you know, in my head you're still five sometimes."

Liz rolled her eyes and added sprinkles on top of her hot fudge. "Mom! I just finished reading *Fear of Flying* last week! I can handle the concept."

"Where did you get a hold of that?" asked Cat, feeling a little uncomfortable.

"Where do you think? If you want to block off

some of your shelves with police tape go ahead, but until then I figure anything on a shelf in this house is fair game."

That was reasonable, Cat had to admit. But she had figured with the huge number of books in the house the odds of her daughter finding one about a woman's exploration into sexual fantasy and experimentation was small enough not to worry about. It was the same copy she'd read herself at about 14 so she shouldn't have felt so freaked out about it. It was simply hard to acknowledge her own baby daughter had reached that place.

Cat said, "Well, I apologize. You could have handled the play just fine, then, and you might have liked it."

"So why did you like it so much?"

How much should she share with her daughter? Some things were too intimate and weird to hear from your mom, and what kind of advice would it be to tell a child that her current opinion was that sex with at least half a dozen men before she settled down seemed like a good sample size, rather than being virgins like her parents were when they met? That was not going to happen. She'd talk about sex another day and go with other themes available to her right then.

"There was a lot to do with what's real and what isn't and how sometimes it's hard to tell the difference," said Cat.

"Dad said there was a baby and that by the end there was never a baby. He kept saying that having a baby and the effects of it on a woman's body were impossible to deny so it didn't make sense. I mean, that's weird, Mom. Either the baby was real or it wasn't, right?"

"Yes and no. I mean, the baby was a symbol to start with, so it was never real. Even if it was real all through the play, it still only existed in the play, so it was never real. No one in the play was real, and the characters made us stop and think about that while it was happening, which was part of what made it so interesting."

"But the play still has to feel like it's representing real things or you can't relate to it, can you? I mean, you really couldn't deny a baby in the real world."

Cat thought about that and ate some more ice cream. "I wish I could say you were right, but, for example, there are genocides all over the world where babies die and governments deny it. If one of those babies were yours, imagine the added trauma of insisting it had been real when officially no one acknowledged it was."

Liz paused and looked into her ice cream bowl as if the spoon and sprinkles were reading her somber thoughts. Cat felt bad. She didn't like the idea of sheltering her daughter, but illuminating evil and horror in the world for her always felt wrong. She should have gone with the sex talk.

Cat added, "Hey, but on the up side, there was a general sense that people should enjoy being young while they are young, because being young can be a

blast. And that's where you are, so there's that!"
She knew it was silly but she hated to see anything
resembling sadness on her daughter's beautiful face.

"But it ends badly for the young people, you
said," challenged Liz.

"Yes, but not for a while. I mean, we all have to
deal with pain and loss at some point because that's
how we grow, but we should learn to appreciate the
good moments while we're in them."

Liz was getting down to the bottom of her bowl
already. Cat felt like a very slow eater by
comparison. There were a lot of ways in which she
thought Liz was ahead of her.

"But why does there really have to be pain to
know something's good?" Liz asked. "I know it
works in your stories or for a play, but in real life?
It seems kinda pointless."

"It's that way in my stories and in plays and in
art in general because all those things try to
encapsulate life in some way, and pain and loss are
a part of life. Trust me, my stories have nothing on
real life when it comes to dishing out pain," said
Cat.

"Then why do you make up more of it? If you
can do anything in a story, why can't you keep
people happy?"

"Well, I kind of do in the *County Vet* books,
don't I?"

"But you don't like writing those."

She wasn't sure how her daughter knew that.
She'd never discussed that with anyone but her

agent. Cat didn't even have the heart to let Nick know how she felt about the *County Vet* books because he thought they were about him.

"I don't really dislike writing them. And even those have an occasional dog being put down or a cat the vet can't save, and do you know why?"

Liz raised an eyebrow at her as she finished her last bite from her bowl.

"Because, if you don't cry over something, you don't know if you care about it. All the happy things in those books can't stand if the sad things aren't there to act as a crutch."

Liz got up and Pogo hopped to his feet. "Well, I'd like to think 'happy' could stand up by itself," she said as she turned around leaving her her bowl nowhere near the sink or the dishwasher. She waved in a goodnight gesture and went upstairs with Pogo trailing behind her as if he were the living embodiment of pure happiness expressly to prove Liz's point.

"We all would," Cat said to herself, and decided not to finish the last of her ice cream. She rinsed out her bowl, and then her daughter's, and went up to join her husband in bed.

CHAPTER TWO

Cat sat on the edge of the pool, feet in the water. It was a good temperature. On days where it was too cold or too warm that could be distracting, and she didn't want to be distracted. It was a quiet day, too, with only a couple of other regular lap swimmers in the pool, but not enough that she'd have to share a lane. On days she had to share a lane, she often bagged the whole activity after only half an hour because at that point swimming was purely for exercise. Today was work. Cat settled her goggles over her eyes and then without any hesitation about adjusting to the water, she dropped herself in and propelled off the wall.

"Into the mines," she thought to herself, although the gemlike aquamarine of the pool—so bright and refreshing—was probably about as far from descending into a mine as one could imagine. But this was where Cat was best able to let her thoughts wander in constructive ways and she could locate elements of the people and places she needed for her writing. She could put the motion of her body on autopilot and with nothing really to see or hear of any significance, the images in her head seemed clearer, which made describing them with words easier.

What she was mining for today was the beginnings of relationships. She had a couple of characters who were still mostly in outline form who needed to meet and fall in love before they could get on with the story she had in mind for them. Reviewing relationship stories from her own life gave her somewhere to start.

Not that she ever used a real situation from her life in her fiction—not really. Sometimes all she took from her mining expeditions was an outfit, a weird meal, or the way someone doodled while they talked.

No one believed that, of course. In every interview, at every book club meeting, at every reading at a bookstore of any size, at least one person wanted to know how much of it was real with the assumption always that most of it had to be. People forgot how much of reading was actively filling in the blanks with their own experiences and their own images, and if they believed she was writing about a particular place or a particular person, that simply became true for them, and they were unwilling or unable to let that go. People wanted to believe she was telling them about herself. But why would she write fiction if she were only replaying events that had already happened to her? What would be the point? They didn't seem to realize the dizzying freedom of being able to completely make things up was where the joy was. The places and people may have a root in some sort of reality in order that they remained relatable, but they did not exist. They could be anything she wanted.

Cat reached the wall at the deep end, circled her body neatly into a well-practiced flip turn, and launched herself back toward where she'd started. How many thousands of flip turns had she executed in this pool by now? She wasn't sure she wanted to know. It seemed like one more way of measuring her mortality. How many flip turns in life do we get?

Relationships. Beginnings. Choices. It begins with the framework from where you make choices. What was hers? Cat had tried her whole life to make the correct choices. She didn't have a religious framework to work from, so she had to ponder everything extra hard because there was no default position. There was no one at an altar or some kind of podium to whom she could defer on an ethical issue that she was too tired to think about. It was all up to her own brain and it was exhausting.

Luckily she had parents she admired and trusted. They used principles based on logic and compassion and experience and their default position always seemed to be love.

Cat had spent many laps in the pool playing in her mind her parents' differing upbringings. Those stories were often useful to mine, partially because the tales had gaps that she could fill in herself a variety of ways.

Her mother's past in particular fascinated her. Diane grew up in a large Mormon family that Cat had never met. The childhood memories she'd heard about were nice enough, but the rules in the LDS church were firm and didn't leave much room for certain lapses. When Cat was young and would ask what made her leave at 19, her mother would distract her with the promise of making cookies or going to a movie. When Cat was older, though, her mom finally did confide in her. Diane had a younger brother named David she was close to. He was gay and she was the only one he'd told. Coming out would have meant losing everything and the stress was too much. Diane was the one who'd found his body in his room. When Cat asked for details, all her mother would say was that blood was impossible to ever completely remove once it was spilled.

Her mother dropped out of the mission she was scheduled for and moved across the country and put herself through school. Diane pursued what she loved, which was teaching high school English. She liked telling Cat and her brother Alex how she met their father the auto mechanic. She'd taken her junker of a car in to the shop next to her apartment to see about a noise, and Paul Devin had told her she had an oil leak. She couldn't afford to do anything about it on a teacher's salary, so he said he'd see what he could do. She was pleased because whatever he'd done seemed to work for weeks until one morning her car sounded awful again and she took it back to the shop. The guy there told her simply that Paul was sick that day and that's why her car sounded bad. That didn't make sense to her until he explained that Paul had filled her car (which was always parked on the street) with oil every morning when he came in to work. She said she couldn't even remember what Paul looked like right then, but that she decided on the spot he was the man she wanted to marry.

Cat loved her mother's stories, and shared her interest in books. Everything Cat read for school her mother would read again herself so they could discuss it. Her mother never made reading seem like work, it was always a cherished luxury, and that was how she inspired Cat to feel about it as well.

There were screaming fights and slammed doors when Cat was in her teens, and that embarrassed her now to think back on, but she supposed it was a necessary part of growing up and becoming her own person. She remembered very clearly feeling as if her parents didn't trust her when they asked her too many questions or wanted to know where she was going. It was insulting and she resented it. She wasn't up to anything bad and they should have known that, in her opinion. She wasn't going to get pregnant or do drugs, so she felt entitled to greater freedom.

Now as the mother of a teenage daughter, she knew better. It had very little to do with trust and everything to do with fear. Sending your baby out into the world alone where you couldn't watch her was like dropping a kitten in traffic and not looking back. Parents saw danger everywhere, and teenagers were much too interested in appearing worldly and brave to have a clue.

Cat's childhood had been normal and uneventful, she always thought, until she hit high school and discovered how many other kids came from families of divorce or serious problems. Then she realized she was lucky. Normal and uneventful were gifts. Life as a kid was stressful enough in terms of learning about everything from yourself to dating to the world around you, without having to worry about having someplace safe to take for granted. To not have a family you could count on when you went home sounded akin to torture as far as Cat was concerned.

Her brother was a science geek and very funny, and they usually got along well. They both resented that their parents had named them Catherine and Alexander so they could call them "great" and find it amusing.

As Cat surfaced for a breath she glanced at the clock on the wall behind the lifeguard. She'd let her train of thought wander further afield than she'd intended. But thinking about how her parents had met was useful. Maybe switch the roles for her characters and have the woman secretly do something nice for the guy over time? Unfortunately that didn't work as well because such gestures made the man seem sensitive but the woman seem needy for some reason. She'd play with it. Why did certain behaviors in a woman look different on a man, and vice versa?

Maybe if the main character's car broke down and nobody knew she was stranded she—Oh, damn it. Cell phones. Cat felt like half her writing time was taken up by trying to work around cell phones. Everyone had everything at their fingertips now, and she kept having to come up with plausible reasons why their phones couldn't help in whatever situations she was constructing. To free her characters, their phones died, got dropped, ended up switched into different bags, got lost in the garbage, or once (in her favorite case) crushed underfoot by an elephant in a parade. Characters set in modern times couldn't get lost anymore, or wonder where somebody was, or lose track of events. It was frustrating.

Almost as frustrating to Cat as real life phones. Liz was addicted to hers, and Nick seemed to think he couldn't function without his, but Cat wanted no part of that. Unless it was an emergency she didn't want people to be able to contact her whenever and wherever. The land line at home was plenty. Although Cat wondered sometimes if Liz even knew where it was since she never used it.

People bugged her about her lack of cell phone use as if she were missing out on something, but she didn't see it that way. Cat observed the cell phone zombies bumping into parking meters and falling off curbs from her view through the windows at the coffee shop and couldn't see the appeal.

People also tried to convince her that social media was a necessity. Cat did try it for exactly one month. At first it was great. She liked seeing updates from her friends back home and reading posts about their kids. But quickly she became overwhelmed by information she didn't want to know about people, and began harboring disapproving thoughts about neighbors she had previously liked. Cat found herself engaged in heated debates online with people connected to her by friends of friends of friends and it was ugly. It was hard in some cases to not take the bait because to remain silent on certain topics seemed the same as condoning them. On top of everything else, social media was plagued by people who couldn't tell "your" from "you're," never mind the nightmarish uses of "there/their/they're" that assaulted her eyes every time she logged onto the internet.

But the real issue was how quickly the distractions of social media eroded her ability to write. After only a few weeks of having her thoughts invaded by scattered but intense input from online, Cat discovered her thoughts were too cluttered to do the one thing she felt she was good at. Her production level ground to a snail's pace as her ability to focus was hindered. Writing became a chore complicated by outside voices. Those voices had to go, so she signed off of all of it and never went back. She still had some form of social media presence, but it was all maintained by some tech-savvy youth on her publisher's payroll.

Technology aside, the main thing that limited Cat's mining expeditions when it came to relationship information was that her own experience was so meager. The stories of how people met usually made people smile, so they were useful stories to have, she just didn't have many personally.

As she pushed herself up and out onto the edge of the pool where she'd started, she realized however meager her experience, thinking back to her early days with Nick still made her smile.

*

Right out of high school, Cat went to a local college that she could commute to from home to save money. She majored in English purely because it was easy for her. Writing papers and reading and literary analysis were things she liked, but she didn't know what to do with in terms of the real world. Teaching didn't appeal to her, and she wasn't interested in journalism. Her parents never pushed her to think about a career, they simply wanted her to be educated and to find something she loved. She told her mom she wanted someone to pay her to read all the world's greatest novels, but her mom always laughed and said if that position ever came up she would beat her daughter to it.

After Cat graduated and moved into a small apartment on her own, she was lonely. She had a job at a local bookstore that didn't pay well, but she had few expenses so she got by. Her mom would happen to come over with bags of food from time to time, and would have mysteriously discovered brand new clothes in Cat's size lying in the back of her closet that she would leave on Cat's bed. Her friends' lives changed so she didn't see them as often. She didn't like going back to her empty apartment at night. Then her mom suggested she take Baxter.

Baxter was the family dog that they'd had since she was in fifth grade. He was a humane society mutt who seemed to be mostly golden retriever. He was floppy and big and silly and his tail could knock everything off a coffee table in a few happy wags. He also had a bark that could scare the hell out of anyone who came to the door or looked at Cat the wrong way, and her father liked the idea of his single daughter who lived alone having the dog as some kind of protection or alarm. Of course, Baxter had never proven he could be of any use in that capacity unless an attacker was afraid of being licked to death, but Cat didn't care. She liked his slobbering, cheerful company.

It helped enormously having the dog with her. Baxter slept on her bed and followed her happily around her apartment, and she even found a dog park within walking distance that the two of them could go to after work. The people there were fun to hang out with, and she loved walking home with her big, silly dog in the dark.

Unfortunately, Baxter was big, silly and old. He had a youthful personality, but he was 16, and his body had about run its course. After he lived with her for a bit over six months, she came home one afternoon to grab lunch and take him out for a quick walk, and he was lying on his side on her tiny kitchen floor. He wasn't breathing right. She couldn't figure out what to do because he was too big for her to lift and she didn't have a car. She didn't even have a vet at that point, and the one by her parents seemed too far away. She thought there was a vet near the movie theater she sometimes went to which was fairly close, so she looked it up quickly and called. Cat dialed in a panic and tried to explain to the woman who answered what was happening.

"Can you bring the dog in now?"

"I don't know how to get him there!" Cat was crying. "I don't have a car and I don't think I can get him down the stairs anyway and—"

"I'm not sure what to tell you, Miss. You'd have to get the animal here for us to examine him."

"But...?"

Car heard a man's voice in the background asking questions, and as the woman explained the situation there was a lot of back and forth that Cat couldn't hear being muffled at the other end. The woman came back on the phone and in an exasperated tone asked Cat for her name and address.

"Okay, Miss. I want you to wait outside by your door. Someone should be there in a few minutes, all right? And please do not tell your friends this is some kind of service we offer."

Cat didn't care about the woman's tone, she was simply relieved. "Thank you! Thank you so much!"

She stroked Baxter's head worriedly for a minute, then she headed downstairs. Soon a car pulled up and a friendly looking man got out. He had light brown hair and hazel eyes and he was wearing a white lab coat. The pin above his pocket read "Dr. Ryan."

"I take it you're Catherine?" he asked.

She nodded and thanked him for coming and showed him upstairs. Baxter hadn't moved. The vet knelt down and gently touched the dog in a few places and started asking her basic questions about when he last ate, and so forth. He seemed worried.

"We really have to take him in to the clinic. I can lift him if you can catch all the doors."

She followed the vet who carefully laid Baxter on a blanket spread out in the back of the car. Cat sat in the back seat so she could pet her dog while Dr. Ryan drove. While he carried the dog into the clinic, Cat ignored the disapproving look on the receptionist's face.

Dr. Ryan asked Cat to wait out front and fill out

some paper work while he examined Baxter. She did as she was told and she fretted in the waiting room.

Eventually the vet came back out and invited her into a small room. There were cats on the wallpaper and a cabinet that was slightly open that seemed to be filled with nothing but boxes of tissues.

"I'm really sorry, Catherine, but I think your dog has had a stroke."

She looked at him and she could feel the wave of tears coming. She didn't say anything because if she opened her mouth the dam would burst.

"You need to make a decision about what you want to do here. I'm afraid there aren't many options because recovery is unlikely, and...Catherine, I gave him a sedative, but he's suffering. You may have to decide to let him go."

She sat down in the nearest chair. The vet pulled up a chair opposite her. Cat knew Baxter was old and had had a nice life, but she didn't want to be the one to have to decide the exact time that life should end.

"I guess...." she started, but then the tears came.

"I— Look, um, I've only been a real vet for a few months and I'm new here and all anyone told me to do in situations like this was to have tissues ready, but... Is there something better? I mean, that I could do?"

Cat looked up with her blotchy tear-streaked face and realized for the first time how young Dr Ryan was. Not much older than herself but lab coats made people seem older somehow. "I don't... I think maybe... Is Ryan your first name or your last?" she asked. She couldn't tell if the name tags were being official or cute.

"My name is Nick," he said. He handed her the box of tissues.

"Thanks, Nick," she said, her breath coming more evenly as they sat together.

When Cat was calmer Nick said, "Why don't you come say goodbye to your dog."

Cat nodded, then followed Nick into the surgery where Baxter was lying on a table, eyes half closed and still breathing in a labored way. She stroked her dog's ears and kissed his head and told him she loved him. She asked if she could stand there with him while he received the injection and Nick said, "Of course. I'm sure he wants you here." She watched as Baxter's eyes flickered from recognition to something empty and she thought she felt broken beyond repair.

For a moment Cat believed Nick might cry, too, but he cleared his throat and said, "I have a few more questions I'm supposed to ask. Is that okay, or do you want me to wait?"

"Yeah, no it's okay," she said softly.

Nick cleared his throat again. "Do you want us to do an autopsy?"

Cat looked in her lap and shook her head. Knowing exactly why her sweet dog had died would not unlock any of the mysteries of the universe, and it would not bring him back, so it sounded useless.

"Okay," said Nick, marking something on his clipboard. "What would you like done with the body?"

She couldn't imagine asking the nice vet to drive her dead dog anywhere. She went with individual cremation and she'd call her mom when she got home and come up with a plan for Baxter's ashes.

He led her back to the small room with the tissues. "Take as much time as you need, and I'll drive you home whenever you're ready, okay?"

She sat for a long time and went through most of a box of tissues. Until that point in her life, she had never lost anything important. The physical aspect of grief surprised her.

Eventually the young vet came back and sat with her. He offered her yet another box of tissues, but she was in a dry spell for the moment and didn't need them. He glanced at his watch.

"Look, I...do you have anyone to be with tonight or anything?" Nick asked.

Cat thought about it for a minute. She had figured she might call her mom and have her come get her, but that was sort of silly since they both were supposed to work first thing in the morning. Part of being an adult and on her own shouldn't mean crying to her mom whenever things got hard, but maybe this was an exception.

She sighed and looked at her lap. She still had dog hair all over her clothes. She felt herself choking up again.

"Hey," he said gently, "I'm done here in like, another forty minutes or something—assuming no emergencies show up. Since I was planning to take you home anyway, can I take you to dinner?"

Cat turned her gaze up at him with surprise. She could not have looked worse if she'd tried and she was perplexed, but he seemed sincere and kind. She could use kindness more than anything else right then, so she said yes.

They went to a little soup place within easy walking distance of her apartment so she could take herself home at any point. But she ended up having such a pleasant time that they stayed until the place shut down around ten. For having taken up a table for five hours, Nick left a generous tip.

For one of the worst days of her life, there were some wonderful memories in it for Cat. Nick was a good listener. He asked about her job (which she hoped she still had after not showing up for her afternoon shift) and her family and wanted her to tell him all about Baxter's life.

Nick was clever with his hands and did origami. He kept squares of beautiful paper in his briefcase and he made her one thing after another since each new creation made her smile. When he ran out of paper he used modified takeout menus. By the end of the night the table was covered with a delicate menagerie of different birds and dogs and cats and monkeys. There were clever shapes and intricate boxes and flowers and a small boat. He tried to lead

42

her through a basic crane, but she somehow couldn't seem to manage it.

"No, fold it toward you," he'd said.

"Toward you or toward me?" she asked.

"Now, how is that part confusing? Toward you means toward *you*!"

"I know, but the last time you really meant toward *you*, and it got all messed up!"

"Just...here, watch me again. This part's called the 'minor miracle fold'."

"Why's that?"

"It just is. Are you watching?"

But Cat found herself watching him more than the paper. He was nice looking. Not like a movie star or anything, but averagely nice. And he was younger than he'd seemed in the clinic. Only about three or four years older than she was.

"Yes," she said as he made careful folds that lined up as if that was the only way the paper had ever wanted to be.

"Now you."

Cat smiled a little and concentrated as she tried to duplicate what he'd done, but the folds were backward again and didn't work.

Nick looked amused and said, "How does that keep happening? Look, maybe if I show you from the same direction."

He slid his chair around to her side of the table so he could sit next to her. She liked having him so close. He got out a fresh piece of paper in a beautiful metallic red and laid it out between them.

He watched as she made the folds and he continued to talk her through it. At one point he reached out to touch her hand when he realized she was headed for a mistake and Cat smiled. When the last fold was correctly in place and a recognizable crane sat in front of her, Cat actually laughed a little.

"Now that's a minor miracle," he said, laughing back.

The next time she saw Nick was when she collected Baxter's ashes. Her mom had driven down with her, and they were going to pick up her dad and her older brother and go out to eat. Then they were going to scatter Baxter's ashes behind the chicken takeout place where he was always finding splintery bones they'd have to wrestle out of his mouth on every walk. Since it was the bones that should have killed him, it seemed like the right place.

While Cat was signing papers at the desk, Nick gestured to her mother that he wanted to speak with her privately. He talked to her very quietly and seriously. Her mother smiled and glanced over at her daughter and then back at Nick who smiled and asked her something and she answered and then they laughed briefly. Another vet came out and told Nick he was needed, so he gave Cat a small wave and thanked her mother and disappeared through the surgery door.

"What was that?" Cat asked her in the car.

"What was what?"

"Why did the vet want to talk to you?" Cat

wanted to know.

"Oh, no reason."

"Well there had to be a reason! What did he say? Was it about Baxter? Was it about me? It was about me, wasn't it? What did he say?"

Her mom smiled and drove and all she would say was that the vet was a very nice young man, which drove Cat crazy.

Nick called her a few days later and asked her how it had gone with the ashes and how she was feeling, and finally asked her to dinner again. She was more than a little pleased to be asked. They ended up at her favorite Indian restaurant which delighted her.

It felt more like a real date than the first dinner had been. She'd thought of that as more of a pity date. This time she was showered and in presentable clothes and there were no tears in sight. Nick seemed less confident and a little dazzled, while Cat was more nervous but animated.

Nick frowned uncertainly at the menu and then without looking at Cat asked, "So, what do you recommend?"

"Oh, I always order the vegetable curry. I keep thinking I should order something else because it's all good, but then I know I'll wish I'd ordered the vegetable curry." Cat watched Nick continue to study the menu. "Have you eaten Indian food before?" she finally asked.

"Not really. So, um, no."

"How about the tandoori chicken?" she

suggested. "It sounds exotic, but it's really just chicken."

"Yes, sure, I'll have that!" he said, closing the menu and looking relieved.

"We could try out different breads, too. Oh, and the mango lassi! That's so good. And if you don't like it I'll finish it for you."

They placed their orders with the waiter who bobbled his head at them before leaving them alone, but this time without origami paper. They sat in silence for a moment as Nick looked curiously around the room, and then Cat asked, "So, this is obviously not your thing. Why did you pick it?"

"Your mom told me you liked this place," he said.

"Is that what you were talking about with her at the clinic?"

"Essentially. I kind of...it's just that I come from a sort of...let's call it a more formal background. I didn't feel right about asking you out again without some kind of permission or approval or something from your parents. I know that probably sounds stupid, but I saw a chance to talk to your mom so I took it. I'll understand if you think that sounds too weird."

Cat smiled. "No, it's sort of sweet. A little weird, too, though, but in my case it's probably not a bad way to go. If my family doesn't like someone then he's out on his ear in my book. And my mom already likes you so I don't have to wonder now, I guess."

"Your mom seemed incredibly nice. I thought she would be from your stories, but it was nice to see for myself."

Cat was pleased. She really couldn't see herself ending up with a man her parents didn't approve of. That sounded sheltered to her, but it wasn't. The fact was, she respected their judgment a great deal, and letting them down would be like letting herself down.

"So," she asked with curiosity in her voice, "tell me of this formal background. Are you royalty?"

Nick laughed. "I guess only if you really extend the definition of royalty to include about everyone. No, it's that my family is Christian to a very strict degree. I've got five brothers and sisters and we were all home schooled for a while, and we were all expected to marry someone from our church eventually. People didn't date without some kind of arrangement. I'm not a part of the church or anything like that now, but some things get kind of ingrained."

"How did that work? The home schooling thing, I mean."

"It didn't work for what I wanted to do. It was fine for a lot of things, but biological science, not so much. I love my family, and it was nice being with them all the time, but it would've been good to know more people than only them and the church group. When I started to set my sights on something involving medicine, I asked my parents if I could go to a regular school and they said 'fine.' I give them a lot of credit for supporting me on stuff they didn't believe in themselves."

"So they don't mind that you're not in the church?"

"Oh, they mind, but they love me and would never cut me out of their lives or something just for that. They hope I'll come back to it, but they know that's my choice to make, not theirs."

"That seems unusually tolerant to me."

"I wouldn't know."

Their food came, and Nick wasn't adventurous enough to try her dish but did like his own, and he was split on the various breads. Cat thought it was funny when he asked if there might be chocolate cake on the dessert menu.

"I hope I can make you laugh like this when I'm trying to on our next date," said Nick looking a bit embarrassed.

Cat thought to herself that she was happy there was going to be a next date.

"What about you?" she asked. "How did you end up here?"

He told her about vet school and how much he loved animals. They didn't have pets at his house growing up because one of his sisters had allergies, but his best friend from the church had dozens. He could never get over that there were so many different ways for creatures to function in the world. The variety was what sent him into veterinary medicine rather than trying to heal people. He explained to Cat in a lively manner how dogs differed from birds differed from lizards in the way they worked inside. Cat thought it would be wonderful to have that kind of clearly defined passion for something.

They even ended up on the topic of their sexual histories a little unexpectedly, which normally would seem a little soon for Cat. They were on the subject of his church again and why he left, when Nick mentioned he'd been engaged.

"Engaged! Well, what happened with that?" Cat asked.

"Oh, well we got married and had eight kids and now we live in France," Nick teased.

"No, I mean it! What's that story?"

"There isn't much of one, really."

"I want to hear it anyway. I don't like loose ends."

"Okay, it's like this. It was drummed into us pretty hard that you weren't supposed to have sex before marriage. We weren't even supposed to hold hands unless we were engaged, so being a teenager in that church group was pretty frustrating. There was this girl at church named Tabitha who was my age and we decided one day that we should be engaged because we couldn't stand it anymore. We were eighteen and it only lasted until I left for college, but we each finally got to kiss someone."

"You didn't have your first kiss until you were eighteen?" Cat asked incredulously.

"Yes! You're going to make me repeat that? Your mother would be disappointed that you're being mean to me."

Cat laughed. "I'm sorry! I'm not in a place to be laughing anyway. I'm sure I'm the only person who left college with a diploma *and* their virginity."

"We're a small club, then."

"Are you serious?"

"Are you *trying* to ruin my night?"

Cat laughed again. "I'm sorry I'm sorry I'm sorry. It could be a nice foundation for our *duprass*."

Nick looked confused. "What's that?"

"You haven't read any Vonnegut?"

"No, I'm not much on reading. Stories, anyway. There was a lot of Jesus reading as a kid and that kind of turned me off of the whole concept."

That disappointed her, but so little else about Nick did that she let it go. She didn't want to look inside a lizard and he didn't want to read fiction, so they could balance each other out a little.

He dropped her off at her place and asked if he could kiss her goodnight. She liked that he was so polite and gentle. He made her feel safe. The kiss was warm and comfortable and she could tell Nick was reluctant to leave, but he did.

The first time Nick told her he loved her they happened to be standing in his old room. Cat was having dinner at his parents' for the first time, and he took her on a tour of the house. His room had been assigned a new function as a sewing space long ago, but there were still old things of his tacked up on the walls such as the periodic table of the elements and pictures of race cars. One second they were standing there in his boyhood space, and the next he blurted out, "I love you!"

It was so unexpected it made Cat laugh. "I love you, too!" she assured him when he looked worried.

They were engaged after only a few months together. One day at the soup restaurant where they'd had their first dinner, Nick asked her to marry him. He'd made a beautiful origami cat and used the ring as its collar and set it on her place mat. It never occurred to her the answer could be anything but "yes."

She told him that night that they should probably not wait until their wedding night to sleep together, lest they find out they were incompatible in some way after they were stuck with one another for life. Nick didn't need any convincing.

That whole period of her life had been a happy whirlwind, but real sex was not like what either of them had been led to expect from books or movies. There were lots of little awkward things all along the process that could be distracting. It was gross when the sheets were wet, and they dealt often with the question of what they thought of as the "trapped arm dilemma." It was still fun, but they were still themselves which could sometimes get in the way. Lots of things usually struck Cat as funny at odd times, but during sex that wasn't helpful. Nick was a gentle person and he was also gentle in bed. That sounded fine in theory, but sometimes Cat thought there should be more.

Overall they decided they were indeed compatible, and they were married in a simple ceremony at city hall with only their families in attendance before the year was out. Cat was 23.

They decided to live in Cat's apartment at first, and assumed they would find something bigger when they had a chance to look. It was close to the bookstore where Cat continued to work, and since they only had one car it made sense. Nick wasn't attached to things particularly, so he got rid of nearly everything from his old place, and they didn't feel cramped in the small apartment. At least, they didn't before the animals.

Nick volunteered at the humane society regularly, but one of the things they needed him to do on occasion was put animals to sleep. If they were in pain or dangerous he could live with it, but once in a while there would be some poor animal whose only crime was being unwanted when presented next to puppies and kittens, and he couldn't take it.

The first time he brought home a dog, Cat thought it was cute. By the time they had three dogs and an elderly cat she was hitting her limit. She cut back to part time work at the bookstore so she could more properly care for the animals. Nick always assured her the pets were there temporarily and he was working something out with the shelter, but some of them seemed to stay a long time. She didn't know how to be mad at him for it, but she didn't want to feel as if she were married to Noah, either.

Eventually her parents ended up with a dog, her brother ended up with a dog, and both managers at the bookstore ended up with cats.

Life as a married woman was unclear to Cat. She worked because she needed something to do, not because she had to. She had lots of time to read waiting for Nick to finish long shifts, but it wasn't the paradise she had imagined. She wondered how long they should wait before having children, and she decided she didn't want to wait.

Before they had a chance to hunt for a bigger place in town, Nick got an offer from out of state. His best friend from veterinary school was taking over his father's practice, and he wanted Nick to be his partner. It was an amazing opportunity and Cat didn't see how she could tell him 'no,' but it meant being far from their families. She'd cried as her mom helped her pack. She also threw up the morning they drove off in their U-haul, but didn't figure out until later it was from morning sickness.

The first few months in their new city were difficult. Nick had to get re-certified for the new state, they were house hunting while living out of boxes in his friend's basement, and pregnancy was hard on Cat. All of it was stressful. When Cat miscarried she blamed herself.

Cat found out she was pregnant the second time the same week they closed on their first house. She was sure with a stable home and a real routine starting to form it would be fine this time, but that pregnancy was even shorter and more fraught. She felt fortunate that Nick happened to be home for lunch when that miscarriage started, because the pain was sharp and breathtaking and caused her to sink to her knees on the living room floor.

Nick called her mother who drove all night to get there. Cat cried and kept asking her, "Why is this happening? Why do I keep losing the babies?"

"I don't know, Honey," was all she would answer.

After her mom returned home Cat was lonely and frustrated. She assisted at the clinic to have something to do, but she didn't have any friends of her own. She tried joining a local book club, but it was disappointing to say the least. They were reading *To the Lighthouse* by Virginia Wolff, and she actually hadn't read it before and was excited. There were two lines that she underlined in her copy that needed clarification for her, but for the most part she felt she had a good enough grasp on it to hold up her end of a discussion. However, the book had proved too challenging for anyone else there, and she found she was the only one who had finished it. She told the women with their wine the story herself as they sat spellbound. They stared at the books in their laps and wondered aloud why they hadn't detected any of the interesting things that Cat had found there. She didn't go back the following month.

The third and fourth pregnancies were similar in their duration and side effects. She was fatigued and moody, but at least neither of those miscarriages were physically painful. The last one she elected to have a D & C procedure done, because the psychological trauma of passing the "products of conception" (as they were so charmingly called by her doctor) was too much.

Nick said, "I think we should stop."

"But we want kids!"

"Yeah, but I don't care where they come from. We could even look into adoption if you want, it doesn't matter to me."

But Cat couldn't let it go.

Their insurance didn't cover any kind of investigation into whatever problem they were having until the fifth miscarriage (a man came up with that rule, Cat decided bitterly) and she wanted to know what was wrong. She felt like she was failing and she wanted answers, even if it meant suffering one more heart-wrenching loss.

But the fifth time stuck. Cat was so shocked by the time she reached 13 weeks she wasn't sure what to do with herself. She had to dig around to find the pregnancy books again and start paying attention as if she were really going to have a baby. Her doctor wasn't taking any chances this time around and put her on bedrest. She wasn't to go anywhere other than to the bathroom or to the hospital.

The pregnancy was uncomfortable and boring, but before she gave birth to Liz, Cat finally gave birth to her own vocation. She wrote her first novel to pass the time. She didn't think too much about it until her mother came out to stay with them to help with the baby once she arrived.

The delivery was traumatic. Elizabeth Marie Ryan was born healthy and perfect, but once all the necessary surgery was completed in the emergency room, Nick and Cat were informed she was the last baby they were ever going to have. It was a beginning and an ending wrapped into one and it made Liz's entrance into the world bittersweet.

While Cat was in recovery at home, her mom stayed with her and helped with the baby and the chores. At some point Cat got up the nerve to show her mom the novel she'd written while on bedrest before the birth. Diane read it and she liked it, and she helped Cat do a thorough editing. Cat found it a pleasant diversion between nursings and diaper changes.

But her mother told her it could be more than that. Diane did some research with her librarian friend back home and found out about query letters and contacting agents and doing manuscripts with proper spacing and courier font.

"I think you could get published, Catherine," she told her.

Cat wasn't convinced. "Mom, it was too easy. I'm sure real writers work harder than that."

"Why don't you think you're a real writer?" she said, holding the properly formatted and printed manuscript in an envelope in her hands. "This sure looks real to me."

"But I don't know how to do any of the business stuff, and I don't really have time for it now," Cat said as she pulled one tiny onesie after another to fold out of the laundry basket.

"I'll take care of that part," assured her mom. "You just take care of that beautiful baby and if you find time, write something else. I'll handle the rest."

Twelve weeks later, right at the point where baby Liz was starting to roll herself over, the letter from the agent arrived. They wanted her book. They thought she was a writer. She decided at that moment she was.

CHAPTER THREE

Cat was a particularly good multi-tasker, but it seemed like her entire household was conspiring to break her concentration right then. She was trying out a new recipe that her mom had recently mailed her, and she was having trouble remembering how much of anything she had measured with the dog jumping around and both Nick and Liz vying for her attention.

Sundays were always odd because usually any plans for the weekend that had to get done were covered the day before, and Sunday was too close to Monday to venture very far afield from routine. And it always seemed to Cat that both her husband and her daughter could do without her for most of the day, but when they each did need something they needed it at the same time. Where were either of them when she got back from swimming or around lunch or early afternoon? Why did they both need her while she had spinach cooking and she was measuring out rice and feta cheese?

Nick was having a laundry crisis of some kind that apparently had to be solved before work the next day. Why he hadn't come to her with what appeared to be dried blood stains on his cuffs when he'd gotten home that way on Friday eluded her. Liz wanted a new snowboard which sounded ridiculous in early March when there were already some trees starting to bud again. Spending that much on something that there were only a few weeks left in the season to use was nuts, but Liz thought differently. She also wanted new boots and bindings while she was at it.

"Mom, I just can't use it this way!"

"Well, whose fault is that?"

Cat had come home one afternoon to find Liz trying to re-wax the bottom of the board herself using a regular iron. The heat controls weren't precise enough for the job and Liz had ruined both part of the snowboard and the iron. Cat had originally considered making Liz pay for a new iron out of her allowance, but the girl was so devastated about the board she let it slide.

"It's not just the wax thing, though! I blew out that edge when I was trying to freeride, but freeriding out here is impossible and I hit that rock. So it's really a safety thing, now, see? The board's too hard to control now. You don't want me getting hurt doing a noseslide or something because my board's screwed up do you?"

"Seems keeping you off the snowboard entirely would be the safest thing yet, so not the best angle to use, Sweetie," said Cat.

"Well, what about new boots? And bindings? There's a sale right now and I could at least get something that matches Anna and Jess better. Please?"

"But we just got you new boots and bindings in December! What could possibly be wrong with them already? How about we rewrap the ones you have like it's Christmas again and you can recapture the thrill of owning them all over."

Nick couldn't quite hide a smirk, but it was easy to see that Liz hated it when her mother tried to be funny.

"Mom, I'm not trying to seem unappreciative, but—"

"Well, you're not doing a very good job."

Nick said to his daughter, "Why don't you look into selling your board if it's so important to you, and you could put that money toward the new one and we could cover the rest. And maybe you could help out at the shelter with me for a week and earn the boots and bindings." He turned toward Cat as if that had solved the issue and presented her again with his shirt. "Should I try something on this myself first, or do you have time to do this by tomorrow?"

"But I don't want to give up my old board," complained Liz.

Cat had reached her limit. She loved them both. They both had to leave before she killed them. The thought occurred to her vaguely that in prison she'd have lots of time to write and someone else would do the cooking. No swimming pool, though, so not worth the manslaughter charges.

"Nick, don't touch it because it just makes twice as much work for me later whenever you do. Liz, go call one of your friends and whine about it that way for a while, okay? We can revisit all of these fascinating topics over dinner in an hour, but just, everybody out for a little bit, please," said Cat.

"But Mom, I—"

"Out! I love you, but I can't think."

Liz slumped out of the kitchen and was already pulling her cell phone out of her pocket. Nick was still standing there. Cat looked at him.

"What part of 'I love you, get out' wasn't clear?" she asked.

Nick smiled. "But I'm not whiny."

"But you're needy, and the distinction is very small right now."

Nick sat on a stool and watched her cook for a minute. Cat was absorbed in what she was doing and almost forgot he was there. But then he said, "So this spinach thing looks great and all, but can you maybe sometime do meatloaf?"

She shot him a look as she reached past him for a dish she needed. As he started to go he put a hand on her hip to stop her from moving around for a moment and gave her a kiss. She kissed him back and returned to the counter to check the recipe again.

Cat got back to what she was doing and thought about an upcoming meeting as she rummaged around the spice cabinet searching for nutmeg. She was getting together with her agent the next day to finalize a new contract. Nick had been looking over her old one while doing a bunch of stuff with their lawyer and had gotten some idea in his head about self-publishing rights. She wasn't quite sure why it mattered because she was a solid asset to her publisher that treated her well and she had no plans to go anywhere and had no need to self-publish, but Nick kept saying something about technology and changes in the industry and hedging bets. Cat just wanted to write and had always left the business details to others, so if Nick wanted to hedge bets that was fine by her.

She had also decided to ask her agent's advice on adapting something into a play while she was at it. Cat had called Tom back a few days after he gave her his card and he was ecstatic. They chatted about a possible collaborative effort, so Cat wanted to find out more about how that might work through her agent before she made any decisions on the matter. She was looking forward to working with theater people.

*

"Well," Michelle said, before asking Cat about Liz or life or anything else they might catch up on in the coffee shop, "Nobody likes this clause your husband wants to add about self-publishing rights, and I don't know what kind of bee he's got up his butt after reading some article that makes him think he knows how publishing works, but we've come up with a compromise that should settle things."

Cat sighed. "Nick's just looking out for me. I never really read those things and it's the one way he feels he can be of help with what I do."

"Whatever. It's a pain. Here's the final version you can show your lawyer before signing and you can mail it back anytime before the end of the month." She handed the large envelope to Cat as the barista called out her name to pick up her latte. Once Michelle retrieved her drink she cupped both her hands around it seeming to relish its warmth as she sat down across from her most famous client. "How's Liz?"

"Oh, you know, she's a teenager and she's got her snowboarding clique that turns into a skateboarding clique as the weather warms up."

"Have you ever taken her out to the Rockies?" Michelle asked.

"Not yet, but she's always clamoring to go. She is a deeply deprived child and the only one in her group who hasn't been there because her parents are evil."

"Yes, well you guys have always struck me as crazed and unreasonable," said Michelle.

Cat smiled. "Most of the time Liz is fine, though. Every once in a while she'll forget she thinks we're on opposite teams and just be herself and talk a little, but it's getting harder."

"That's so typical, though. I mean, honestly, Cat, were you any different?"

"I was perfect!"

"That's not how your mom tells it!" Michelle said. "Have you talked to her recently?"

"Not as recently as I'd like."

"You should really learn to use the ridiculous array of social media available to you and stay in touch better. She's trying to figure out who keeps leaving garden gnomes in her little free library, which you would know if you had an Instagram account. Plus you should be doing some of your own promotion."

"That's what you're for."

Michelle took a small sip of her drink and savored it a moment. "Yeah, well, technology is changing everything."

"You sound like Nick."

"Please, I am not over the hassles I went through for him on this contract so don't talk to me about Nick for a while, okay? Hey, where is the bathroom in this place?" said Michelle as she set down her cup and picked up her purse.

Cat pointed Michelle in the right direction and sat back a moment with her tea. That's when she started listening to the conversation happening behind her in the next little sitting area.

64

"No, Stephanie, you're amazing. Honestly, how can you think that?"

"But then, why? I don't get it! Everything seemed so good, right? I mean—"

"I know, I know. It has nothing to do with you. If anyone could make it work right now it would be you! It's just not fair to someone like you to have to deal with this, but the timing is bad. Maybe when I've got things worked out on my end I could still call you?"

There was nothing but sniffling for a moment.

"But why can't I help?"

"Because an amazing girl like you deserves someone who is all together, not someone who needs fixing."

"But—"

"Just give me a chance to be worthy of you, okay? If some lucky guy snatches you up before I have a chance to make things right, then I'll just have to deal with that as my loss, but you deserve the best, Stephanie, really."

"I guess.... Couldn't we just try and—"

"When the timing is better we can. You're amazing for wanting to help. You'll always be special to me, and.... "

Cat didn't notice when her agent sat back down and started talking again. The breakup at the table behind her was fascinating. She wished she were positioned in a way where she could get a peek at the couple without it being obvious, but it wasn't really possible. There was something familiar about their voices, but she couldn't place it.

The girl had to be pretty young to be falling for all of that, but the guy was good. Cat was sure whatever puppy-eyed facial expression he was likely using was putting it over the top, but the words alone, she knew, on paper would look false. She understood enough about dialogue to know what carried its weight on a page and what needed other elements of expression to work. Cat wondered if she handed the girl a transcript right then if she would be able to see all of it more clearly and maybe toss a drink in the guy's face instead of accepting it all so blindly. It probably wouldn't matter to the girl. People believed what they wanted to believe, and the girl obviously wanted to believe whatever lines she was being fed right then.

Michelle snapped her fingers at Cat who hadn't realized she was back. "Hey? Remember me? The one you invited out here?"

"Sorry!" Cat laughed. "I...never mind!"

"I don't know why we ever have meetings in public places. You are hopeless!"

"People ask again and again about where I get my ideas, but if I stop to observe the world a little it's a federal crime," said Cat.

"Can't you maybe observe the people you're supposed to be paying attention to, for a change? Then we'd all be happy."

"You got it. My next book is all about an agent named Michelle, anyway, so that works out fine."

"Don't you dare! I don't want to show up

anywhere in your writing. There's a vicious streak in you that would cause me to worry for myself in one of your stories." She shook her head a little as she sat back in her seat and sipped her coffee.

"I'd protect your fictional self, I swear! Until the ending, anyway."

"Okay, fine. Ignore me and skewer the people sitting behind you instead."

"Ha! So, moving on to other business, how about we talk about adapting one of my existing stories into a play?"

"That sounds interesting," said Michelle, sitting forward again. "Talk to me."

"I introduced myself to the director at the Avenue, and—"

"That cool looking theater down the street from here?"

"Yes, that's the one. Anyway, he put the idea in my head that maybe I could write a play, or at least adapt something dialogue-heavy I've already done into something. It's not an idea I've ever considered before, but the more I think about it the more I like it."

Michelle finished the last bit of her coffee, looking at the empty cup as if it had betrayed her by not lasting longer. "You know, from a writing perspective I can totally see it. I can get you in touch with a couple of editors who specialize in plays and screenplays. Shoot me a short list of which pieces you're thinking of and I'll look into the licensing and rights." She started to gather her things together, then gave Cat a look somewhere between tenderness and concern and added, "From a personal perspective? I think it would be good for you to get out more and doing something collaborative would be great."

Cat was startled. "Hey, I'm out! I'm here almost every day!"

Michelle paused, then smiled affectionately and said, "Yeah, this doesn't count. I think theater people might be good for you."

Cat wasn't sure what to do with that. She gave Michelle a small hug goodbye over the coffee table between them, then watched her leave from her spot at the loveseat.

Cat settled in to do some editing. As she was feeling absorbed in the task of removing the word "very" from as many places as possible in her recent chapter, she became aware that a man was standing across from her.

"Excuse me, but aren't you Catherine Devin?" a familiar voice asked politely.

Cat glanced up from her laptop and felt her jaw actually drop slightly when she saw the handsome face that belonged to the voice. It was Brian Smith from the play standing there wearing a small smile and way more clothes than she was used to seeing him in. His eyes were bluer than she remembered.

"Yes, I am," she answered finally.

"Hey, I am a big fan of your work. Particularly the short stories. *Trees in the Water* is one of my favorites."

Was it Cat's turn to speak? She was pretty sure that's how that worked, but she was feeling star struck. Brian Smith looked different out of character and in normal clothes, but was definitely still the man who had occupied so much of her mind of late. She thought about all the nights she'd gone home from the play imagining her hands on his body and wondered if she were blushing. She felt dirty, since she'd taken this polite boy and objectified him in a manner that she'd spoken out against many times when it was done to women. But wow, he was handsome.

"Well, thank you very much! Most people who come up to me only know the *County Vet* books."

"I've read all of those, too, but the more abstract pieces you do are very interesting. You have a particularly good ear for dialogue. Have you ever considered writing a play?"

"You're the second person to ask me that recently," said Cat.

Brian laughed a little. "Well how many votes do you need before the motion passes?"

"I'm actually a fan of your work, too."

"Yeah?" Brian looked pleased.

"Yes, you were in the Albee play. You were...amazing." He smiled and sat down across from her, setting a script and notepad down on the table between them.

"Well, thank you. That part was challenging. The other male role? The Man? That one was more interesting, though. He had all the best lines and he had to go from engaging to sinister which is more fun to do."

"Why couldn't you do that one?"

"Too young, still. Maybe in ten years. Right now I'm in a niche of shirtless roles I guess."

Well of course he was. Cat found herself marveling at details of him that she wouldn't have been able to see from her seat at the theater. There was a bit of stubble on his jaw and she wanted to touch it enough that she decided to literally sit on her hands. "I wondered what it must have been like for you and that girl to arrive at wardrobe expecting outfits and instead have clothes taken away."

Brian grinned. "It's cold, but it keeps life simple." He tapped the script on the table and added, "I'm hoping Iago wears more than his pajama bottoms, but you never know how creative directors feel like getting with Shakespeare these days."

"Hmm. Well, maybe there's a bigger budget for *Othello*."

"One can only hope."

Cat caught herself blatantly staring again and mentally shook herself out of it. "You really were great in the Albee play. I saw it a few times and I can't believe you could cry like that in exactly the same place each performance."

Brian said, "Yeah, that entire second act was a bit draining because I was supposed to be upset for essentially the whole hour. The tears take practice, but I can do them on cue. It just takes preparation beforehand and some time to shake off afterward, but it's part of the job. It's a weird job, but I can't think of anything else I'd rather do. I've always admired writers, myself."

"Really?"

"Yes, I minored in English and wrote my thesis on Joseph Conrad. I spend whatever spare time I've got with a novel. And when I read I try to read everything that author wrote."

Cat smiled and said, "Well, you haven't read everything of mine, Verlac."

There was a brief flash of both irritation and surprise on Brian's face which made Cat feel like she should apologize, but then he said, "You know, most people could dredge up that Conrad had written *Heart of Darkness* from their high school days, and possibly *Lord Jim,* but I don't think anyone's ever tossed me a reference to *The Secret Agent.* I'll admit to feeling a little outclassed." This would have made Cat fill a bit bad except that he also offered her a crooked smile that was completely endearing. "What of yours do you think I haven't read?"

"It's just that my first novel went out of print a long time ago and didn't do well at all. I think the only copies left are on the shelves of family members, so it's my only book that I never see on Amazon. My publisher never even bothered with a digital version."

"Wait, so *Bending Chance* wasn't your first novel?"

71

Cat was pleased that he did seem to know her less popular work. "No, it actually wasn't, but most people think it was. Wikipedia even has it wrong because the facts there are some kind of group consensus, so the one time I tried to correct it they changed it back the following week. *Bending Chance* was the first one that made it into paperback, eventually. The real first one didn't go anywhere, but it got me rolling."

Brian was lost in thought for a moment and Cat found herself with the opportunity of looking at him again the way she would have if he were on the stage, in front of her simply to admire but not interacting. He snapped out of it and gave his full attention back to Cat. "Where can I find it? I'd be curious to see what got you rolling."

"I have no idea. Other than on my shelf at home. I suppose I could lend it to you sometime if you promise you won't break the spine."

"That would be great, but I really like to own copies of what I read, so give me a chance to see if I can track one down. Sounds like a proper literary quest. What's the title?" He handed her a pad of paper and a pen.

"*Almost There.*" She took the pad of paper and the pen he offered her and noticed all kinds of intriguing notes about the character he was preparing to play. She wrote the information he wanted in the bottom right corner of the page, but then she wanted to keep reading Brian's notes. "Um...."

"Yes?"

Cat glanced up from the notes. Wow he was handsome, she thought to herself again. For a writer she was finding it pretty pathetic that the best thing her mind kept coming up with was "wow" over and over.

"Can I look at your notes here a second, if that's not too nosey?"

"I don't mind a bit."

Cat was interested in the backstory he seemed to be creating for one of Shakespeare's greatest villains. He'd made Iago the bastard child of a drunken wench and a sadistic sheepherder. There were notes about how many women, or possibly men, the character had been with both before and after his marriage. There were lists of the different ways Iago might have caught Othello cheating with his wife, or ways in which he wished he could be with Othello, in addition to odd details like a penchant for neatness and pulling the wings off flies as a child.

"Do you do something like this for every character you play?" she wanted to know.

Brian shook his head. "No, not really. I just don't get Iago's motivation. I suspect he's jealous and wants a woman—or possibly a man—he can't have, but really it's anyone's guess. The play is weirdly vague in that area, because Iago's suggestion that Othello slept with his wife and the whole being passed over for a certain military position in the beginning, don't seem enough to justify the extent he goes to for revenge. I figure he got onto a bad path to start with and no one cared enough to correct it, and it spiraled out of control finally."

"That's interesting. I always chalked him up to pure, unadulterated evil. Some characters are simply bad."

"Well, it's hard for me as an actor to have pure evil to go on. Other factors help if I want him to seem believable."

"Why is that?"

Brian looked at her quizzically. "You know, I've honestly never had anyone ask real questions about what I do. I either hang out with other actors who already sort of know, or sometimes when people are flirting they ask, but it's obvious they don't really care so I don't genuinely get into it."

Cat felt herself blushing furiously but decided to hold his gaze in the hopes that would somehow keep him from noticing how hot her skin was getting.

Brian continued, "I guess, for me anyway, if I have to stand around with a particular expression on my face while someone else is doing lines, real thoughts help create real expressions. People bring several small qualities to their face or body language that as a whole add up to something specific, and I can either try to keep track of all of those things and recreate them, or put myself in that mental place and it just happens—assuming I pick the right thing to think about."

Cat understood that very well. She'd simply never tried to describe any of those things using her own body. She watched people's expressions carefully and found ways to use them on the page.

"And pure evil isn't useful to think about?" Cat asked.

He shook his head again. "Not for me. Besides, what does that really mean? Evil isn't really evil until it causes something bad. Easier to concentrate on the bad thing, or sometimes its opposite, for like, if you are *pro* evil as a character."

Cat contemplated that. Brian had crossed one leg over the other while he was speaking so that his left ankle rested on his right knee. The wear pattern on the bottom of his sneakers didn't go with the fairly new appearance of the rest of the shoes. He must walk a lot. Maybe it was hard for a young actor to afford a car, or maybe like a lot of younger people nowadays he didn't drive. "That sounds like a lot of work."

"No, that part isn't hard, really," said Brian. Cat noticed his brow crease slightly when he caught her gaze as it was leaving his shoe. He continued, "It's easy to stand up there and simply think how much I hate my—hate someone, and my body does the work for me." The small frown hung on his face another second before he selected a smile instead and said, "Or, I could save some effort and grow a mustache to twirl, and bingo! Instant evil."

That made Cat laugh. Nervous as she was, at least she felt like she was holding her own in the conversation. Or so she hoped.

He gave her a crooked smile and stood as he picked up his script and Cat handed him back his notepad. "It was really great meeting you," he said. "I wish I didn't have to get going, but I have a bit of preparation to do for the play that's happening before this one. Maybe I'll see you around sometime?"

"Well, you've discovered my spot, so I guess you will," said Cat trying not to let the pitch of her voice wander too high. "This is like my office in the early afternoon, so writing doesn't feel so confining."

Brian looked down at her and extended a hand. "Yeah, well, Catherine, my schedule's often open around now, so maybe we can continue this conversation again soon. You can help me run lines."

She took his hand and thought how even his grip felt young and warm. "Call me Cat," she said.

Cat couldn't concentrate on her work after the young actor left. She realized that he had neglected to tell her his name, but she already knew very well it was Brian Smith. Compared to his headshot in the program on her nightstand at home she preferred him better up close and in color.

She liked to believe if she were single and in college again that she would have the nerve to talk to someone like Brian at least as well as she'd just done, but she knew she wouldn't have. People liked to think that if they could go back to an earlier stage of their lives and do it over knowing everything they knew now that it would go better. Cat knew for herself that wasn't true.

She'd found that out in an odd way when she visited her daughter's seventh grade class a couple of years back. Cat had been invited to be part of a career day that focused on the arts. One parent was a musician, another a potter, another did photography for the local paper. Cat was the resident writer, and she went feeling unprepared since there was no way to display what she did, but she got through it. Then she joined Liz for lunch in the cafeteria before heading home. Cat and Liz ended up sitting across from a bunch of geeky looking little boys, and at one point one of them glanced at Cat, turned to his friend next to him, and whispered something. Then they laughed.

At that moment Cat's body simply reacted as if she were in seventh grade again. She was embarrassed and self-conscious. It was ridiculous, since she was older and wiser and her popularity or happiness did not hang in the balance of what those boys thought. She couldn't even know for sure they were laughing about her, but her gut reaction was to curl up and hope to disappear.

That was when she realized she would fare no better if given a second go at childhood. Context was everything.

What people thought they would be armed with if they went back to do it again was confidence. But confidence was an illusion. They believed as they got older that they got better, but in reality they customized their environments to suit their comfort levels. They chose with whom to socialize instead of ending up next to their alphabetized partner in line. They chose their transportation instead of enduring the cruel hierarchy of the school bus. They selected where to invest their time and didn't worry about being tested regularly in all subjects. She didn't care what people tried to tell her, trigonometry did not come up in her post-school world and she was fine with being bad at it now that she could be. She didn't have to talk to anyone who ate paste. She could choose where to sit, when to go, what to eat, whom to talk to, and what to do nearly all the time. If she were forced back into junior high among the whispering boys it wouldn't matter how much she knew about running a household or getting a book published. She would be an insecure mess all over again.

The real fantasy would be to combine the best of both worlds. To have youth and opportunity again, but in a customized present. Life didn't work like that, but to really be herself as she was now, and still be available and of interest to someone like Brian Smith, that would be…exciting. But that wasn't reality.

Cat closed her laptop and looked at it fondly. That was why she enjoyed being a writer. Her head, and therefore her computer, was filled with any reality she liked.

CHAPTER FOUR

Cat hadn't thought about her first book in a long time. She had gone home after mentioning its existence to Brian at the coffee shop and found one of her own copies on one of her many bookshelves. She didn't open it; she held it a moment and studied the cover. Her mom had been so proud when it came out. Cat had been, too, but nothing like what her mom felt. Her mom had done all the parts that Cat considered the hard work, such as much of the editing, finding an agent, and dealing with the business end of things the way Nick did now. All Cat had done was make up a story. In her mind the credit for the novel's presence in the larger world belonged to Diane Devin, rather than to her.

It hadn't even mattered to her mom when the

book tanked and hit remainder tables practically before the pages had time to cool. Her daughter was a published author, and Diane now had a book by her to put on her shelf alongside some of the literary creations she held most dear.

When Cat's writing took off into a full-blown career, Diane remained proud, but never seemed quite as proud as after that first publication. Cat had certainly written better and more successful books since, but there was something about a first time that contained a special thrill.

As she glanced along the shelf that contained an advance copy of everything she'd ever published it occurred to her that she didn't know if Nick had ever read all of her books. The *County Vet* ones, certainly, but *Bending Chance*? Or the short stories? She didn't think so. He'd gotten through the first novel slowly and was so upset by it in the middle that he'd put it down for over a week before making himself finish it. He advised her against sending a copy to his mom.

"What's wrong with it?" she'd wanted to know.

"Nothing's wrong, really, that's not fair. It's just, you know, sad."

"Your mom can't handle sad? She's got a dead guy nailed to a cross in every corner of her home! How much sadder can it get? Besides, it's not like it's real."

Nick had frowned and looked uneasy. "But, see, that's kind of the problem. You could write anything, but you chose to write something like that. My mom's not going to understand how your mind could've gone there in order to write it down."

That had made Cat angry, but she kept it contained. "What about you?"

"What about me?"

"Can you understand how my mind could've gone there?"

Nick considered it. "No. Honestly, no I can't. It seems unnecessary."

"It was a plot device!"

"You killed a kid!"

"No, I *made up* a kid, and she met an untimely end! It's fiction!" argued Cat.

"But, you made a conscious decision to have her die and put her parents through hell and—"

"Her *fictional* parents through *fictional* hell! None of it happened, Nick!"

"But you made me feel it like it was real. Why would I want to go through that?"

It was the greatest compliment and the greatest insult she'd ever received. She'd succeeded in making something feel real and been told that she shouldn't have bothered all at once. How do you respond to that? You don't. You cry and leave the room and make your husband feel bad by giving him the cold shoulder for the rest of the evening. Then you make up before going to sleep, apologizing out of necessity.

She placed the book back where it lived on her shelf, and set her mind to figuring out yet another dinner.

*

Cat came to look forward to running into Brian at the coffee shop nearly every day. She didn't get much work done there anymore, but the conversations were worth it. She justified her time with Brian in her mind as research since there were many details she could see using someday in a book. He told her one afternoon about the history of the Avenue Theater, describing the hidden doors and passageways and odd nooks and closets that were the staple of any old theater, and she figured that was useful enough material that sitting there with Brian still qualified as work somehow, even if staring at his cheekbones did not.

She'd never met anyone with a memory as good as his. She could bring up books he hadn't read in years and he could recall all of the important characters. Cat had to admit, though, that as great as the conversations were, often he would be in the middle of some impassioned description and she would simply admire his arms or his chest or the way his neck met his broad shoulders. Brian didn't seem to mind repeating himself when she would admit to having not heard him. He usually gave her a look that was somewhere between bemused and understanding, as if it were a writer thing he should accommodate. It was a lust thing, but he didn't need to know that.

Even if he hadn't been as fun to look at, Cat would have enjoyed their conversations because he caught things no one else had to her knowledge. She made some crack about writing the *County Vet* books on autopilot and Brian disagreed.

"The anagrams," he said simply.

"What?"

"In the names. I know you put thought into those books because there are so many anagrams. Once I caught the first one, I noticed you put them in everywhere. It's this thing you do that made me realize you have kind of a love-hate relationship with writing those particular books that's probably more like hate-hate."

Cat grinned. No one had ever pointed out her anagrams. She thought of them as her own private jokes. "I wouldn't go that far, but yes, that's something I do to entertain myself a little as I go. What was the first one you caught?"

"Seth Poreum," said Brian.

"Oh, the guy who brings in his beloved bird...."

"Yeah," said Brian. "It was such an unlikely name, so when I realized it rearranged into 'Prometheus' I laughed my ass off. All I could imagine was the fate in store for that poor dude once he brought home his bird, now that it was all healthy and ready to peck and peck and peck...."

It was a moment that made Cat happier than her first good review.

One afternoon they were having a particularly nice discussion as they were drinking their tea and laughing, when Brian said casually, "You know, I finally got a hold of a copy of your real first novel."

Cat's eyebrows went up. "Really? Where did

you find that?"

"Oh, the internet is a wonderful thing. You troll around enough you can find anything you desire." Brian continued to drink his tea and didn't seem inclined to say anything more. Was she being teased?

Finally Cat said, "Well?"

"Well what?" She *was* being teased.

"Did you read it?"

Brian looked amused. "Yes, of course I did. I read it straight through the other night, cover to cover." He drank some more of his tea.

"And what did you think?" asked Cat, shifting in her seat with impatience.

"Oh! Sorry, it's great. I just assumed you knew that and didn't need to hear it from me."

Cat smiled despite herself. She hated that she cared what other people thought of her work, but she didn't know how to shake that either. It pleased her when someone she liked appreciated her writing. It was such a lonely, isolated profession without much opportunity for meaningful public recognition. When she constructed a particularly nice paragraph, there was no one around to appreciate her efforts. She liked that a young man who knew his literature found something of value in what she'd done.

"I'm glad you liked it. It was my first attempt at any kind of fiction, so it has a naive quality to it that's kind of fun to look back on."

Brian leaned forward a little. When he talked at

any length he made graceful gestures with his hands that Cat found appealing, and she could see he was preparing to let them move.

"I think especially for a first novel it's really good. I like that it starts off gently, and all the elements of how you handle dialogue later are there. I liked very much how many small threads are tied together over the course of the story. I usually keep track of little details here and there and get disappointed when an author doesn't do anything with them later. It drives me crazy, actually, to drag all that information along through a whole book and to never get to use it. You tied up nearly all the loose ends."

"Nearly all?"

Brian gave her his crooked smile. "You never did explain where the main character gets her first name from."

Cat smiled back. "Some things we never get answers to. That's information I decided Maddie would never have, and the reader doesn't get to have it either."

That apparently interested Brian. "Do you know?"

"That's the funny part about a writer's brain, isn't it? I get to decide things and in that universe it becomes true. The minute I choose to answer that question in any possible way, it becomes real in a sense, so I honestly never pondered the question."

"How can you not? That's like asking someone not to think of pink elephants."

"No, it's like asking someone not to *name* the pink elephants, and that's a murky business because there are lots of choices," explained Cat.

Brian pondered that a moment. "So," he said finally, "when you work, then, how much do you plan out in advance? How do you know what choices you're going to have to make?"

Cat considered the question before finally answering, "It depends on the project, I guess. Some things are very freeform and I see where they take me, and other things are very structured. The *County Vet* books are highly organized before I begin because they need a certain balance to work. They're more about the story. The short stories are not, because they're usually character driven, and sometimes characters decide what they'll do without you."

"How is that possible? You control everything they do, so how do they have any agency?" asked Brian.

"I don't know," said Cat. "They just do. I come up with certain parameters, and then one thing leads to another, and sometimes they lead me somewhere unexpected."

"Hm." Brian seemed as if he was turning several things over in his mind.

Cat opened up her laptop again. "Like, come see," she said as it booted up.

Brian moved across to her loveseat and sat next to her.

Cat clicked around and opened up a couple of

files. "This is a typical outline I use. I've got large sections of the next *County Vet* book done, and I use the outline to go back and fill in the spaces that still need to happen to hold it all together. The reader expects them to flow a certain way and this keeps me kind of reined in."

Brian was absorbed as he studied the screen. He was sitting very close. He smelled good. She wondered if all he could smell on her was chlorine.

"And then here," she continued, opening a different window on the desktop, "is a character sketch for a new story. I gave her a full name and a birthday and a place of birth, etc., and by the time I decide all her hobbies and habits and everything, she kind of starts moving on her own. I'll decide what kind of situation to put her in, and based on all the things I already laid out, she'll react to it. Some of it I make up, and some of it writes itself."

"That's really interesting, Cat," said Brian, still leaning in to better see the screen. Then he sat back a little and looked at her, but he made no move to go back to his original seat. "Did you learn to do that in school?"

Cat shut her laptop and scooted herself away from Brian just far enough that she could turn to face him better on the loveseat. "No, I don't have any formal training in creative writing. This is just how I do it. I have no idea how other people work, to tell you the truth."

Brian looked surprised. "But, how do you know what to do?"

"I don't know. I just do it. And it makes me happy and it comes easily so I keep doing it."

"Huh," he said. "That sounds a little freaky, actually."

"I am what I am," said Cat, who realized with his arm extended the way it was over the back of the loveseat now she could not sit back again without his arm essentially being around her. She scooted slightly forward.

Brian cleared his throat. "So, Cat? I know I said before a while back that some of your work sounded like it could be adapted into a play, but that's especially true of some stuff from your first book. More like a screenplay, actually."

"You really think so?" Cat was flattered.

"I do. I also noticed that I fit the physical description of the Zander character, so I'd like first crack to play him if it comes up if you don't mind."

Cat paused. She supposed he did look like Zander. Actually, it was uncanny, now that her attention had been drawn to it. What did that mean? She dismissed the formless thoughts suddenly darting around her head. Brian was attractive in all the ways that appealed to her, but he wasn't her Zander.

Cat forced a smile. "I guess so, sure. I don't know how that kind of thing works anyway, so don't quit your day job."

Brian said, "I'm sure your agent knows. You should look into it."

"Maybe I will."

They sat in a silence that was unusually awkward for them before Brian cleared his throat again. "So, really, now. I can be Zander. I read through everything to do with his character very carefully and I think I get him."

He sort of gazed past her briefly and he adjusted his posture and put a slightly different set to his jaw. Then he quoted Zander's first couple of lines from chapter one.

"*Duck Soup*! Wow, we saw that, what? 14 years ago, is it? I don't think I've gotten to take you to a movie since.... God, since before Annabel was born. How did we go five years without going to a movie?"

Cat froze. She felt something in her stomach tighten. It was like seeing a ghost. No not a ghost, someone fully back from the dead who shouldn't be there. How did he do that? Of all the characters she'd ever created, Zander was her favorite, the one who was too good to be true. Too good to be real, and now he was sitting next to her, close enough to touch if she chose.

He gave her a Zander smile, which dissolved into a Brian smile again.

"See?" he said.

Cat felt as if all the air had been sucked out of the room. She didn't say anything.

"I was thinking that, if you wanted to, we could trade lines. You could be Maddie."

Cat still didn't say anything. Had that really happened? Had Zander really been there? She didn't know what to think. There was a strange pressure somewhere behind her eyes. She felt like she wasn't seeing things right.

Brian went on, "That way you'd see how well it works off the page. Plus, it could be fun. Like an acting lesson! I'll be your coach."

Cat looked straight into his eyes but wasn't sure what she was seeing.

"Can you do that again?" she wanted to know.

Brian seemed happy. "Sure! This time, though, when I say '14 years ago, is it?', you say 'I'm sure we're not that old, so I'll pretend I didn't hear that,' okay?"

Cat nodded slowly, eyes fixed on his face. He concentrated for a second, and then there was Zander again. He said his line, Cat said hers, and they continued on a bit with Brian feeding her more dialogue as they went.

Cat felt as if she'd entered the *Twilight Zone*. She didn't know if this was good, bad or crazy, but the longer they did it, the more it became fun. She lost all track of everything until a school bus passing by the window caught her eye and she checked her watch.

"Oh my God, I had no idea it was so late! I have to get going before my daughter gets home from school."

Brian looked up at her as she stood and quickly gathered her things. She was agitated but still remembered to put her usual tip in the jar at the counter. She paused for a second before rushing out the door and glanced at Brian. "Um, thanks again. It was...it was fun."

"See you around!" he said with a small wave.

"Okay." And she left without looking back.

Cat drove home in a daze. She reminded herself repeatedly to snap out of it so she wouldn't get into an accident, but it was hard. She kept thinking back to those long afternoons trapped in her bed while pregnant with Liz. She had been so turned on by everything during her second trimester, and it seemed like forever before Nick could come home each night. Cat had poured all of her sexual energy into fantasy, and when the available figures from movies or television or novels didn't suffice, she'd made up Zander. She'd felt guilty at first, because it seemed so much like cheating on Nick. It would have been nice if thinking about Nick had satisfied her at that particular time, but it didn't. And she decided that it wasn't possible to cheat on someone with yourself, which was really what she was doing when she thought about it, so she let the guilt go.

She and her imaginary lover had fun conversations and walks in Paris, and when she had to throw up in the bathroom again and again she imagined him with her being concerned and saying all the right things. Zander found her irresistible and charming and the sex was wonderful. He made her mind a pleasant place to be at a time when it was the only place she could be.

When Nick came home one afternoon with a laptop wrapped with a ribbon, she couldn't imagine at first what he expected her to do with it. His original idea was that she could surf the web and e-mail people and feel more connected to the outside world. He set up everything so all she had to do was plug in and go, but beyond reading the paper online there wasn't much she was interested in.

Then she discovered the word processor. She started out by writing down her Zander fantasy stories as a different way to think about them, and she always deleted them before Nick came home. She discovered writing made the days go much faster.

Then she decided to make up more people whom maybe she didn't have to delete every night. She thought about how much she missed having friends to talk to, so she invented two friends and let them talk instead. She poured into her story all her fears about actually having to raise the baby in her belly. Eventually she decided to give Zander to her main character. She missed him and wanted him involved in a project that seemed to be developing into something important. She retooled him to only love Maddie and it was a little like a breakup.

She hadn't really thought about Zander in that way in a very long time. Cat realized that he was younger in the book than she was now. She didn't want to picture him aging, so he hadn't, but it seemed unfair that she had to.

Cat pulled into her driveway and sat in the car for a moment. It had been incredible watching Brian act Zander out. She had a crazy flash of herself lying on her bed like a teenager and calling him up and asking if he wanted to come over. She wanted to prop Brian up at the footboard and make him be Zander over and over like she was rewinding an old tape.

Liz knocked at her car window and made her jump.

"Mom?"

Cat was embarrassed for having been startled, then reached over to grab her bag off the passenger seat before opening the door to get out.

"Hey, Sweetheart! How was school?"

"Fine, I guess. What were you doing?" Liz had a questioning look on her face that she got directly from Nick. Lots of Nick's features and facial expressions were easy to see in their daughter. No one would ever question his paternity.

"Just thinking."

They walked together to the front door, each with her own bag slung over her left shoulder.

"About a new book?" Liz asked.

"Actually, about an old one. Someone told me today he'd read my very first book. The one I wrote when I was pregnant with you. It's just funny to think back like that and, I don't know...remember who I was then."

Liz seemed already bored with that topic and wanted to know if she could go to McDonald's with some friends rather than eat another home cooked meal. They had the same argument they always had about good nutrition and family time and Liz ended up in her room with her cell phone and the dog while Cat started pulling things together to make another dinner no one seemed to want.

She opened the fridge and realized there was chicken she needed to use up, and half an onion. She pulled those out. She could roast some broccoli... she thought there was some whole wheat pasta still in the pantry....

Almost on cue as she started heating a bit of olive oil in a pan, Pogo appeared at her feet. The only time that dog loved her more than he loved Liz was when Cat was cooking chicken. She rubbed his head and asked, "Would you like a chunk of broccoli?" Pogo's ears drooped and he looked at her as if she'd lost her mind. Cat laughed and then continued chopping. She knew Pogo wasn't going anywhere until it was clear all hope was lost that the chicken might hit the floor, and then he would go right back to shadowing Liz.

If only Cat could teach the dog to report back. She monitored Liz through scraps of information that came through the laundry room via unchecked pockets, and occasional eavesdropping when her friends were over, but unless Cat wanted to tap into her daughter's phone she knew she wasn't getting a clear picture of whatever Liz might be up to. Cat wasn't ready to go that far into spy territory.

Still, maybe she should. Teenage years were hard. Being young in general was harder than most people wanted to admit. Cat had always considered herself above romanticizing those years since she remembered how hard they could be, but closing in on 40 was having an effect.

That was surely part of Brian's appeal, the fact that he made her feel she had access to that earlier version of herself again. The person who could have taken a different path. Maybe she was seducing herself into believing those different realities were still open to her. She pushed that idea to the side and started chopping what was left of her onion into pieces that were probably too small.

CHAPTER FIVE

The acting lessons began slowly.

The meetings at the coffee shop went from
being a semi-regular thing to part of each of their
daily routines. Sometimes Cat would try to do some
actual work and Brian would stretch himself out on
the opposite loveseat and read. But little by little
more of their time turned to Brian trying to teach
Cat about how to do his craft, even if neither of
them thought it was going particularly well in terms
of actually getting Cat to act.

"Seriously, Cat, how can you be that observant
about people and not get what I'm saying?" he
asked, slumping back in his seat while looking like
he was trying hard not to laugh. "I mean, do you
know how many classes there are on learning to see

how people behave in certain circumstances? You could cross signals by using your voice one way, but your body another, blah blah blah, and you get all of that already. For a lot of people that's the hard part and you've got that shit down. But then..."

"What am I not doing right this time?" Cat asked, amused that he looked annoyed but wasn't really annoyed.

"I don't know, you're so inhibited about doing anything consciously with your body. Let's go back to concentrating on only your face." Brian sat up. He was straight across the table from Cat and he leaned forward with a small grin.

"Oh, not smiling again. Brian this makes me feel so stupid."

"You can do it. I mean, come on, you've got a beautiful smile to work with. Your parents obviously sprang for braces, so let's make sure they got their money's worth here."

Cat laughed and smiled for real.

"See?" said Brian. "That. When the smile reaches your eyes it looks real. If you smile without it reaching your eyes you look like a psychopath."

"Who did you get your lessons from, Tyra Banks?" Cat resisted the urge to stick her tongue out at him. As young as he made her feel sometimes, that was regressing too far.

"Yes, you're really funny. And, no, her thing is about smiling with just your eyes. You're not up for that yet."

"Why not?"

"Just trust me. Okay, so relax your face, and when I cue you, pretend you're smiling at someone next to you. Ready?"

"No."

"I don't care, do it anyway. Go!"

Cat turned to the imaginary person on her right and bared her teeth a bit while feeling ridiculous. Was acting really just not caring that you looked like an idiot?

"Lordy, Cat, seriously, haven't you ever had to fake a smile at a dinner party or something? Why are you making your eyes wider?" Brian laughed and rocked backward again.

"I'm not!"

"You are! God, this is insane. All you have to do is think of something funny, and you find weird things funny all the damn time, so why can't you make your invisible friend funny? Wait, let's just..." Brian got up from his side of the table and seated himself next to her. "Okay, smile at *me*. Go!"

Cat tried another nervous smile with lots of teeth but a self-conscious look in her eyes that would convince no one of any true mirth. Brian apparently couldn't resist literally tweaking the situation, and he reached out and tickled her side. Cat let out a tiny shriek of surprise which caused someone waiting at the counter to glance over. But she did laugh, and she did truly smile.

"Yeah, *that*!" said Brian. "I want that."

"Fine fine fine. Can we run lines again? I like the parts of acting that are really about reading, not doing the body things."

"You know at some point we're going to combine those parts, right?"

Cat took those words someplace else in her head for a moment.

"Wait, so now you're smiling at nothing," he said. "This is like herding—"

"Don't say it. So, really, can we just do lines for a bit now?"

Brian looked at her closely for a moment, as if he knew something she didn't. "Sure," he said finally. "So... Do you want to be everyone but Iago in *Othello*, or do you want me to... for us to be Maddie and Zander again?" He didn't bother reaching for his script on the table.

"Do you mind?" asked Cat.

"Not at all, but I was wondering if you'd mind maybe writing some new scene for them to do?"

Cat cocked her head a little. "What do you mean?"

"I don't know. Maybe actually get in some practice at writing an actual play by having them do something new? We've read through certain parts of chapters so many times, but it's not structured right for this, really. Aren't there, like, places in between where they could walk together and discuss the future or something? Where the action doesn't get interrupted because you're in someone's head instead of doing stuff?"

Cat mulled it over in her mind momentarily. "Sure, I could do that."

Brian grinned. "That would be great! So maybe in a week or something we can—"

"No, give me a minute," said Cat. She had her laptop open already and was typing quickly.

"Wait, what? What are you doing?"

"I'm writing a new scene. Should take about fifteen minutes? Give or take?"

"How is that possible?" Brian looked incredulous.

"I told you, I'm a fast writer. It won't be perfect and if it's worth saving I'll fix it up later, but drafts are fast, so if you don't mind reading a draft...."

"Damn. I mean, it takes me forever just to get one good page down."

Cat stopped typing and looked up from her computer at him. "Wait, Brian, you write?"

"No, I very slowly put words together on pages that never turn into anything. It's hard."

"No it's not."

"Yes it is!"

Cat was dumbstruck. "How has this not come up before? Why are these lessons going only one way? Okay, this we are discussing later, but right now let me finish this."

She started typing again quickly, and at some point when she realized Brian was simply watching her with a slightly stunned look on his handsome face she said, "Brian, maybe go get us more tea and see if there are any oranges left for sale on the counter."

After closer to twenty minutes Cat seemed

satisfied that she'd come up with something ready to try out. Brian sat pressed against her slightly so he could read the words off her screen, rather than asking her to hand him the laptop so he could quickly memorize what was there. As he tested the lines quietly in his mouth close to her ear Cat tried to keep her breathing slow and even.

"Huh," said Brian, after he'd read through it all twice. "That's...that's kind of amazing. That works."

"It's almost like I'm a professional or something," said Cat. "Maybe I could make a living at it."

"Oh, come on, you know that's weird. Did you already have that in your head or some part of it planned?"

"Kind of, since I know the characters already and what they are likely to say. You plunk them in a park and you know Maddie's going to look at the trees and Zander will look at the composition of the path and keep monitoring Maddie to make sure she's okay. I just let them do their thing."

Brian started to ask her something when suddenly Cat looked at her watch.

Brian sighed. "Is the imaginary school bell that's hooked up to your temporal lobe going off again?"

Cat really didn't like to remind Brian that she was married and had a teenage child, but sometimes there was no way out of it. "Yeah, well..." Cat never knew what to say when she had to go home to be there for her daughter and to make dinner. "Tomorrow?"

"Tomorrow."

After a couple more weeks of playing the roles of Maddie and Zander at the coffee shop, the guilt was getting more intense and somehow this translated into Cat deciding to finally make Nick that meatloaf.

"So you made what now?" he asked as he kicked off his shoes in the front hall after work, leaving them in a jumble halfway onto the mat with his daughter's sneakers.

"Meatloaf. You're always asking if I can make your mom's meatloaf, so I dug out that recipe card she wrote out for me years ago and actually did it," said Cat as she set out the asparagus she'd made to go on the side. She turned toward the stairs and yelled, "Liz! Your dad's home! Come on down to dinner please!"

From a distance they heard, "But I already went to McDonald's with my friends!"

"What? When?" Cat yelled back, deeply annoyed.

"While you were out at the grocery store!" called down Liz.

"Well why—? Wait, just get down here, I am tired of yelling up the stairs!"

"Why should I come down if I'm not going to eat?"

"Oh, you're going to eat!"

Nick dropped his jacket over a chair that was fewer than two feet from the coat hooks, and came to the table, unfazed by the conversation being shouted up and down the stairs.

"Fine!" yelled Liz as she noisily made her way down to the dinner table, Pogo at her heels.

"Great. Finally. Sit. We're having meatloaf."

"Why?" asked Liz.

"What do you mean, why?" asked Cat.

"Like, why? You never make meatloaf. What's wrong with it?"

Before Cat could respond in a way she might regret, Nick jumped in. "I think she means, is it my mom's actual recipe, or did you substitute mushrooms or something for the meat?"

"Seriously?" asked Cat. "I can't make meatloaf without it being suspicious? Should I just save myself the hassle and stop making dinner altogether from now on?"

"Yes," said Liz.

"No! No, Liz tell your mother you didn't mean it. You're being really rude," said Nick.

Liz shot an exasperated look at her mom, but then glanced at her dad and said quietly, "Sorry."

Cat sighed and started slicing up the main course. "I'm sorry too. Although I'm not sure for what." She decided secretly it was for putting pureed carrots into the meatloaf.

*

As much as Cat felt she should probably find a way to back out of the arrangement, she was enjoying her time with Brian every day too much to do anything about it. Then he suggested maybe she should try a real acting class.

"I can't do something like that! It's too...I don't know! I'm not that brave."

"I think you're a lot braver than you give yourself credit for. When you do Maddie at this point it's natural and convincing so you can obviously do a character. You just need time on a real stage to get used to it."

"I don't know. I think some people can do it and some people can't. I'm in the 'can't' group, and that's fine because people like you who can, need someone out there to buy tickets and clap," said Cat.

"Well, anytime you're up for it, I have a key to the Avenue and we can go stand on that stage by ourselves and you can try it out."

"Now, that just sounds scary," said Cat.

"It's not any scarier than anything we're doing now, I swear!"

"For you."

Brian studied her a moment. Then he moved across to the loveseat to sit next to her and said, "I've been working on a new interpretation of a Maddie and Zander scene—the one at the end of chapter five. Do you want to try it?"

Cat shifted in her seat.

"I don't know, Brian, I haven't gotten any work done lately and really should be trying to finish this chapter I'm on, and...."

Brian simply launched in anyway. He took a second and adjusted his posture and gave her a warm, confident Zander look. "Hey, I was wondering what happened to you after you put the girls to bed. Come see something for a sec."

In the book, Maddie goes over to Zander at that point and sits in his lap, and Cat was tempted to slide herself on over, but she stayed glued to where she was. It blew her mind all over again that after inventing hundreds of people compiled from her scraps of observation and her own imagination, that one of her first could be sitting next to her. And not just any character, but the perfect character. Looking at Zander gave her goosebumps. It was hard for her sometimes to remember it was really Brian.

Cat opened her mouth to say something, but nothing came out.

Brian was still in character but deviating from the story. "What's wrong? Cat got your tongue?"

The pun snapped her out of it. "Look, I...I don't think we should be doing this here anymore."

Brian was back and Zander vanished. Cat was sad to see him go. "Which? The 'this' or the 'here'?" Brian asked.

"What?"

"You don't want to do *this*, or you don't want to do it *here*?"

"I'm not sure. Both. Neither."

Brian looked at her thoughtfully for a moment. "Well, I think we should walk down the street to the Avenue. It would be nice to stretch our legs a minute, and I can show you what the stage looks like when it's deserted and you can conquer one of your fears."

Cat was unsure. How far did she trust this man? Boy, really. He was like a trinity to her, consisting of Boy, Brian and Zander.

He gave her the crooked smile that was so cute. "Come on," he said. "I think it would be good for you."

It suddenly occurred to her why that smile was so endearing. Brian's features were so perfect he was in danger of appearing cold, like a Greek statue. The lopsided smile broke up the otherwise flawless symmetry of his face and made him seem approachable and real. Cat wondered if he knew that and used it consciously in the world and not only on stage where necessary.

She glanced at her watch and decided she was well past the point of being productive that afternoon, and there was still over an hour before she should be home when school let out. Why not try something new? If she was seriously considering trying to write a play she should learn more about it. It was research.

She started packing up her laptop and took a last sip of her tea. "Okay. But don't expect a song and dance number because even in private that's not happening."

Brian laughed and grabbed his own stuff, and held the door for her as they left.

The Avenue Theater was locked up and lifeless at that time of day. Brian took her around the back way and opened a door that led to the backstage area near the dressing rooms. He flipped a couple of switches on a board near some pulleys, and lights popped on all focused at the stage. It was eerie with no one in the building. There was a set that looked like a living room complete with a couch and a rug and a television. Brian stepped out amongst it all like he actually lived there, which in a way he did. He gestured for her to come join him. She walked out into the lights but was seized by a sense of dread.

Cat was too nervous to sit on the real stage set, even in a completely empty theater. Brian wasn't going to push it, but he finally coaxed her into sitting backstage where some of the props were waiting in the wings, including a bench with cushions on it.

"See? Nothing to be scared of. It's the same as playing house when you're a kid, only with bigger and better stuff," said Brian, and he took a seat on the bench in the shadows.

"I suppose." Cat was nervous. She suspected she was projecting most of her fears about the dangerous game she'd been playing with Brian onto the whole theater scene. Part of her felt she should go home, but another part of her thought that if she wasn't technically doing anything wrong, why shouldn't she be entitled to some fun? So her mind had been straying from her husband more than usual. It was her mind, and he wasn't entitled to everything in it. She didn't want to know about his fantasies. If talking with an actor helped fulfill some of hers, where was the harm?

Brian sat on the bench patiently.

Cat joined him and they sat there together for a moment, and eventually Cat said quietly, "Can you do Zander again?"

Brian smiled and turned toward her slightly. "Yeah?"

Cat nodded.

"What kind of scene do you want to do? Something from the book, something new?"

Cat wasn't sure. He did Zander so well sometimes it amazed her that she had come up with the character without ever having seen Brian. Of course, when she had invented the character, Brian would have only been nine years old. That made her wince.

"You know, we could.... I don't have a problem with doing the scene of their first kiss," suggested Brian.

Cat was startled. "What?"

Brian laughed a little. "I'm an actor. You've watched me kiss people on stage. You know it doesn't have to mean anything! It's just a very compelling scene in your book and it doesn't scare me to do it. I have that whole chapter memorized. It might be an interesting experience for you, is all."

Cat's mind was racing. She wanted to, but it was definitely over the line. Kissing someone in her mind was one thing, but to make it real was wrong. She couldn't do that to Nick. Nick trusted her. Nick loved her.

"I...I don't think that's a good idea, Brian, I mean, I'm...." Cat couldn't bring herself to say the word "married," but she wasn't sure why not.

"That's fine," said Brian without a hint of judgment in his voice. "You know, we could do the scene and leave out the kiss. It's all the same to me."

Cat thought about that a moment. That didn't seem wrong. If they didn't actually kiss, it wasn't betrayal or cheating. Part of her realized it still wasn't good, but she thought she could live with it at least. It could be interesting. She knew it would be fun.

"Umm...."

Brian simply started. He put on his Zander smile and squared off his shoulders a bit more. He appeared a little uncertain and started quoting from the middle of chapter three. "So, which bed is mine?"

Cat looked into those beautiful blue eyes and found herself saying quietly, "The one by the window. Here, let me move all this stuff."

Brian softly and unobtrusively started reciting the narration verbatim. He could seamlessly come forth as Zander for a line or two, then go back to narration without it seeming affected or odd. Cat listened to her story being recited to her and it reminded her of being read to as a child. She felt comforted by the familiarity of the words combined with the strange thrill of the dark. She didn't always remember exactly what Maddie's lines were here or there, but Brian always adapted effortlessly.

Finally, the scene rolled around to Maddie showing Zander her sketches while they sat on her bed in her dorm room and they were supposed to kiss. Brian leaned in slightly and met her gaze and then he waited.

Cat couldn't move. He was so close she could feel the heat from his body. She didn't know what to do.

Then Brian started whispering to her. "You've always wanted to kiss Zander, haven't you? What would that first kiss really feel like? It's just acting. Your body is just a tool. Exploring new experience through acting is no different from doing it on the page, because it all starts in your mind. If you've already kissed Zander in your mind what's the harm? You created him. He belongs to you. If I can simulate that kiss so that you can finally feel it, it's still an experience you created. I'm just following your direction. Zander is yours, and you know I understand how you want him. Don't be afraid. Don't let this opportunity go to waste. If you want to kiss Zander and have him kiss you back, this is the time."

Cat felt dizzy. Maybe it wasn't wrong. It wasn't like an affair; it was one kiss in a theater. And she wouldn't really be kissing a real guy, she would be kissing Zander and Zander was hers and she carried him around with her everywhere anyway. She might never have a chance like this again. What would she regret more? One small kiss, or a missed opportunity? Her husband never had to know. Was there really any harm?

Brian leaned in a bit closer and said even more softly, "When you're old and grey do you want to look back on this moment and remember a kiss, or regret that you never found out something you always wanted to know?"

That finally pushed Cat over the edge. It was such a small thing, and the world would not be destroyed over such a simple thing as one kiss. She closed her eyes and leaned toward him slightly.

Brian leaned in the way Zander would have, and held her face in his hands gently. The kiss was soft and warm and sent shock waves up and down Cat's body. It was exactly the way she had imagined it should be, but it was alive and real and not like the phantom kiss she'd always conjured up in her mind. She kissed him back and felt a clawing in her body like something wanted to get out.

Brian slowly pulled his hands back and waited. He smiled when she opened her eyes again and said, "There, now was that so bad?"

Cat shook her head. She felt guilty, but it had been wonderful, and she couldn't undo it now anyway. That die had been cast and she had to live with it, for better or worse, so she may as well try to make it for the better.

Brian laughed a little. "One fewer hurdle to jump! I'll make an actor out of you yet, you'll see."

She smiled, but she didn't feel well. "I'd better go, Za—*Brian*. It's getting late."

He gave her a concerned look. It was a very Zander look and she couldn't tell if he was trying to do it that way or not.

"Hey, are you all right?" he asked.

Cat nodded but didn't say anything and her eyes were cast vaguely toward the floor.

Brian put a hand on her shoulder and moved his head around until he caught her gaze and she was looking straight at him. "Hey, listen, if you weren't ready for that I'm sorry. We don't ever have to bring it up again, okay? Are we still friends?"

Cat looked at him and felt confused. "Is that what we are?"

"Uh, sure," he finally managed. "Sure, if that's what you want."

Cat had no idea what she wanted. She could still taste him on her lips and part of her simply wanted more of that, but part of her was screaming at her to go home to.... Why couldn't she remember her husband's name? Nick! It was Nick and she had to go home to him. She had to go home to him and kiss him with the same lips that had just kissed Zander-come-to-life. What had she done? Part of her wanted to take it back and part of her wanted to do it again. She felt like she might rip in two.

"Cat?"

She didn't speak.

"Cat, hey, I'm playing a role, but if you'd rather just deal with the regular me at the coffee shop I'm fine with that. We can do or be whomever you choose."

She made herself smile but knew from earlier "lessons" she was doing it wrong. "I'm okay. I just...it would be nice to be as free as you are in the real world. I'm only used to being free on my laptop, and it's...."

Brian waited for her to finish, but she only said the word "lonely" in her head.

"That's okay. You don't have to explain yourself to anyone as far as I'm concerned," he said. "We only get one life that I can tell, and I don't want to miss any of it. I'd hate to see you miss out on any of it. You should never feel guilty about living the kind of life you want. It's yours."

Cat sat quietly for a moment. She was going to have to think that over.

"I have to go," she finally said.

Brian touched her lightly on the arm. "Are we okay?"

"Yeah, sure. I'm...I'll see you at the coffee shop sometime."

She got up and headed for the door. She didn't know if she wanted him to follow her or not, but he didn't. Cat couldn't decide if she felt like laughing or crying, so she did neither.

CHAPTER SIX

Cat decided not to go back to the coffee shop. She would work at home.

Her head was reeling. Instead of puzzling through her normal work problems as she swam or sat at her desk she kept circling back to how she could be with Brian and still have it be fair to Nick as if that made any sense at all. Was the kiss a bad thing or not? Of course it was bad. What rational person wouldn't think it was bad? But she didn't want it to be bad.

She had made love to Nick once that week, but she couldn't decide if she should be using all the sexual tension she was feeling or suppressing it, because she didn't want him to suspect anything. In the end Nick had done what he usually did and

114

didn't seem to notice anything out of the ordinary. Cat found herself in bed afterward feeling cheated and resentful.

On top of everything she could feel her 40th birthday coming up on the calendar as if it were stalking her. Part of her had never really accepted that she wouldn't get her youth back at some point. The rest of her life was going to be exactly like this but older and older and even more familiar. It made her desperate and frustrated. She also felt greedy and ashamed. She could not have asked for a better life and she still wanted more.

Why did it have to be wrong to explore something that was purely physical? If she got a massage because it made her body feel good, that was okay, but simply because she wanted someone to rub other parts of her too, suddenly it was a condemnable offense.

Of course, did she feel Nick was entitled to the same feelings? Certainly not. The idea of anyone else pawing all over Nick was disturbing and unacceptable. That should have clarified everything for her right on the spot, but then her mind wasn't particularly clear anymore. It was a quicksand of desire and guilt. She was aware of a whole different biological clock ticking and it was deafening.

Eventually she had to venture out into the world again because she had a meeting with Tom Olsen at the Avenue. According to the note Nick had left on her desk, the director had supposedly narrowed his play idea down to two short stories he wanted to discuss with her, and he was still interested in the idea of doing something with the *County Vet* books which she was hoping to discourage (although Nick had that part underlined to show he approved of the concept). The whole time she was getting dressed for the meeting she couldn't decide if she wanted to run into Brian or if she didn't.

When she walked into the theater her heart was pounding and she didn't feel well. She didn't see anyone there at first, but then spotted a stagehand backstage who was able to point her toward the director's office. Cat went around to the small room in the back and found Tom.

"Hello!" he said cheerfully as he looked up from his desk. It was covered with heaps of paper in precarious piles. Cat couldn't imagine trying to work like that. She didn't even like it when her computer desktop appeared cluttered.

"Hi," she said as she glanced around for a clear surface to sit on.

"Oh dear, I know, it's shameful, isn't it? Let me find you a spot." He removed a stack of old playbills from an overstuffed armchair and she sat down and crossed her legs.

As Tom went back behind his desk and fussed with more piles he said, "I really think you could have something here. Either the story about the woman stranded overnight at the truck stop, or the one about the couple getting the wrong baby and deciding to keep it could be incredible on stage! They both take place in limited settings so they work in a static environment, and the conversations are compelling."

"I still don't have a clue how to add in things like stage direction," said Cat. "And so much happens in the characters' heads that's necessary to understanding what's going on that I don't see how it would make sense as something to watch."

Tom nodded. "I understand what you're saying, but there are ways around that. Plus you have to give the actors some credit for getting into a character's head and communicating what they're about without having to say anything sometimes."

Cat certainly knew that was true. She could hear other people starting to file into the building and someone talking by the stage.

"So, Catherine, I have a proposal. I have a couple of scripts here for you to read and get a sense of how a play is laid out in a form we can use, and then you pick the story you want to adapt and take a stab at it. Don't try to make it complete, just take it as far as you're comfortable, then we can work together to fill in the blanks."

Cat nodded. That sounded not only doable but rather entertaining. Tom handed two scripts over to her. The one on top was *The Play About the Baby*.

"I think it would be an exciting experience for you to see your characters come to life," said Tom with a smile.

Cat looked at him a moment and finally said, "I'm sure it would."

As Cat left Tom's office she wondered how long

it would take before her seat was engulfed with paper again. The activity on the stage caught her attention as she passed it from the wings. The stage was lit and there were several people on it. She stood to watch for a moment. They weren't doing real acting; they were standing around while people called things out toward someone standing in the audience and the lights changed slightly. She walked closer out of curiosity and didn't notice that she was standing in a patch of light a bit offstage.

She spotted Brian. He was in shorts and a t-shirt, and he seemed to have some kind of part as a delivery guy. He had boxes he was supposed to carry and bend down for, and they kept making him stop and hold still while people made adjustments and decisions she couldn't see. He was particularly beautiful to look at on stage. He really belonged there.

At some point Brian was laughing with another person standing near him when he glanced over and saw Cat. He smiled and gave her a small nod.

Cat felt her stomach flutter, then clench up. She glanced around briefly for her backstage bench but it wasn't there now. She looked at the plays in her hands and began flipping through one of them as she walked toward the door to the street.

She hadn't gotten more than about half a block from the theater when Brian ran up next to her.

"Hey!" he said, panting a little as he slowed down by her side.

"Hi," she said, trying not to sound nervous.

"Don't you have work to do in there?"

"I'm done for a while. I only have a small walk-on part in this one. I'm more of a prop than anything else, but at least they gave me a shirt this time."

Too bad, thought Cat.

They walked a bit in silence, sort of hurrying but for no apparent reason.

When it was clear Cat wasn't going to speak Brian finally said, "So what are you up to?"

"I have some plays to read through so I can figure out how to adapt a couple of my short stories for the stage."

"Which stories?" he asked with interest.

"*Refills on Everything* and *Keeping Amber*."

Brian nodded as they continued to walk. "Good choices. Particularly the truck stop story—lots of good roles in that and you'd only need one set."

"Boy, you really do know my work," said Cat.

"I do."

They walked on in silence a bit longer and their pace slowed as it started to become obvious that Cat didn't have a destination. They were a long way from the coffee shop.

"So, you haven't been around," Brian finally said.

"Busy," replied Cat without looking at him.

They stopped at an intersection where they remained for a while since Cat couldn't decide which way to go.

"Hey, I know you usually need to eat around

this time," said Brian as Cat kept studying each of the various directions available but not moving. "I know a place you might like where I can grab a burger but they also have, like, kale things."

"I really should read through these scripts. I don't have any idea what I'm doing." Cat finally looked at him.

Brian smiled. "All I do is read through scripts! Let me help. I see you even have the Albee play. I could recite that to you while you read it and you could get a sense of how someone interprets what's happening on the page in order to use it on a stage."

Cat was unsure.

"Strictly business," said Brian.

Damn that crooked smile, thought Cat. "Fine! Fine," said Cat as she watched that smile broaden.

Brian led her off to an area she was more likely to drive straight through if she were on her own. It was gritty in a way her more manicured side of town was not. At a walking level the grittiness turned out to be artsiness and youth. A few times Brian would nod or wave at people he apparently knew. Cat wondered what the two of them looked like together. Maybe people thought he was out with his aunt.

They reached a small restaurant on a corner with bad art for sale on the walls (all of which were by the same artist who was apparently in a blue thermometer period, which made it appear to Cat as if a variety of winter fundraisers were being tracked everywhere), and found a table in the middle of the room. As they sat, Brian handed her the menu since he didn't need it.

"You promised me kale things I believe," said Cat as she studied it. Was the print extra small, or was she starting to need glasses? God no please not glasses yet.

"Bottom right—lots of stuff there I never get but you might like."

"What do you get?"

"They've got a really good cheeseburger, and if Ashley is here she always gives me extra fries."

Cat didn't like Ashley.

"Well," she said, "How about I meet you halfway and do the veggie burger? And you can have my fries if Ashley's not here."

Ashley wasn't there, but magically Sophie (with a heart over the "i") knew to put extra fries on Brian's plate, and he also got a shake he didn't order.

"Shall we look over these plays?" Brian asked between bites.

"Sounds good," said Cat.

*

Almost immediately they fell back into their old routine at the coffee shop, minus the Zander/Maddie acting practice. They didn't discuss it, or the kiss at the Avenue. They were friends, and friends hung out in public, and that was totally fine and acceptable and there was no reason to feel guilty about any of it, right? Right. Didn't matter what she did with her friends in her mind. That was none of their business.

Brian finished the play with his small walk-on role and was busily preparing for *Othello* so Cat saw him less for a while. But he had a day off before the first full rehearsal and after a few minutes in the coffee shop, where he kept glancing out the window at the beautiful weather outside, he convinced her to take a walk with him instead of sitting inside. They were a few blocks past the Avenue in a new direction where there was more sun, when Brian took off his jacket. Cat noticed a stain on his t-shirt. She frowned.

"What?" he asked.

"Nothing, it's just, you've got a bit of something...never mind."

He looked down at his chest with surprise. "Damn! I need to do laundry and I wasn't paying attention this morning. Do you mind if I run up and change my shirt?"

"Run up where?" asked Cat.

"My apartment's right there. Why don't you come on up with me? It will just take a minute and then we can walk over to the bookstore together."

Cat was torn. "Why don't I meet you at the bookstore?"

"You can if you want, but really, it won't take more than two seconds. Besides, shouldn't I soak this or something? Do you know what to do?" He scowled at his shirt and scratched at the stain.

Cat peered at his shirt for a moment and said, "It looks like ketchup. Cold water and a decent stain remover might work, but on light cotton like that you might be stuck."

"Maybe I'll douse the whole thing in ketchup and it will be uniform."

Cat laughed. Maybe a quick trip up to Brian's apartment wouldn't hurt. She was curious to see where he lived anyway, and it would just be for a minute.

Brian unlocked the door at the street between a law office and a florist and they walked up the narrow staircase to the second floor. The next thing she knew they were standing in Brian's small apartment together. The windows were open wide to let in the spring sunshine and some air, and the busy sounds from the street filtered up from below.

Cat was astonished at the number of books. It might not have been as big as her own collection, but packed into a smaller space it looked close. The place was tidy and there wasn't really anyplace to sit other than on the daybed which seemed to separate the kitchen area from the rest of the room.

"Give me a sec, okay?" said Brian as he set his keys down and proceeded to take off his shirt. Cat tried not to look startled and marveled for the thousandth time how actors could be so unselfconscious with their bodies. Of course, with a body like that, why wouldn't he be? When Brian had his arms up over his head she found herself following the line of his side down to his hip. There was nothing remotely flabby there, only taut beautiful skin over muscles where she was sure her husband didn't have any. Her husband. What would he think of this? He would be panicked, she realized. The thought caused her pain and she glanced away from the alluring young body and back toward the door.

Brian tossed the shirt into a very full laundry basket in the corner and walked off into what she assumed was the bedroom. He left the door open and called out to her, "Have a seat! It's going to be a moment before I find something clean."

Cat looked around at the books instead. There were shelves on every wall, some of them makeshift things out of cinder blocks and two by fours. Most of it was fiction, there were a lot of plays, and there was one bookcase that consisted of biographies and textbooks on psychology and philosophy. All of it was carefully alphabetized and neatly arranged. Cat couldn't resist looking through the D's, and sure enough, there was a whole shelf of her work. Several of them were paperbacks, but most of the short story collections were in hardcover. It was kind of nice to see. The only other person she knew with a shelf like that was her mother.

She gently pulled the copy of her first novel off the shelf by coaxing it out from behind and then holding it past the sides of the spine. People pulling at books by crushing the top of the spine and prying on it was one of her pet peeves. None of Brian's hardcovers looked as if they'd been mishandled in that way. She flipped through to the back, and then carefully returned it to its home on the shelf.

"See, I told you I have all your work!" said Brian coming up from behind her. She turned to see him putting on a dark blue t-shirt. Cat felt a pang as she watched the fabric slip over his well defined abs. She shouldn't be there. Brian had been remarkably good at continuing to interact with her while seeming to have tactfully erased the whole incident from the theater, but that made him more attractive to her, not less.

Cat laughed. "Well, not quite, but it's close!"

Brian raised an eyebrow and looked at her disbelievingly. "What am I missing now?"

"Oh, it's...never mind. You have enough."

"No, tell me! I really want to know."

"Well, it's just that among the many problems along the way with that first novel, there was a change made halfway through printing. My editor decided to add an extra chapter I'd written, so most of the books go up to chapter 16, but your copy only goes to 15."

"What?"

"It's good, though, for you I guess! You have the rare copy, so if it's worth anything, yours is worth more."

"Not to me!" protested Brian. "I need to know how it ends!"

"It's no big deal, really. The extra chapter doesn't change things much."

"Can I borrow a copy from you?"

"I suppose. Tomorrow I'll—"

"Can we get it now?"

"No!" laughed Cat. "That's silly. You don't need it right this minute."

"But I hate not knowing the endings to things! I've finished novels I couldn't stand just because I still had to know the ending. And now, you're keeping me from the end of a novel I actually liked!"

"Well, that's your problem!"

Brian cast a concerned look around the floor briefly as if the missing chapter might appear there if he concentrated enough. "Listen," he said, as he took her by the hand and led her over to the daybed to sit down with him. "Can you at least tell it to me? Then waiting might be easier."

Cat felt a little bad at how amusing she found all of this. "It's better read."

Brian groaned. "Now you're just being a tease on every level."

"What does that mean?"

"Never mind," he said. "It's just, the story was over! There was a symmetry to the chapter structure so that it ends as it began with the two friends talking in a restaurant. There was nowhere else for the story to go!"

Cat was stunned. No one had ever noticed how she had organized the book before. Not that she'd talked to a lot of people who had read that book, but still. She was deeply impressed, and she felt both a little closer to him and a little exposed.

She sighed. "It goes backward. Because, you're right. The story was done. I just wasn't ready to let go of those characters yet, so I wrote an extra chapter entirely on a whim that was never intended to be included because it didn't further the plot. I wanted to explore what that first couple of exciting and awkward months after Maddie and Zander's first kiss were like, but it came out really well and I ended up showing it to my editor. She loved it and thought it deserved a place in the novel, and when I told her I couldn't imagine where, she suggested the end. That way, after you've seen everything they go through, it's kind of bittersweet to visit them again at a fresher and more hopeful time. That was the idea, anyway. I'm still not convinced it actually works, but I like that the chapter got out there."

Brian was deep in thought and he wasn't looking at her.

"Huh," said Brian, finally. "Writing's an interesting process, isn't it? I mean, I know novels don't come fully formed right out of people's heads, but it's so hard for me to picture them in pieces and parts that need to be arranged and rewritten. When they're done well they seem like they must have always been that way. It's amazing what you do. I wish I could write."

Cat had never thought of herself as having any particularly special skill. She always figured any decently educated person who wanted to and could find the time could write if they chose. Maybe that wasn't true.

"I'm sure you could write if you tried," assured Cat.

Brian gave her a small smile and squeezed her hand. Until that moment she hadn't realized he was still holding it.

"No. No, I've tried, actually, but I can't focus well enough. Anything open-ended like that.... When I'm doing something else, like a play, I can see where I'm headed and can concentrate on a goal. But writing, since I don't know the end, I...I don't know."

"Then start with the ending," suggested Cat.

Brian looked at her like she was crazy. "That's the same problem in reverse! Finding the beginning is just as hard as finding the end."

Brian seemed sad. It felt impossible to Cat that anyone so young should be sad, but she knew that was wrong. She remembered what it was like to be young and sad. Sad didn't discriminate based on age.

"Hey," she said, and found herself touching his cheek with her hand. "If it's something you really want, I could help. Start small. We could map out a storyline together and you could do simply the writing part, and see if that gets you started. I can't believe there is anything you couldn't do if you really wanted it."

At that moment, between his grip on her hand and the way he was breathing, she realized what he really wanted was her. She thought she could feel his heart beating faster. Or was that just hers? She didn't know. He looked at her intently.

"Cat...." he said quietly. "Please, Cat, I need to

kiss you now."

"But...." she started. He put an arm around her and pulled her close. He began nuzzling her neck and she didn't want to stop him.

"Call me Zander," he said in a raw whisper as his lips moved up her neck. "Just call me Zander if it helps, but please...."

Since the kiss in the theater, Cat felt she'd crossed a line. She wouldn't get any credit for backing out at this point anyway. All sins were equal, weren't they? But she didn't believe in sin. That should have made it easier.

She may as well feel guilty about what she really wanted to do.

"I...." She closed her eyes and felt his chest pressed up against her and his hands gripping her back. Cat didn't want to resist any longer.

"Just say it!" he said. "Call me Zander and it will be okay!"

"I can't...." she said. But she thought it.

"Then don't say anything." He kissed her mouth with urgency.

The freshly put on t-shirt came right back off, and he reached up under Cat's shirt to unhook her bra with a practiced ease. She pulled her own shirt off and started fumbling with his jeans. This was the point when she always figured people who cheated could stop themselves. There was so much awkward stuff to do dealing with clothes that she always thought there was little excuse for being distracted by pure passion. Now she knew that was wrong.

The fumbling with and the removal of clothes was not pedestrian at all but thrilling. It was like the way she had unwrapped presents with joyful abandon as a kid. They pawed and pulled at each other's clothes while trying to keep their lips in full contact the whole time.

There was something both indecent and exhilarating about being there in the middle of the room in the afternoon with the windows wide open. She heard a car horn from somewhere down on the street, and the rush of traffic. She heard voices of people going about their day oblivious to what the two of them were doing.

Brian's hands roamed her body and his lips followed. Cat found every part of him was pleasurable to touch and she marveled at being able to see him naked in full daylight. He was all energy and power and heat, and she wanted all of it.

There was a bowl full of condoms tucked under the daybed and Brian reached down without looking and fished one out. Cat lay back and watched him put it on. During the pause she had one last flash of it not being too late to back out, and she realized that was ridiculous. It was way too late. There were things she needed and she intended to get them.

Brian pressed himself back down on top of her and ran his tongue in places that made her shiver. Cat tried to guide his body in ways she was used to, but he wasn't having any of it. He went at her with a hunger that scared her in a way she didn't know she wanted.

They were both sweating in the heat of the afternoon. Cat could smell chlorine from her skin mixing with Brian's sweat as their bodies slid against each other faster.

She found herself thinking that next time they could— But the last piece of her rational mind interrupted, *"Next time?"* and she squelched it. She put all of her concentration into enjoying the physical experience she was having and came as close to shutting down the verbal part of her brain as she'd ever been able.

When Brian came he cried out and practically collapsed on her. He lay there breathing hard, in no hurry to leave her. He seemed like he might fall asleep.

Cat had no intention of letting that happen. He'd had his fun. Now it was her turn.

*

It was getting late. The light had shifted across the apartment in such a way that Cat could tell hours had passed since she'd gotten there, but she had no idea how many. The daybed was a disaster of pulled up sheets and covers and Brian was splayed out on his stomach, one leg and one arm over the edge, in very deep sleep. Cat had found a small airline blanket off to the side that she'd pulled over herself when she'd gotten cold.

She lay looking up at the ceiling, wedged in close against Brian, one of her legs draped over part of his back. For the life of her, Cat didn't know what should happen next. Could she leave without saying goodbye? He looked so peaceful and wiped out she didn't want to disturb him, but she really needed to go. She needed a shower before her husband got home. That thought sounded devious, but also necessary.

Cat wished she could stay there. Part of it was for nice reasons. She recalled other times in her life when she wished time would leave her alone and let her enjoy a moment endlessly, like the first time Liz fell asleep in her arms on a Sunday morning in her bed. She was so small and so perfect and Cat wanted to be warm and snuggled up with her like that forever. There was the first slow dance with Nick at his older sister's wedding. Cat had felt special and happy, and when the song ended they both swayed together in the dim room a moment longer. There was the time after her second miscarriage and her mom had come to be with her and they took a walk. In the midst of all that sadness, there was a clear moment of connection between them where she felt she understood the true depth of her mother's love for her, and she remembered wanting not to take that last turn around the block toward the house because she didn't want that walk to be over.

Part of it was fear. She was afraid to go home and either hurt Nick directly, or lie to him and hurt him indirectly. She was afraid of getting caught. Cat realized she was afraid of herself. If she was capable of this, which she would have sworn up and down only a few months ago that she was not, what else was she capable of? She didn't know and she was scared to guess. She was afraid of facing tomorrow as this new person she didn't know yet.

Cat decided she should pick up some Chinese food on the way home so she wouldn't have to cook, and that she would tell her family she was on some sort of creative roll that required her to isolate herself in her office for the evening. They would buy that. They weren't aware of any reasons not to.

She carefully slid her leg off Brian but he didn't stir. She smiled a little to herself. He had seemed so surprised when she took charge. She'd made a conscious decision to take full advantage of Brian's stamina. He was positively fatigued by the end and she didn't think he could move now even if the fire alarm went off. She wondered if he thought she was trying to kill him with sex. It wasn't a bad way to go, actually, if the sex was that good.

Cat took a minute to gather up her clothes which seemed to be everywhere, and she never did find one of her socks. She quietly got dressed, gathered up her her laptop bag, and left. She felt she was too old to be leaving notes. He would figure out she was gone all on his own.

She walked in the slanting sunlight back to her car by the coffee shop. Her skin felt like it was buzzing. She got into the driver's seat and sat there for a long time. Maybe she should drive to some new place altogether and start over as a waitress where no one knew her. That sounded easier than going home. The clock on her dashboard said it was after five. She didn't know if she could beat her husband home at this point. Cat could smell Brian all over her, but would Nick be sensitive to something like that? She closed her eyes, took a deep breath, and started the car. She picked up Chinese takeout at the place where they had celebrated a few anniversaries, and where the waitress had once managed to stick a candle in a fortune cookie for Liz's tenth birthday.

While she waited for her order she went into the bathroom and tried to get a read on how she looked. She looked like she'd been having sex all afternoon. Her mouth was rubbed to the point of looking tender, her hair was mussed, and she thought something seemed different about her eyes but she wasn't sure what. Maybe it was guilt—that whole "window to the soul" thing. She went hopelessly after her hair with a brush and finally wrangled it into a ponytail.

When Cat got home she came in through the back door into the kitchen. She could hear loud music coming from Liz's room upstairs. She didn't see any evidence of Nick yet, but he could have come in through the front way and dropped his things out there. Pogo came running up, tail wagging enough to wiggle his whole rear end, but when he smelled her he backed off a little and started to bark.

"Pogo!" she scolded. "What are you doing?"

"Cat, is that you?" called Nick from the other room.

Cat felt like something seized in her chest briefly. "Uh, yeah," she called out. "Sorry I'm late! I brought takeout from Wong's."

Nick came into the kitchen. He was in the process of removing his tie, so he must have gotten home minutes before. Pogo was still barking at her.

"What is wrong with you?" said Nick with a smile, bending down to wrestle with the dog a little. "*Now* you decide you don't like cats?"

He started to stand up and she sensed he would give her a quick kiss. Cat wasn't ready for that yet, so she moved to get out plates and silverware and kept herself in motion on the opposite end of the kitchen.

"Where were you so late?" asked Nick as he started to unpack the food from the bag.

"Oh, uh, just around," she said, trying not to look at him.

Nick laughed a little and he started to peek in each of the boxes to see what his wife had picked out. "You sound like Liz! Will I find you skateboarding next to the library, too?"

Cat laughed, and wondered if she were too loud. She had no idea how to act like herself. She observed everyone else, but she didn't know a thing about how she moved or spoke or reacted.

"Yeah, no, I got a new idea today and decided to try, uh.... I just walked around a lot. It helped me think and I needed to observe people on the street."

Nick was happy to discover a container of cashew chicken and was looking for rice to go with

135

it. "Huh. Sounds fun. What's the new idea?"

"The new idea?"

"For your book, that had you walking around all afternoon."

"Oh, it's, uh, kind of vague at this point." Cat was certain any second Nick would look at her and simply know. She felt as if he should be able to see every spot where Brian had placed his lips on her only hours before.

"Well, what's the central theme? You usually decide on that first, don't you?" He went to the sink to grab a glass of water to go with his meal and gestured that he could get one for her, too.

Cat shook her head. He really didn't suspect anything. "The central theme is the idea of people looking right at one another and not really seeing each other at all."

Nick nodded. "Sounds interesting. I'll take a dozen copies!"

Cat smiled weakly. "Um, Nick, I'm going to hole up in my office tonight if you don't mind. I need some time to think, okay?"

"Sure, Catnip! I don't mind. I've got some journals I need to spend time with tonight anyway, so I don't think you'd have seen much of me either way." He walked past her to call Liz down for dinner, and before she knew what was happening, he gave her a quick peck on the lips on his way back to the counter. She waited for accusations that were deserved but didn't come, and then she started heading for her office.

"Aren't you going to have any with us?" he asked while filling up his plate.

"I'm not hungry right now."

He smiled at her. "We'll make sure to save you something, okay?"

Cat simply looked at him a moment. He was so dear, and she hated herself deeply right then. "Thanks."

As she started to leave the room he called after her. "Hey, Cat?"

"Yeah?"

"You look great today."

She forced a smile to show him the compliment was appreciated, and she made a conscious effort to have it reach her eyes. "Thanks."

On the stairs, Cat passed her daughter, who gave her a brief greeting as she headed toward the kitchen. Cat walked down the hall to her office. She went in, locked the door behind her, and curled up in a ball behind her desk where as quietly as possible she cried and cried and cried.

CHAPTER SEVEN

Cat took a shower before she went to bed. Her own shower felt unfamiliar since she usually showered at the YMCA after swimming. She had a gym bag with the shampoo and conditioner she liked, her favorite hairbrush, body wash, face wash, puff, razor, and body lotion. None of those things were in her actual shower. She would have borrowed Liz's things but her daughter had her own bathroom down the hall closer to her room, and Cat didn't feel like going all the way down there now that she was wet. She looked at Nick's stuff, which was sparse. There was a bar of soap, and some dandruff shampoo. No puff, no bottles with the suggestion that flowers or fresh fruit might be involved somewhere. It would have to do.

It was a little after two in the morning, and even her daughter had gone to bed hours ago. Cat scrubbed at herself harshly with the bar of soap.

She was experiencing the strangest combination of feelings she had ever known. The sensation of guilt was palpable and she was disgusted with herself. She was officially a bad person and she didn't want to be. Or maybe she was bad all along and this just proved it. Something came back to her from her very first conversation with Brian about evil not really counting for anything until it caused something bad. This was bad.

At the same time, as she ran the soap over her body, she could recall her afternoon with Brian and feel something she didn't have a good word for. Somewhere beyond happy. It was happy combined with something selfish and something thrilling. Something she wanted again.

She didn't know what she should be doing next. She decided all she could do was play things by ear minute to minute and deal with it as best she could. Cat did not know what to do about Nick. Was it cruel for him to know? Yes. Was it cruel for him not to know? Yes. The problem was she had done something cruel, and there was no way out of it.

Cat scrubbed herself hard with the soap starting again from her feet and working her way up her body for the fourth time. She mulled over advice on pop psychology shows that ran the gamut. Some people insisted if you cheated that you mend your ways and keep it to yourself. That sharing information was a selfish way of sharing the pain so you didn't have to drown in it alone like you deserved to. Others said the aggrieved party was entitled to know what they were in the middle of so they could judge for themselves if this was a situation they wanted to work on or not. That people should have all the necessary information they needed to make informed decisions about their relationships and their lives. None of it erased what she'd done, so she felt like none of it was really helpful.

Cat stayed in the shower until she believed Brian was sufficiently removed from her skin, but she could still feel him there. She liked feeling him there. She wanted to shake all of her memories from the afternoon off as much as she wanted to replay every detail over and over.

She dried herself, put on some pajamas her mother had sent her for her last birthday that had drawings of sock monkeys all over them, and crawled into bed. She stayed as far over on her side as she could and lay there with her eyes open. Nick stirred, and when his foot bumped against hers he unconsciously rolled over and put his arm around her. Her mind raced and she didn't pass out until nearly dawn.

Cat again avoided the coffee shop. Weeks of working at home made her stir crazy, but at least she would actually make her *County Vet* book deadline. She considered looking for a new place to work in the next town over.

After much back and forth in her head she concluded that no one needed to know her secret. She would resume life as a wife and mother and put her experience with Brian behind her. That was kindest to everyone, and the guilt she suffered was deserved and she would accept it and find a way to pay penance. Maybe donate a wing to some kind of animal hospice center, or let Nick get a second dog.

Cat managed to avoid making love to her husband for almost two weeks before she thought he was starting to seem concerned that something was wrong. Then she worried that she was overcompensating by making herself too available for a while.

It wasn't as strange being with Nick again as she'd feared. The contrast was huge, but Nick was so familiar that she could just step back into that well-practiced dance without much effort. She noticed that she could predict exactly where his hands would go and when. She could tell in the dark when he was about to kiss her. She knew precisely the right moments to roll over or move faster. Cat was tempted to change the routine, but it was too soon. She would introduce new ideas at a safer distance from where she'd acquired them. The thrill of the unknown had been amazing with Brian. She'd had no idea from moment to moment exactly what was going to happen. She didn't know if there was a way to reproduce that with Nick. Part of her didn't know if she wanted to. There was something scary about that idea. She didn't want to not know

Nick. She wanted to continue to get to know Brian, but that was not a smart plan.

She got a call at one point from the theater that she assumed was Tom, but she didn't return it. Part of her worried it may really be Brian trying to find a way to contact her, dangerous though that would be. The idea of going back to the Avenue was too complicated. She didn't trust herself anymore and she was trying to make things right, even if she was the only one who knew about it. That was the bed she'd made and she was going to lie in it with just her husband.

But then Nick came home with a surprise.

"*Othello*?" asked Cat as she looked at the tickets he'd put into her hand.

"You liked that other play so much I thought you really should get to do more of that. I got us seats for opening night on Saturday after my shift at the clinic."

"Both of us at the Avenue?"

Nick laughed. "Yes, both of us! Did you really think I hated going to a play that much?"

Cat was not sure what to do. Maybe it wouldn't matter. Certainly she could attend a play unnoticed and go back home without anything happening. That had to be possible. It was going to have to be. "But, have you seen any Shakespeare before?"

"Not really. We read an abridged *Romeo and Juliet* in high school, and I tried to read *Hamlet* on my own without much luck, but I'm armed this time!" He pulled a black and yellow booklet out of his briefcase. It was old and battered and appeared as if it had lived a very long time on the shelf of a used bookstore.

"Cliffs Notes?" asked Cat dubiously. She had never even held a copy of Cliffs Notes in her hands, let alone read one. They were literary blasphemy in her mind. A way to distill the essence of a great work while bypassing what made it great. She pursed her lips.

"Hey, it's helping me so I can follow the play a little better. I'm getting a lot out of it actually. The real thing ought to be really good, and I'll have something more intelligent to say about it afterward other than 'What was that?' on the way home."

It was a bad idea. She was frantically trying to think of a way out of it, but her "acting lessons" hadn't reached how to play sick enough to avoid a night out with her husband. "Thanks, Sweetie," was all she could think to say.

"Great!" he said brightly. "But I get to pick the restaurant this time, too. We're having hamburgers and I don't want to hear anything about anyone's arteries while we're there."

The drive to the theater on Saturday was an odd switch. Nick really had done his homework and was genuinely excited about seeing *Othello*. He kept telling her about certain plot points to watch for, and the how the setting fit into history. Cat kept reminding him that yes, she knew about Desdemona and the handkerchief and about the wars between Venice and Turkey. She wondered if she were this

143

dull when she talked about literature. Poor Nick. Maybe she should finally look inside a lizard if she could find one.

They got to the Avenue Theater in plenty of time to find their seats. They were good seats on the floor left of center and toward the front. Cat fidgeted. Nick looked happy and ready to settle in for the first three acts. The lights dimmed, and out onto the stage stepped Brian and another man. Cat caught her breath.

Iago and Roderigo strode about and exchanged unkind descriptions and gossip about Othello. Brian was convincing from the first line. It gave her chills. He cut such a beautiful figure under the lights. She had been with that figure. She probably could be again if she chose to. That knowledge made how she saw Brian onstage entirely different from the last play.

By the time of the intermission at the end of Act Three, Cat couldn't sit still any longer. She stood up to stretch as Nick said from his seat, "The sets are amazing. Costumes, too."

"Does that mean you're having trouble following it?" asked Cat looking down, her arms extended up over her head for a moment to get her circulation going.

"No, I can follow it. It helps to know ahead what is supposed to be happening, otherwise yeah, I think I'd be a bit lost. It's good, though. Even if I didn't know what was going on there is a lot to see."

Stretching in place was not doing it for Cat.

"Want to walk around with me a minute? This one's a long intermission. They're hoping to sell a lot of wine and overpriced brownies."

"No, I've been on my feet all day. Sitting is fine with me right now. You go. Sneak me in an expensive brownie if you can."

She cast him a look that said she was not enabling that addiction if she could help it, and headed for the lobby. The crush of people by the bar was not conducive to a good stroll, so Cat wandered alone farther back near where she knew some of the dressing rooms and storage closets were on the other side of the wall.

Brian had told her about all kinds of odd doors and closets and passageways that were necessary for being creative with different productions, and she knew there was a secret door back in that area. She was curious to see if she could spot it. She was looking for any kind of open seam in the wallpaper that would give it away when she heard a voice whisper from close by.

"Cat!"

She turned and was startled to see the wall she had just passed was open a crack, and there was Brian. The makeup which was so natural from a distance was heavy and grotesque up close, but didn't really distract from his handsome features.

"Brian, I—"

"Come here," he whispered and held out his hand.

Cat hesitated, but curiosity got the best of her

145

and she stepped closer to the opening and he pulled her inside.

Before she even knew how to react, Brian pulled her a few steps down a corridor into a small closet and shut the door.

"Brian! I need to go, I have—"

"Shhhh." Brian turned her so she had her back against him. He held her to him tightly around the waist with one arm and groped her slowly with the other hand and whispered in her ear:

"She that was ever fair and never proud,
Had tongue at will and yet was never loud,
Never lack'd gold and yet went never gay,
Fled from her wish and yet said 'Now I may,'
She that being anger'd, her revenge being nigh,
Bade her wrong stay and her displeasure fly,
She that in wisdom never was so frail
To change the cod's head for the salmon's tail;
She that could think and ne'er disclose her mind,
See suitors following and not look behind,
She was a wight, if ever such wight were,—"

But he substituted Iago's infamous punchline to his description of the perfect woman "To suckle fools and chronicle small beer" with "To come and kiss me in secret here."

Cat closed her eyes and drank it in and enjoyed the sensation of feeling his hands in places she shouldn't let them go.

They stood there in the tight space for a moment and Cat pretended she was in a play herself and this was a tiny universe where such things were acceptable. She forgot everything about her life for an instant, but then the panic started to creep back in.

Brian said quietly from behind her, "Please don't stay away, Cat. I have to get back and be ready for Act Four, but.... don't disappear on me again. Please?"

Cat didn't answer him. She heard him open the door, and she opened her eyes. He led her back up the little corridor and he checked a monitor. There was a camera in the hall outside that allowed you to see anyone in that area. That was how he had known she was there. When the coast was clear he opened the secret door and guided her gently out. By the time she turned around he was gone again.

She glanced around and figured out the camera was in a fancy light fixture. She stared directly into it for a moment, then she headed in a daze back out toward the lobby. The lights were flickering to signal people it was time to return to their seats. Cat stood in indecision. She caught a glimpse of herself in one of the decorative mirrors in the lobby and wondered if she looked more rumpled than she should. There was a bit of stage makeup by her ear. She picked up a napkin from the bar and wiped it off. She was one of the last people in the lobby and the lights were flickering again. She got back to her seat right as the lights were going down to begin Act Four.

"What happened to you?" whispered Nick.

"What?"

"What took you so long? Where's my brownie?"

"I just—" But the stage lights came on and the play resumed. Cat watched Brian warily and wondered if he could see her from up there. Nick held her hand at one point and she worried he would notice it was clammy. She watched Iago kill his wife and it made her shudder. By Othello's closing words before killing himself the crowd was ready to jump to its feet with applause. Cat sat where she was.

Nick was happy on the way home, but tired. "That's a long play. But I got it this time. Betrayal, death, alienation...but...."

"But what?" asked Cat, who hadn't contributed much to the conversation. Her mind was elsewhere.

"Well, the actor who played the villain, Iago...."

Cat stumbled slightly but Nick didn't notice. "What about him?"

"He was great in the part, but, shouldn't someone that bad *look* bad? He could be a movie star or something. Isn't that the wrong way to cast that?"

Cat waited a moment before answering. "Because," she finally said, "When evil is in an attractive package you are less likely to recognize it. Even if it's sitting next to you."

"Hm. I guess that makes the betrayal thing easier to pull off then, doesn't it? I think I can see that."

No, she thought to herself. No, you can't.

The next morning, Cat pulled the Sunday paper

off the porch and flipped to the section with the local reviews. There, of course, was a picture of Brian, looking dastardly and handsome, and there was also a much smaller shot down below of the people playing Othello and Desdemona. They were good, but not as photogenic. She wondered if anyone were as photogenic.

The reviews glowed to the point they were almost embarrassing. Brian Smith was described as dynamic and charismatic and the one to watch. They praised the Avenue for not casting him as Cassio, the obvious choice for someone with his gorgeous visage, but trusting him with the large role of evil incarnate. The reviewer said Brian actually made you believe he was capable of manipulating people purely for his own incomprehensible and wicked amusement. Quite a feat. Everyone should look forward to next season with bated breath.

Liz had spent the night at a friend's and still wasn't home yet.

Cat asked Nick, "Should I give Bella's mom a call?"

Nick rifled through the paper in front of her to find the sports section. "No, it's kind of early. They were probably up late and need to sleep in anyway. Why, do you miss the eye rolling?"

Whatever messed up business Cat was dealing with inside her head about her marriage, as partners in parenting she had no doubts. She counted on the team she and Nick were when it came to raising Liz.

"Actually, while we have some time alone, can we have a parenting meeting?" asked Cat.

Nick put down the part of the paper he'd been looking through and asked, "What's up?"

"What do you think of Liz lately?"

"What do you mean?"

"I mean, do you trust everything she's telling us right now?" Cat asked.

"Well, she barely tells me anything, but I trust the 'hello' she gives me in the morning."

"Really, I want to know. I'm getting an odd feeling about her recently but I don't have much to go on."

"Like the cigarette thing again?"

"No, after we found that pack she was holding for Jasmine there hasn't been anything else along those lines," said Cat.

"Well, I can't imagine she'd lie about going to another party after you caught her the last time," said Nick.

Cat had known what their daughter was up to, despite the relay of phone calls to the library to form her alibi. She had politely and sweetly greeted Liz at the door when she got home and presented her with a blank thank-you card and a pen. Liz was puzzled until her mother explained that when you go to a party you always thank the host in writing. Liz had flipped out and started denying everything to a degree that even Nick could see was over the top and that Cat had been right. Cat patiently waited for Liz to calm down and then she explained that

Liz would write the note and let her proofread it, but that this time they wouldn't have to mail it. If there was ever a next time, she would. Liz cried and refused until Cat explained, again with great calm, that without trust they had nothing, and nothing meant nothing as in no cell phone, no snowboard, no internet, no clothes of her choosing—nothing. Liz sat down and wrote a card to her friend Chad from her biology class, thanking him for the beer which she didn't actually try and for introducing her to more than two dozen new people while his parents weren't home. Cat corrected one punctuation error, handed her back the note, and sent her to bed.

"It's something, though," said Cat.

"What kind of thing are you worried about?"

Cat shook her head. "I can't tell yet, but I want you to keep an eye out for anything odd or anything that doesn't match something she says."

"Okay. I'm not sure what I'm looking for but I'll do my best," assured Nick.

The truth was, Cat didn't trust her own instincts. She needed Nick to help monitor their daughter a little better because her own moral compass had dropped in the middle of a discount magnet store and was spinning wildly in all directions. She didn't know if she was suspicious of Liz because there was some reason to be, or if she was projecting.

And she knew as she watched Brian in the second half of *Othello* the night before that her moral authority was gone. She had come to a decision. An awful decision, but one befitting the themes played out on the stage before her.

Life was too short and she wanted everything. She wanted her home and she wanted her career and she wanted Nick and she wanted Brian. She didn't want to get to the end of her safe little life having never grabbed for the things that made it worth living. If no one knew, which no one seemed to, then no one got hurt. Nick could die one day content that everything was as it should have been, and if no one told him otherwise, why shouldn't he? Her reality was different from his regardless, so what did it matter how different it really was? If her reality included mind-blowing sex and a private book club rolled into one, that was her decision. She could keep Nick happy and also work at keeping herself happy. She was a great multi-tasker, so it could be managed.

But she would need more acting lessons.

CHAPTER EIGHT

Once Cat made her decision and accepted the fact that she was selfish and shallow and bad, a calmness swept over her. Now that she was not going to struggle with her conscience on this issue it was merely a matter of logistics and proper planning. She was good at those things.

She started down her new path by superimposing it upon the old one. She went back to the coffee shop Monday after swimming. They were pleased to see their most reliable customer had returned and asked her if she had been away or ill. Cat thanked them for thinking of her, and said no, all was well, she'd simply been pulled a different direction for a while. They offered her a complimentary muffin to welcome her back, but she declined it and ordered her usual tea.

Cat sat in her familiar spot and organized herself. She pulled out her laptop and started reading through the fragments of puppy and kitten stories that she was going to try to string together in a way that made them seem different from the last strung together batch of puppy and kitten stories.

She wasn't more than ten minutes into her work when she felt a strong hand caress her shoulder.

Brian smiled down at her. "You came back!"

Cat looked up into his handsome young face. Was this really what she wanted to do? She thought she'd been through all that, but now she wondered again. It was so easy to see what was wrong from a detached, rational vantage point. It was another thing entirely when a different, more neglected part of you asserted its own rights and wanted equal time. Why should one side always dominate? Weren't there more parts to her than her rational mind?

Apparently there really were, because when no one was in view for a moment, Brian bent down close to her and nuzzled her ear, and the part of her that loved it started campaigning for the rest of her to cast its vote in favor of more. He kissed her earlobe and ran his tongue lightly around it and whispered, "Let's go."

She didn't have to ask where or why, that was all understood. There was one last flicker of resistance in her that almost caused her to stay put, but Brian was so close and so warm and the promise of another afternoon with him was too irresistible. She gathered her things without saying a word and followed him back to his apartment.

There was no pretense this time that anything other than sex was on the agenda and they simply headed straight for his bed. It wasn't as frenzied as before, but it was intense and much more methodical and thorough. They didn't speak once. They rested for a while, and then started exploring each other again. By the time they realized they were really done for the afternoon, Cat noticed it was after three.

"I have to go," said Cat simply as she started hunting around for all of her clothes.

Brian propped himself up on his elbow and watched her. Whenever she passed closely enough to reach he would try to gently draw her back toward him, but she chose not to be distracted. Her scheduled fun was finished for the day and she had other things to do. Brian cocked his head a little as he watched her in her single-minded purpose. She had mentally left his apartment already and was compiling a grocery list in her head.

"Cat, I—"

"Brian, I really have to leave now." She stopped once she got her shirt back over her head and looked at him. "Are you free tomorrow?"

Brian hesitated and finally said, "Sure."

"Great. Should I try to get something done at the coffee shop first, or should I come straight here?"

"I suppose it makes more sense for you to just

come here."

"Sounds good! See you then." And she let herself out.

Cat walked the half mile back to her car in the fresh May air. She felt like she could relate to spring inside and out. She stopped at the store on her way home and grabbed a few extra things for dinner. She had decided to add steak to her vegetable stir fry. Both Nick and Liz liked steak. She observed other men in the store and thought to herself that there wasn't another one there who was even remotely as good-looking as Brian. It gave her s peculiar sense of satisfaction.

She went home, checked in on her daughter, made her meal, greeted her husband when he finally arrived, ignored the barking of the dog, and fed her family. She even tossed Pogo a bite of meat to shut him up, which seemed to work. When a creature's needs and desires are met, there is serenity, she thought to herself.

Cat cleaned up, worked on her laptop for a while in her office, kissed her husband on her way upstairs and told him not to wear himself out. She decided for once not to ask Liz to please turn her music down. She stretched herself out while she had the bed to herself for the time being and decided it had been a good day. "Good" had a loose definition nowadays.

Cat went straight to Brian's apartment every day that week, but on Friday, following his Thursday night performance, Brian was still kind of wiped out. He was not in the same willing mood he had been in on the previous days, and he was a little petulant. This was not part of Cat's new plan and it aggravated her.

"But, Brian...." she said, as she slipped her fingers inside the waist of his jeans and gripped them in an attempt to pull him toward her. Brian didn't budge.

"Cat, I'm really tired, and I don't—Stop! Stop, already, that tickles!" Cat completely ignored what he had to say and sent her hands wherever they wanted to go.

"Cat!" He took her hands in his firmly and made her pay attention. He smiled in a bemused way.

"What?"

"I told you I'm not up to it today, okay? I've got performances all weekend which take a lot out of me and after you leave I feel like I've done push-ups for a straight hour. I need a break."

Cat looked at him a moment. She sighed and started to turn to grab her bag when he gripped her hands again.

"Hey," he said, "You don't have to *go*."

Cat was confused. "But you said—"

"I know what I said but I don't know what you heard. Just because I don't feel like screwing around right this minute doesn't mean I don't want you here. We never talk about anything anymore. I miss hanging out at the coffee shop and arguing about books and—"

"Arguing?"

"*Wuthering Heights*."

"Oh, yeah. That is *not* a love story! I don't know how can you say—"

"Yeah, *this*! I miss *this*, Cat." He looked in her eyes and smiled hopefully.

Cat thought about it. "I guess." It was a nice thought to go back to talking again. Not what she thought of when she considered a torrid affair, but talking about books was seldom a negative. "What do you want to talk about?"

Brian sat on the daybed while he pondered the question. She liked watching him think. It was one of the few times he let his guard down and his face could simply be what it wanted to be.

"You know, Cat, I was kind of hoping you might follow up on that idea to help me write a story myself. If you're still willing to teach me."

Cat looked at him sitting there. He seemed frighteningly young at the moment. "You want me to be your tutor?"

Brian laughed. "Not when you say it like that! You have to raise an eyebrow at the end or wink or something." He pulled her onto his lap and kissed her arm from her hand up to her shoulder. "Then when you say it, you'd be my sexy, naughty tutor, and that's much more fun."

Cat was smiling again. "Okay, okay. You have your laptop handy or do you want to work longhand?"

"Laptop."

"Fine. But we're holding class in your bed and I

don't grade on a curve."

Cat was sort of amused by this odd turn and Brian seemed happy. She removed her laptop from her bag and took it into the bedroom. She found an outlet and got herself all plugged in and ready to go. A moment later Brian climbed onto the bed next to her and propped his own computer up against his knees.

"What do we do first?" he asked eagerly.

"You're sure you don't want me to fuck your brains out?"

"Monday. I'll put it on my calendar."

Cat sighed again. She gazed longingly at his body. "It's only fair that if you're going to make me do my kind of work, you have to do your kind of work, too. Take your shirt off."

"What, am I auditioning for *A Streetcar Named Desire*?"

"Yes, Stanley. Just do it already."

Brian grinned and stripped off his t-shirt. Cat started her word processor and opened a new file.

"Okay, let's see. Your problem was that you need more parameters to work inside so you know where to go, so I'm going to decide certain things for you, and we'll decide other things together to make it easier, all right?"

"Okay."

Cat started typing herself a list.

"Now, I'm going to ask you to come up with details and you jot them down in your own list. Ready?"

"Ready."

"You get one major character. Is it a man or a woman?"

"Um...a man."

"Young or old?"

"Old."

Cat decided she didn't want to know what he thought of as "old" so she didn't ask for more clarification on that point.

"Is he white? African-American? Middle Eastern?"

"White."

"Rich or poor?"

"Hmm," said Brian. "Once rich, now poor."

"Married? Single?"

"Divorced."

"Okay," said Cat. "Give him a name."

Brian thought a while. "Alan. Alan Michael...Jones."

Cat thought: Leave it to a "Smith" to come up with "Jones."

"All right. Now, Brian, take a minute and write a paragraph in general about this guy. Very dry stuff like his birthday, the clothes he usually wears, any odd features to his body, that kind of thing. Don't get deep, here. This isn't the story, it's merely the guy we're going to stick in it. Got it?"

"Got it." Brian happily set to work.

Cat pulled up her *County Vet* book that she'd been neglecting and worked on a snippet about a boy asking if Hamster Heaven was anywhere near

160

Cat Heaven and should he be worried for poor Snickers up there. They worked quietly with the sounds of typing softly filling the room.

"Done," said Brian.

"Okay, now—"

"You don't want to see it?" asked Brian.

"There are lots of things I want to see, but not that," she said.

Brian looked confused. "But how—?"

"Trust me. This first story is all yours. There is no pressure because no one ever has to see it. That's my first rule of writing. Just write and figure out if anyone should read it later. If you worry about that now you'll be paralyzed. If it's not fun to write for yourself, you have no business writing at all."

He sat quietly for a moment and then he shook his head. "You know, this is so backward for me. Everything I do is so... exposed. How much stuff do writers do that nobody ever sees?"

"You have no idea."

Brian looked at his screen then back up at her. "Okay, so what's next?"

"Let's do the setting next. This is a very short story, so think of it like a one act play with a minimal set. What is something you feel you know a lot about?"

After a long pause where he seemed to be examining and rejecting various choices he finally said, "Riding the bus."

"Good," she said. "Your setting is on the bus. Tell me where the guy is going."

161

"To work."

Cat regarded him carefully. "Does he actually want to get there or not? Is he dreading going to work or looking forward to it?"

"He's dreading it."

"Okay, set the scene. Write a paragraph—or two if you want, I don't care—describing this guy on the bus."

"But what's the story?"

"I thought you were going to trust me! Do I have to make you take your pants off, too?"

Brian gave her an exasperated look and got typing, but after a few minutes he stopped. "The creative writing class I took in college wasn't like this."

"And for you it didn't work, did it?"

"That's true." He tried typing again. He paused. Then he sounded like he was deleting things.

Cat sensed he was in trouble and stopped what she was doing.

"Stuck?" she asked.

He nodded.

"Okay, let me think for a second," she said. Cat glanced around the room at the poster on his wall and the things on his dresser until an idea hit her. "New angle. I'm going to hand you a story line and you're going to write it. You need to get something flowing and eventually it will be easier to get on a roll. We'll come back to your old white guy on the bus later. The only way to write is to write, so let's get started."

Cat closed her laptop and moved herself across from him. She sat between his feet and rested her arms on his knees and looked at him over the laptop. She smiled. Brian tried to smile back but mostly seemed conflicted.

"Once upon a time...." she started softly. Brian grinned. "There was a young, handsome actor named Ryan. He was cast in a play where he had to ride a unicycle, but he didn't know how. His career would be perfect if he could master the damned unicycle, but it wouldn't come. So one day a strange woman with a glass eye said she would make it happen if he promised to be with her at the end of his career and he agreed. The unicycle play was a hit, and he moved on to better things, but he got greedy, and by the end felt too good to be seen with the woman with the glass eye. She was angry and revoked her spell during his farewell unicycle performance. He fell off it and died with her cursing over his broken body. They buried him with the unicycle. The end."

Brian stared at her, utterly dumbfounded. "What was that?"

"What was what?"

"What am I supposed to do with that?"

"Whatever you want. But it has a beginning a middle and an end, so all that's left is stuff to fill in however you feel like."

Brian looked like he didn't know whether to laugh or cry.

"But, Cat! It's...."

"It's what?"

"Well, first of all it's silly."

"Hey, I did not come over here today with this kind of lesson plan in mind. I had different things to teach you. Excuse me if my horny energy is interfering with my writing muse, but it's not actually that silly! It could be as scary or light as you choose to make it."

"How can you say it's not silly? And actually, you just stripped down *Faust*! But you made Gretchen a unicycle for some ungodly reason, and the devil a woman with a glass eye! What is that?"

"'Of course it's *Faust*. All 'sell your soul' stories are really *Faust*."

Brian stared at her in disbelief. "So you can rip off *Faust* and not be bothered by that?"

"Why should I be? Goethe ripped it off from someone else."

"But...."

"Brian. There are no new stories. Not really. We all tell the same stories over and over. Do you know why?"

He shook his head.

"Because we all live the same lives over and over. There is nothing you have done or I have done that someone else didn't do before in some way or another."

"But each experience is unique."

"That's the paradox," said Cat. She reached around in her head for a good example. The best one she knew had to do with having a baby, which was something she was loath to remind him she'd done. She didn't feel like entwining her two worlds even in conversation, but it was all she could come up with.

"Look, Brian. When you have a baby, it's the most remarkable, miraculous, special thing in the world. It's unique in every way, except that it is the single most common experience people have. You live that paradox every day as a parent."

"Yeah, well, I have no reason to be impressed by the experience of parents," and he looked at her unhappily.

"Why, what was up with your parents?"

Brian was decidedly gloomy. "I don't want to talk about it."

Good, thought Cat. It sounded like more than she wanted to deal with right then.

She sighed. "Okay, forget about parents, just focus on individuals. We all live the same story: we're born, we live, we die. Beginning, middle, and end. The details make each story unique, but the arc makes it universal. We can't help but tell the same stories again and again, because the arc is the same again and again."

"But at what point is it cheating?"

"I guess when you steal the details, too. I mean, really, if I wrote out the unicycle story myself and you caught that it was *Faust*, you would feel like you were 'in' on a literary reference. But Gretchen wasn't a unicycle in the original poem, so the detail makes it mine. I get to be thought of as clever or crazy, not a thief."

Brian started to close the laptop. "I think I'm done. Maybe we should—"

But Cat was on a mission now. This could work, she just had to find the right way. She grabbed the top of the computer and pulled it open again gently. "Not yet. Give me one more chance, okay? Scrap my unicycle story. It's too distracting. We're going back to your guy on the bus."

"But...."

"Shhhh. Listen." Cat talked soothingly the way she did when she volunteered to work with animals at the clinic. Sometimes animals needed to be kept calm after surgery and before their owners could come take them home. She was good at getting them to relax in the unfamiliar environment.

"Here's your whole story. The guy is on the bus. He's going to work. He doesn't want to. The last line of your story is 'He stepped out of the bus.' That's it. If a detail scares you, I'll talk you through it. It doesn't have to be good and I don't plan to read it. You can even delete it when we're done. It's just an exercise."

"But it isn't a story! Nothing happens."

"Oh, unlike the big car chase scene in *Waiting for Godot*?"

That got Brian to smile again.

"Good. What got you stuck before?"

"Um...I pictured him on the bus at night and then I couldn't figure out what kind of a job an old guy would be going to at that time."

166

"Ah. How fixated are you on the nighttime thing?"

"It's just how I see it."

"Well, if you want to keep it I see two solutions. Either find him a job that fits that, like he's an elderly night watchman somewhere, and maybe it's a pity job since he's old. Or, imagine he's up so early it's dark out still. Maybe in winter when the days are so short. Both ways keep him on the bus in the dark."

Brian looked more relaxed. "Okay," he said. "But what about the lack of story?"

"The guy is the story. It's a bus journey, and all stories are really journeys because journeys are a metaphor for life. The whole we're born, we live, we die thing again. Don't worry about the story. I already gave you the last line. Just work your way up to it. Whatever you do is not wrong. It's your story. He can commute by bus to the moon if you want. You get to run that little universe however you see fit, and that's the fun of it. If a detail trips you up again, I promise I will have an answer."

"An answer without a unicycle?" asked Brian, smiling a little.

"Well, I can't promise that, they're on my mind now, but I will do my best."

Brian sat quietly, lost in thought. Slowly he began to type again.

She didn't really know how to teach what she did, but it was interesting having to explain it in a way someone could use. She hoped it had been of any help at all.

When Brian appeared as if he was safely rolling along, Cat got up and got herself a glass of water, but what she really wanted was wine. Or maybe a beer. She checked the fridge, but it was all old takeout boxes.

She called out from the kitchen, "Brian? Do you have anything to drink that's not water?"

"Like what?" he called back.

"Like wine maybe?"

"I don't drink, Cat."

"Like, ever?"

"Like never. It's, um… It goes back to the parent thing."

And that was a place she still didn't want to go, so she drank her water and didn't ask questions.

She came back into the bedroom and opened her own laptop again. She positioned some pillows so she could lean up against Brian while each of them typed. Cat got back to work on her puppies and kittens and actually kind of wished she were writing the bus story. She was even a little tempted by her unicycle story, despite Brian's rejection of it. She could see it as a Tim Burton movie in her head. But she buckled down and told herself her fans were waiting, and Michelle wanted the book by mid-September, so she'd better make herself finish it already.

They sat that way working for over an hour before Cat needed to get going. She had to drive Liz somewhere right after school and she didn't want to be late, but she didn't want to say that out loud.

Brian didn't notice as she started packing her computer away. When he finally did look up, Cat had her bag slung over her shoulder and was leaning in the doorway of the bedroom, watching him.

"So, did that help at all?" she asked.

"I think it did! Thanks, Cat."

"And I'll see you Monday?"

"Same place, fewer clothes. I promise."

Cat smiled and headed out the door. She had mixed feelings about the afternoon. She had convinced herself that taking advantage of the opportunity Brian presented for a last chance at great sex was somehow not completely horrible. It was simply bodies doing what bodies wanted to do. She had enjoyed her previous conversations with Brian, but assumed it had been a pretext for sex and were not necessary now. But he was serious about wanting access to her mind, and something about him having her mind and her body at his disposal seemed like too much. Somewhere in that mix lay her soul, probably, and she wasn't sure she was ready to make her own Faustian bargain. But maybe she already had.

The following week Cat and Brian started falling into a new routine. Cat didn't always go straight to Brian's apartment. She would go to the coffee shop and work and at some point he'd meet her there, and they would negotiate what to do that day. Some days they just talked, other days she

169

helped Brian write, and there were even days he would come hang out near her while she worked and he read. Other days they would simply head straight to his place and enjoy themselves. There was nice variety in it, which kept all of it fresh. For a while.

The more time Cat spent at Brian's apartment the more she had to start factoring in certain details. She had to bring her own soap and shampoo there so she didn't smell like the products he used (and ultimately didn't smell like him, although the dog always knew no matter what she did). She wound up stocking his fridge so there was something decent in it when she was hungry (although she was denied wine because Brian's aversion to alcohol was so intense). She also ended up treating stains on his laundry and soaking them in the sink on occasion, which was about the unsexiest use of her time she could imagine, especially when she compared it to how her role as a stain consultant had gotten her into his apartment to begin with.

But beyond the ways repetition in an environment dulled her appreciation of it, repetition with Brian was taking a toll on how she interacted with him. As a fantasy figure she knew nothing about except for the parts of him he wanted her to see, he was magical. He was nothing but charm and sex. But you can't share a bathroom with anyone for any length and maintain that illusion. And as beautiful as she found his feet, she drew the line at helping him clip his toenails at one point when he

170

asked.

The biggest bone of contention with Brian seemed to be Liz. They usually didn't talk about Liz, but she came up whenever Brian complained that Cat seemed to drop everything to do things for her "all the fucking time" in his words. There was jealousy there, which surprised Cat, since Brian seemed indifferent to Nick's existence. Any accidental reference to her husband didn't faze Brian at all. But not so with Liz.

"Why can't she just deal with whatever it is herself?" Brian wanted to know when Cat received a call from her daughter at an unusually early time of day which interrupted everything.

"Because she forgot her project on the kitchen table and it's due today and she needs it in less than an hour," said Cat, putting clothes back on that had only been off for a few minutes.

"But, isn't she supposed to be learning responsibility or consequences for her actions or some other crap parents care about instilling in their kids?" asked Brian.

"Yes, but it's also a big part of her grade and she did the work and everyone slips up and I think the consequence would be out of proportion with the offense. Why are we even discussing this? It's my job to be there for my kid, so let it go, okay?"

Brian glowered from the bed. "Well, when I was a kid I had to do everything on my own and I was just fine, so you should let her sink or swim already."

"Yes, and you don't have any hang-ups or resentments about any of that at all, do you? Worked out great. I'll be sure to pick up your book of parenting advice when it hits the shelves," said Cat as she angrily forced her feet into her shoes.

Brian was silent for a moment and then asked, "Are you at least coming back later?"

"Probably not, because by the time I get out there I have to do some errands that are already out that direction, and then Liz needs to go to—"

And under his breath Brian said, "All hail Princess Liz! Keeper of her mother's heart and dominatrix of her time."

"What did you just say?" asked Cat from the doorway as she was grabbing her keys off the table where Brian's mail collected unopened for weeks at a time (and bothered Cat to no end).

"Nothing," said Brian. "I'll see you when I see you I guess."

This was not the kind of double life Cat had been planning on leading. This was... work.

In the meantime, however, the play collaboration started and that was a joy. She had decided on the truck stop story, which Tom was thrilled with, and they agreed to work on separate sections. Cat would rework and come up with additional dialogue, and Tom would sketch out all the stage direction. Cat handed him a draft of her part, then he added in his, and it went back and forth for a while, each time becoming more cohesive with the idea that at some point they would both agree on at least the bulk of it and they could have a session or two together to get it finished.

It also meant that Cat was hanging around the theater for legitimate reasons and it was one less thing she had to feel she was lying to her husband about. Most days she told him truthfully everything that happened there, because not much outside of real business did. She and Brian talked together in the theater, but were careful never to let anything look too cozy. Except for an occasional orgasm in a closet, Nick knew everything about what was happening in her new theater world.

One afternoon, a few hours before a performance, she and Brian were hanging out together in the first row facing the stage. An attractive young woman with blond hair was walking across it at one point when she noticed Brian sitting there. She stopped and appeared cross.

"Hi, Cassie," said Brian.

"Hi yourself! Where the hell have you been?" she asked.

"You know me. I'm around."

Then Cassie started doing what looked like angry sign language at him. Much to Cat's surprise, Brian started signing back. They had what appeared to be an animated argument in complete silence for about two full minutes when Cassie finally stalked off.

"What was that?" Cat asked.

"You don't want to know," said Brian.

"I mean the signing part. How do you know how to sign?"

"Oh, that! Well, Cassie is one of the interpreters for the deaf that the Avenue calls in if someone makes a request for one before a show. There are a few of them, actually. Anyway, Cassie and I went out a few times when I first moved here and I picked a bunch of it up from her. I liked it enough I took some courses. It's a lot like acting, really. I don't have much opportunity to use it, but it's a lot of fun. Most of it's not as vulgar as what you just saw."

Cat was struck by the whole scene. It got her thinking about Brian's past with women in a more concrete way which she knew very little about. It also explained the lovely gestures he tended to make with his hands when he talked. She wondered how unconsciously he might be translating for himself and if there were ever people who read sign visually eavesdropping on them from across the coffee shop.

Othello wrapped up a successful run toward the end of May, and then Brian's schedule was wide open until casting and rehearsals for the new season were set to start in August. With the extra time, as the weather got warmer and more pleasant, Cat and Brian even developed a habit of taking walks together downtown and exploring different neighborhoods. It was on one of those walks in mid-July that Cat discovered Brian had slept with three other women after the first time he slept with her.

"You what?"

"Cat, it's not like you were around. How was I to know I'd ever even see you again? You dropped off the edge of the earth for a while. You wanted to know why I think we need the condoms and that's why."

Cat was still shocked. She figured he had slept with a lot of women, but how many? The topic had come up because she was getting tired of using condoms. Stopping to deal with them disrupted their rhythm and they made him taste funny afterward.

"Besides," he said, "What about pregnancy?"

Cat blanched. "Trust me. That's not an issue."

Brian didn't pursue that and instead said, "Well, Cat, I get tested all the time, so if the only big concern is disease, I'm not that worried."

"When was the last time you went to the STD clinic?" Cat wanted to know.

"STI."

"What?"

"No one calls them STDs, it's been, like, STIs forever," explained Brian.

"Whatever. When was the last time you got tested? Before me? After those women? When?"

Brian thought for a second. "I guess...a couple of weeks before you. I suppose it has been a while."

This was beyond annoying. It was a fast way to diffuse any magic from the relationship. She felt like she wanted to take care of that uncertainty as rapidly as possible and get it off her mind.

"How long does it take?"

"Not long to do, but then you have to wait about three days for the results. We could go now if you like, I don't care."

"That's about the most unromantic thing I've ever heard," grumbled Cat.

Brian looked irritated. "Did I ever promise romance? And hey, it's not like you have some great foundation of purity to stand on at this point. I mean, shouldn't you be using condoms to protect 'Jack' the wonder vet?"

Cat shot him an angry look and he immediately cast his eyes to his shoes. She didn't know what to say to him, so they stood there in an uncomfortable silence.

"Look," he said finally, "This is seriously the longest relationship I've ever had, so I don't know what I'm doing. I don't know what this is. I don't want it to stop... but... I'm sorry. I didn't.... Let's go to the clinic. It's less than a mile walk and it's near some cool shops you might like. I can pop in, get tested, and then you can feel better, okay?"

"Okay," agreed Cat. This was an odd landmark in this new territory she'd entered. They didn't really talk on their way there. Brian held the door for her and once he stepped inside the receptionist glanced at him and turned her head toward the area behind her.

"Brian's back!" she called. "Hey, Honey, how're you doing?"

"Hey, April!" he said, as he took the clipboard she handed him and started casually checking off

176

boxes. Two young women in lab coats appeared from somewhere in the back and smiled at Brian and they all started chatting. He knew everyone by name, including the janitor.

Eventually someone noticed Cat there and the woman at the desk asked, "Do you need anything ma'am?"

"I, uh...." started Cat.

"She's just visiting," said Brian as he handed the completed forms back to April.

April cast Cat a peculiar look, and then she turned back to Brian.

"Well, you cute thing," she said to him, "why don't you just head on back with Mary and she'll take your blood today, all right?"

Brian and Bloody Mary headed into the back together, and Cat could hear him asking her about some class she had been taking. It was hard for Cat not to notice what a cute couple the two young people made. What did they make of her presence there? She didn't know and she didn't want to know. She took a seat in the small waiting area and ignored the television. None of the magazines looked interesting.

She was starting to wonder all over again what the hell she was doing. She enjoyed Brian, she really did, but what kind of guy is on a first name basis with everyone at the STD—ST freaking *I*—clinic? In a normal relationship you wanted to know more and more about the person you were with. In this case, the more she knew the less comfortable she became.

Cat thought about Brian telling them she was "just visiting," and she realized that was exactly what she was doing. When you visit a place you skim what you like from it as best you can, but you are not a part of it. You don't become invested because you will be leaving again for the life where you are truly involved and committed. Brian's life was a place she was just visiting.

She tried to find anything worth reading in the magazines on the waiting room table, but they were not aimed at her. It struck her with an unsettling clarity that they were aimed at her daughter. The one on snowboarding Liz even subscribed to online. Cat was still sorting through the disturbing implications of that when Brian returned with Mary laughing next to him. He had a bandage on the inside of his right elbow.

Cat got up and met him by the counter. April studied her again, and then her eyes opened wider with recognition. "You're the lady married to that nice pet doctor on the other side of town, aren't you? The one who writes all the books!"

Cat felt glued to where she was standing but every part of her was screaming that she should run. The mounting panic she was feeling was the closest she'd ever known to pure terror.

"Yeah! I had my dog in there last week. Got bit pretty bad by my neighbor's dog, but your husband stitched him up real good! Nice man, that pet doctor. Had a picture of you up on a shelf with some of your books. Good picture. Looks just like you."

"I...." but Cat's mouth had run dry and she was starting to feel unsteady.

Brian glanced at Cat, then herded her toward the door while he waved goodbye and said in April's direction, "Yes, she's working on a play that I might get to be in if I'm lucky."

"Well, no one gets luckier than you, Brian Honey," she said. She looked from him to Cat again and frowned slightly.

Out on the sidewalk, Cat was on the verge of a meltdown.

"Cat, calm down!"

"Calm down? *Calm down?* What was I thinking? Why am I being seen with you? If I were writing this in one of my books I would never have the protagonist be stupid enough to walk around town with her lover as if it were fine!" Then she clapped a hand over her mouth and hissed angrily, "And she would definitely be smart enough not to yell about it on a public sidewalk!" She was feeling shaky and frightened.

Brian started to move as if he meant to put his arms around her, but then seemed to think better of it.

"Cat?"

She looked at him but didn't really see him.

He waited another moment. "Cat, what do you want to do right now?"

She wanted to breathe normally, that's what she

179

wanted to do right now. She shut her eyes and thought for a moment. "I...I want to go to my car."

"Do you want me to walk you there or do you want to go alone?"

"I think..." she said eventually, "I think I should go alone." But she didn't move to go anywhere yet.

"Cat?"

"Hm?" She gave him another look that didn't actually settle on him anywhere. He waved a hand in front of her eyes.

"Are you going to be okay?"

She started walking then, and said more to herself than to him, "I haven't a clue."

CHAPTER NINE

Until her brush with potential discovery in the STI clinic, Cat hadn't seriously grappled with what the possibility of getting caught would mean. It would be a nightmare. It had all seemed so easy she got lulled into a false sense of safety.

Actually, until she started scheduling time to meet Brian, she hadn't realized how little her life intertwined with anyone she cared about who would notice anything had changed. Nick worked long, fairly predictable hours. Liz had either been in school, or once summer started there was skateboard camp until four which Cat drove her to and from herself, so she knew where her daughter was at those times. Most of the other people in her life whom she considered herself close to in her mind were not close in proximity. No one who saw her with Brian cared, so it had been easy. She wondered if she'd had more of the people around her whom she considered touchstones, such as her mother or her old high school friends, if she would have been so inclined to make the choices she had recently. Brian filled a space that she had carved out unwittingly.

Cat concluded that she was going to have to end it. Maybe not that minute, but probably before her birthday in September. That gave her about a month and a half to let Brian down gently. She would be extra careful about not getting caught, and she would enjoy what they had even more since she knew it was going to be over soon.

How long could such a thing go on anyway? Six months? A year? Ten years? There was no possible future in it for either of them. Even if she wanted to hang onto Brian, who knew how much of her body would remain appealing to him once she got into her 40's, and what about her 50's and 60's?

She had a life she liked. Cat hadn't realized how much until the picture of it getting torn away from her outside the STI clinic with Brian had entered her mind. If she had the chance to do her life over, this was still the place where she would have liked to end up.

The unexpected thing for Cat was how humanizing Brian in any way had killed the fantasy. When he was an unattainable god on a stage she couldn't imagine getting enough of him. Then when she'd had him and he was still playing a role, it was incredible. Then over time she got to know his habits and his quirks, and she had to take those things into consideration when dealing with him, both to be practical and to be kind. Lately she'd felt like she had two husbands to keep track of and it was annoying. No wonder polygamy only ever worked for men. What woman in her right mind wanted to monitor the needs and requirements of extra men?

Brian was still handsome to a degree that was stupefying, but there were moments she didn't notice that at all. She was too busy being irritated by something to enjoy him in blissful ignorance. For one thing, he ate junk, which didn't seem to make a lot of difference at the moment, but when it caught up with him it was not going to be pretty. He was dedicated to a very specific workout routine at his gym with arms on some days and legs and abs on others. That was fine, and he looked great, but he didn't ever want to use that body for anything other than acting or sex. He wouldn't swim with her or consider going on a hike somewhere and he didn't even know how to ride a bike. Cat was interested in being healthy, not just looking that way.

And what about whatever the story was with his family? It sounded bleak, what little she knew. It shouldn't matter since she certainly never expected him to take her to his familial home for Thanksgiving dinner, but it was disconcerting nonetheless. As far as she could tell he had no real past, and he somehow dropped down fully-formed at the Avenue one day.

His alcohol aversion was also irritating. It was fine with her that he didn't drink. Cat was not much of a drinker herself so she couldn't care less. But if she had so much as a sip of wine with a meal he refused to kiss her, and that was odd. They stopped eating Italian food together because she liked wine with it, and that was a sexual deal killer for Brian every time.

And the book thing was really getting on her nerves. He had to read everything by an author and she couldn't imagine what the point was. Not everything by an author was worth everyone's time, especially when there were so many great things out there to read. She could almost understand only reading the one best thing by every author, but any restrictions or rules on reading like that were anathema to Cat. If you were doing research on someone and needed to have the whole scope of what they did to understand their development and life, that was one thing, but for everything? It was useless! It had gotten to the point where she had stopped recommending books because it was too frustrating.

The last one she suggested was *The Handmaid's Tale* by Margaret Atwood. It was one of Cat's favorite books and she had wanted Brian to read it because there was one section in particular she wanted to be able to refer to and have him know what she was talking about. But it was a mess.

"Why are you reading *The Edible Woman*?" Cat asked him.

"It was Margaret Atwood's first novel."

"But that's not what I asked you to read. I wanted to talk about *The Handmaid's Tale*." Cat had trouble hiding her impatience.

"I know, I'll get to it. But I'm not looking forward to it, if this one's any indication."

"Well, the book is fine for what it is, but I could have told you it wasn't up your alley!"

"Yeah, well, it's quite the long feminist path you've sent me down so thanks a lot."

"I didn't send you anywhere but toward *The Handmaid's Tale*! Which it doesn't look like we'll get to discuss for a month if that stack is any indication. What has she written, a dozen novels?"

"Thirteen that I can find. God, this book is dull," Brian complained.

Unbelievable. There were times she wanted to slap that pretty head of his around.

She had toyed with the idea of tricking Brian into reading a short story she knew he'd love by Richard Bachman, and then letting him figure out for himself that it was really written by Stephen King under a pseudonym. She thought Stephen King was a terrific writer, and that he did the most convincing female characters from the point of view of a man she'd ever come across, but Brian was a snob about books and didn't want to go near any of those horror novels. She thought the real reason was that the sheer number of them that seemed to run endlessly with their black covers down the aisle at the bookstore was too much for him. An unabridged copy of *The Stand* alone would probably kill Brian, and Cat decided he was too beautiful to die.

The sex was great. That was hard to ignore. But the personal end of the affair was getting distracting and threatening to overshadow all of her fun. The possibility of Nick getting hurt loomed larger the longer things went on, and Cat had resigned herself to finding a way out before any more damage could be done. After a little more sex, though, since she couldn't imagine there was much of a difference between being blamed for two months of cheating versus four. There was an all or nothing quality to it that rendered that point moot.

There was one sticking point regarding Brian that she hadn't decided what to do with, exactly. Cat had recently returned a call from her agent expecting it to be related to publishing the play when it was done. She got a surprise instead.

"Cat! Once I realized you were open to the idea of adapting some of your work I started contacting people, and, well—there could be a movie!"

Cat was stunned. "For what book?"

"The one you told me to think about—that first one with the mom and the dead kid? Last time I called to bug you about your deadline you said you thought it could be resurrected as a movie, so I pitched the idea at a recent meeting and they loved it!"

"Really?"

"Yes! It's got two good roles for women in their thirties that certain actresses should scramble for, and it's a guaranteed tear-jerker with some funny lines on either side. The husband role is like a dream part because he's so appealing but gets to emote and still seem like a guy's guy. They were crazy about it!"

"Huh."

Cat could feel Michelle's irritation through the phone before she even spoke again. "Well aren't you excited? I mean, I've already got a screenwriter lined up to do the adaptation, but you get final veto power, I'll make sure of that. I have a good feeling that it may actually happen!"

"Yeah, no, it sounds incredible, Michelle. I just.... Can I recommend someone for a part?"

"What, you want your favorite television star in it or something so you can meet him?"

"No, I just know a local actor already who would make a great Zander, and it would be great if—"

"Cat, it doesn't work like that. I'm sure whatever studio picks it up will have their own ideas about casting and maybe need a certain person to make it worth their money. If they cast Tom Cruise I don't want you pulling an Anne Rice stunt and make waves you want him out."

"But—"

"One step at a time! It's a long process and we're like in the prenatal stages and you're talking college graduation. If someone wants your say in

187

any of that I'll keep it in mind and let you know, but I wouldn't set your heart on it."

Cat tried to keep her mind from darting in too many directions. "Well, as it happens, I do have some more dialogue for that book that came way after the fact. If you think the screenwriter would be interested in seeing any of it—"

"Yes! Send it! If it's on your computer you can e-mail it to me and I'll pass it along."

Cat was excited by the possibility of her first novel ending up on screen. It also made her a little nervous and she worried about it getting altered too much, but Michelle did say she was trying to make sure she kept some creative control, so that could work out.

Of course the main thing her mind kept going back to was Brian. What should she tell him? He didn't just look the part, he inhabited it in ways she thought were genius. He even used a slight trace of an East Coast accent muddled with elements of the Midwest added in that was perfect. Beyond the way he used the character for sexual role play, he had actually worked hard at finding all the nuances necessary to make Zander exactly right. Maybe another actor could do that, but it wouldn't be fair. The problem was it didn't sound promising in terms of her having any real sway, but maybe later when she knew what powers she might actually be granted she could tell him something with more certainty. The movie might never even happen at all, so it seemed cruel to potentially get his hopes up anyway. She would wait.

The next few weeks were hard for her, knowing she was planning to break up with Brian and not being able to share her news about the movie with him. They had sex, they hung out in his apartment, and she tried to just enjoy him and let certain irritations go. They didn't take walks together or go out to eat anymore, and that kept Cat's fear of discovery in check.

They even finished his story, finally. And it was good. Cat had originally thought they could do dozens of things from lots of angles and perspectives, but Brian didn't work like that. He was a cautious writer, handling his words on the page like grenades that he was holding the pins in. Cat kept reassuring him it was not intended to be a masterpiece, it was only a character study for practice, but he took it very seriously, so she did, too.

Brian picked at the story on and off over a total of many weeks, and eventually he convinced Cat to read it. It surprised her a little. The old man, who had once been very handsome and rich and married, was now decrepit and poor and alone. He had been wasteful in his dealings with money and people and now he was living with the consequences. He was headed to work in a fancy building where he did night watchman duty, but over the course of the journey we come to learn that his successful son has acquired the building where his father works but doesn't recognize him. It's implied by the time the old man steps off the bus that after work he plans to kill himself.

Cat wasn't sure what Brian was drawing on for his ideas, but he seemed satisfied with how it had come together. She had made some suggestions about reorganizing certain sections and taking out things that sounded redundant, but she left the final edit to him and he was happy. Cat was pleased to have made him happy.

But something about finishing that story caused Brian to open up for a change about his family. Not much, but enough to make Cat worry for him. They started off talking about names, and she told him about how when she first read his in a program it had sounded fake.

"No, it's my name. I thought about going with my full name 'Brian Michael Smith' to kind of give it more rhythm, but it's good. I never have to worry they'll spell my name wrong in reviews."

"So, you used your own middle name in your story?" asked Cat.

Brian shifted a bit in the bed next to her. "Sort of. Alan Michael is my dad's name."

"Wait, so, Alan Michael 'Jones' the old tortured guy in your story is your dad?"

"No. My dad would never figure out the world would be better off without him."

Cat sat not knowing what the right reaction should be. Did she dare ask about his mom? But then Brian went there on his own.

"And then who knows whatever happened to my

190

mom. How long do drunks last, anyway? I guess that's kind of like suicide, but it's so fucking slow."

Cat was out of her depth. That was territory for a therapist, not her. All she could think to say was, "I'm sorry."

"Yeah, well. Fuck 'em."

So there was that.

Then one Saturday afternoon in early August while Nick was out of town for a weekend symposium on heart worms, and she had already dropped off Liz at skateboarding camp for the day, Cat was settling in for some serious editing work when she got a call on her cell phone. That was wildly unusual since only her husband, her daughter and her mom had the number. She had the thing purely for emergencies and it almost never rang.

She quickly fished it out of her bag assuming either Nick or Liz were hurt and bleeding somewhere and was perplexed to find out it was Brian calling.

"Cat! I'm so glad I caught you! I need a favor."

"How did you get this number?"

Brian sounded taken aback. "What?"

"I just, I mean.... How did you get my cell phone number? I don't even remember it." Cat was bewildered.

"You have it written on the back of the phone on a piece of tape."

"When did you even see my phone?"

"I was going through your purse a few weeks ago because I needed some laundry quarters. I didn't think you'd care. Maybe I should be giving you phone lessons instead of acting lessons. The rest of the world finds texting useful."

Cat found herself gripping the phone too hard. Nick never went into her purse without asking. But that was Nick, wasn't it? This was Brian. Brian who had gone through her purse and was now calling her on her fucking emergency-only cell phone.

"Well, what is it, Brian? I'm in the middle of something."

"Oh."

"What is the favor?"

"It's, well—Cat, I have this shoot for a modeling job kind of out near where you live, and I'm supposed to return the lighting guy's car."

"What are you even saying to me?"

"There was a thing, over by me, with a bunch of these guys who are working the shoot today and they were drinking, and one of them ended up leaving his van here assuming I would just drive it over today."

"So drive it over there. You want my permission?"

"No, Cat, I don't drive."

"What do you want me to do about it?"

"I was hoping you could come drive me out there."

"Then how am I supposed to get back?"

"Oh, see, there's a different car I'm supposed to drive back because one of the makeup people lives by me and is getting a ride with her friend somewhere else and asked if I'd just take her car back. See?"

"What? How did you get yourself roped into driving two different cars when you don't even drive?" Cat was mostly irritated that the logistics of it were so incredibly stupid. Could no one under 30 plan anything properly?

"Please, Cat? I normally wouldn't ask, but it would really help me out."

Cat held her phone a minute and wondered if her breakup moment had come, but decided that was too insensitive to base it purely on her own convenience.

"Fine. Are you at home?"

"I can be wherever you want me."

Cat realized that mere weeks ago the same sentence would have aroused her. Now it was simply the sound of her time getting sucked up.

"Your place is okay. Wait downstairs and I'll be by soon."

Cat headed out. She felt put upon. It was the first time she was ever headed specifically to Brian's apartment where she wasn't looking forward to getting there. How could he go through her purse? And why did he feel entitled to some kind of weird chauffeur service from her? It was like...Liz.

She pulled up and saw Brian looking attractive on the sidewalk with a backpack slung over his shoulder. It was interesting how people's faces looked one way if you knew them, and another if they were strangers. She remembered running into her dad one time in an unexpected place—a shoe store in the middle of the day because one of his laces had broken—and she and one of her friends happened to be shopping there that afternoon. A man walked in who looked ordinary, but whose ears stuck out in a funny way and his nose was crooked. It wasn't until her friend said, "Hey, Mr. Devin!" that she realized it was her dad. He transformed right before her eyes and all she saw was the lovable face she adored. She tried to look at him objectively again, but it wasn't possible. Understanding altered perception in ways you couldn't control.

Brian had his own personal Brian look now. He was still handsome, but not actor handsome like he had been before. He was complicated and predictable and smart and annoying and fun and cool and self-absorbed. He was Brian and his face had meaning to Cat. She couldn't remember the image from before at this point. That stranger's face was lost to her.

Brian pointed her toward the green van parked a few spaces ahead as she got out of her own car.

"Please tell me you have keys and aren't expecting me to hot wire anything," she said.

Brian held up a set of keys with a keychain in the shape of a small sneaker and handed it over. He climbed in the passenger side, and once she was settled in behind the wheel adjusting the mirrors he gave her knee a squeeze. "Thank you so much, Cat!

This means a lot to me, and favors like this won't be some kind of habit, I promise."

Cat tried to smile. "Where do we go?"

"You know that big man-made lake in the middle of the park near you?"

"Uh-huh."

"Well, it's out there. They're using the lake as the backdrop. Usually I do modeling jobs in a studio, so it's interesting to do one outside. They lucked out with the weather, I guess."

"I guess."

Brian glanced over at her as they drove. "Are you pissed at me for something?"

"What? No, Brian, I.... You just caught me on a day when you weren't in my plans. I had the house to myself for the first time in a while and there was a bunch of stuff I wanted to get done before I ran errands. I'm a bit preoccupied is all, so it's hard to relax."

"Well, maybe after the shoot we can go somewhere and find a way to relax together. Maybe somewhere at the park—we've never done it outside together before."

"Are you *crazy*? It's bad enough I might be seen with you in this stupid van, but you want me to cheat on my husband out in the open in my own area of town on a beautiful day when the park will be *full*?"

"Whoa! Hey, Cat, I was joking! Half-joking anyway. What's wrong with you today?"

"Sorry," said Cat. "I have a meeting this

afternoon with Tom to go over the play again and Nick is gone all weekend."

Brian was quiet for a moment, and then he asked, "So your house is empty?"

Cat wasn't sure where he was going with that so she didn't say anything.

Brian asked instead, "When do I get to look at the play?"

"Whenever you like, really. I have to stop off at home and grab it before I take you back to your apartment, so you can skim it on the drive, even, if you like."

"Sounds good. Hey, we're getting close! The photographer said she'd be on the North side of the lake."

"The area with the artificial beach?"

"That would make sense. It's a swimsuit ad of some sort. It shouldn't take long and then we can switch out the cars and go."

Cat sighed. This was not how she had planned to use her Saturday, but it was gorgeous out, and the experience could be interesting.

They found the site of the shoot, which wasn't hard with all the equipment set up for additional lighting and all the pretty people standing around. Cat found herself an unobtrusive spot under a tree not too far away and had a seat. It was a warm day with a pleasant breeze and no clouds in the sky, and it did seem like a nice idea to sit back and clear her head for a while.

There was a makeshift changing area that Brian

ducked into and came back out of a moment later in blue swim trunks. Cat watched as he settled in at the makeup table and chatted with the woman who worked on him. Two different women took their turns in the changing area and put on stylish swimsuits. Cat hated even the idea of swimwear that you couldn't actually swim in, and these suits looked merely decorative.

Modeling was not particularly interesting to watch. There was a lot of standing around and making adjustments to everything. Brian simply stood with his back to the water and turned his head when asked and flashed his perfect smile from time to time. There were a few different costume changes, and the women took their turns. At one point they were all asked to pose together and look as if they were having a fabulous time, which they did effectively and could shut off in an instant.

Cat found herself watching the other people in the park instead. There were children in shorts running and old people walking and couples pushing strollers. She saw young skateboarders that reminded her of her daughter. There were people on bikes and other people walking dogs. There was a heavily pregnant woman walking slowly alongside someone Cat assumed was the woman's mother. There was a middle aged couple talking seriously together on one bench, and an old man feeding birds from another to the delight of the small child next to him. She was struck by all the phases of life represented at the park, and it hit her that they all had value and they were all beautiful in their own way. If everyone looked like the models by the water, the world would be extremely dull.

Brian was sent back to the makeup table for something and the two women were posing together. Cat wondered if Brian had slept with either of them. She wondered if he'd slept with anyone else since they last talked about it before the STI clinic incident. It wouldn't have surprised her, and frankly she didn't have a leg to stand on if she had an objection. Maybe under different circumstances she could have ended up more like Brian. It shocked her how much the basic workings of their minds were alike, but she suspected she had been loved and cared for in a way he couldn't even relate to, and that had affected their choices in life.

They hadn't done any Zander/Maddie scenes in a long, long time. She had been having sex with the real Brian and not a role for months, and she didn't know how she felt about it. She'd been observing him long enough to know that there were two Brian Smiths. One was a role he played out in the world. He was effective in it. He calculated when to use what smile and exactly how to position his body to facilitate whatever goal he was trying to obtain. This was the Brian Smith everyone saw over ninety-five percent of the time.

The last five percent she had an exclusive backstage pass for. This Brian was scared. He tried to hide that even from her, but she was around him too much when his defenses were down. Even someone as talented as Brian couldn't act all the time. She'd seen the real Brian and he was someone who struggled with self-doubt and feelings of inadequacy just like everyone else did. She found herself worrying for him more like she worried for her daughter, and that made her uneasy. And despite his charm and his ability to apparently find sexual partners with little effort, he was isolated. He was liked at the Avenue, but he didn't have anyone to talk to there. Not about anything personal or real. That loneliness was part of what they recognized in each other.

She thought about Nick. They had loved each other for so long she had felt acclimated to it. Cat thought about when they first met how little they had in common, other than a general sense of compatibility. They had an easy kind of love that was large enough to render differences that would seem insurmountable with anyone else, irrelevant.

There were more parts of Brian that she understood because they were so much like herself, but she didn't learn much by talking to herself. She and Nick had simply shared so much over time that they had built commonality between them through a conjoined history. She should have been trying harder to talk to Nick instead of assuming it was too late to find interesting common ground. It was natural when you found something you liked to want to repeat it, but compile that over years and years and it lost its meaning. Routine was what had made her stop looking at Nick the way she should

199

have. Maybe they should break up the routine. Maybe if they found some new activity to try they could see each other in a new light and use their compatibility to their advantage again.

Cat was afraid of getting older and afraid to die, but it started to occur to her that those things were going to happen anyway no matter what she did or whom she slept with. Whenever she was afraid, her impulse was to cling to Nick, but he had felt like part of that sinking ship when it came to aging and death. It was hard to forsake a lifeboat just to stand on the deck of the Titanic with her husband, but maybe they could learn to sing together on the way down into the sea.

She glanced at Brian looking perfect but with a life completely unconnected to the one she'd built. Suddenly it hit her that a consequence of bad choices could be to die alone.

Brian eventually finished up, wiped his makeup off with a towel, and got changed. He came bounding up to Cat by the tree.

"Did you see me?"

"What are you, four?"

Brian laughed. Apparently getting through the successful shoot had put him in a good mood.

"Well, I have the keys for the car we're supposed to take back, so can we go pick up your play now?" Brian asked. "Unless I can talk you into sex in the bushes over there," he added as a joke.

"The play seems less prickly. Let's grab it and then I have to run you home."

They pulled up in front of Cat's house in the rundown blue sedan, which she simply left on the street since they'd be leaving again so soon. She hadn't intended to let Brian in, but he was already getting out of the car and it made her uncomfortable to order him to stay like a dog.

Cat unlocked the front door and he followed her inside.

"This is beautiful," said Brian, stunned by the size of the house. Cat started to tell him to just wait there in the foyer when Pogo came bounding in. The little dog stopped several feet from Brian and started to growl.

"Whoa, I didn't know you had a dog," said Brian backing slowly away toward the living room.

"Pogo!" said Cat. "What is wrong with you lately? He's a sweet dog, really," she said looking over at Brian before scooping the little dog off the floor as he continued to bare his teeth in Brian's direction.

"Seems like a real peach," said Brian who was now far enough into the living room to get distracted by the huge number of books. Cat figured Brian could stay put there for a moment, and she tossed Pogo into the backyard which was fenced, but the little dog simply scratched at the door. Cat would worry about him later.

She headed upstairs to look for the things she needed in her office which wasn't going to be easy. It was as if the things associated with Tom Olsen were contaminated with some strange spell that moved things into messy heaps. Cat was organized, but somehow the plays and rewrites and notes and work she'd done with Tom were in bits and pieces everywhere.

As she started compiling what she needed, she heard the front door open and close and she assumed Brian had finally gone back to the car. God, please don't let him introduce himself to any of the neighbors. Wouldn't that be a disaster? She'd have him safely back at his apartment soon. She kept rummaging until she thought she had it all, and started down the stairs.

Cat was halfway back to the first floor when she heard voices coming from the living room. One of them sounded like Liz, but it couldn't be Liz because Liz was gone for the day. She wasn't due for Cat to pick her up for three more hours. But it *was* Liz. And apparently Brian hadn't left because Brian's voice was down there, too. And who was the third voice? The third voice was male and asking something about why the door had been left unlocked. There was more Cat couldn't make out so she moved farther down the stairs to listen.

"Yeah, it's just weird to see someone else pull books off a shelf the same way my mom does," came Liz's voice.

"You kind of have to pull them out like that, I mean, do you know how much this thing is probably worth? It's signed!" said Brian.

"Yeah, there's a lot of stuff like that around. When I had to read *The Great Gatsby* for school my

202

mom bought me my own paperback version because she didn't want me handling hers."

"I can see that," said Brian. "Some things shouldn't get ruined. And a book like that you should be able to read the first time by cracking it open wherever and dragging it with you outside and laying it flat on your bed while eating cookies or something. It's more fun with your own paperback."

"We don't have cookies," said Liz.

"I suppose not," said Brian.

Then the third voice said, "But, like, I thought you said no one would be home."

"Come on, Chad, I told you my dad's out of town and my mom's car's not here—she always takes an hour at the grocery store and then she has some stupid theater thing to do again so there's lots of time before she comes to get me at skate—"

"But, like, why is this guy here? Why are you just talking to some burglar?"

Oh Chad, because no one calls the cops on a hot guy holding a book, thought Cat.

She finally moved to the bottom of the stairs where she could see them in the living room. Brian was leaning against the built-in bookcase with her copy of *Sanctuary* in his hands. He was slumped down a little and leaning forward to be in better eye contact with Liz, who was standing only a couple of feet in front of him. Brian looked absorbed, the way he always did when he talked directly to one person and drew him or her (usually her) in. Chad looked nervous and was positioned as if he wanted to go but didn't want to leave Liz there.

At one point, when Liz glanced over at Chad, Cat thought she saw Brian's eyes travel lightly over the length of her daughter's body. Something in Cat felt like she had just hit the bottom of a drained swimming pool head first. For the first time she realized that Brian was closer in age to her daughter than to her. That in only a matter of a few years, Liz and Brian would make a much more plausible couple than the two of them ever had. She felt sick. She looked at Brian and wondered what the point had been for him. Liz was easily Girl from the play, who was a siren of youth, and as much as it pained Cat to admit it of her baby, she was sexy, just standing there in her innocence and her desire to be taken seriously. That left Cat in the role of Woman. She remembered watching Brian recoil from the touch of Woman on stage and how she had felt personally hurt by that. It was such a relief when he did desire her the way she had hoped for, but now it seemed absurd. She was not in the same league with her daughter on that score and it made her.... It made her a joke.

But she had parental business to take care of and she could nurse her own ego later.

"Liz!"

All three people in the living room looked up quickly. Cat worried Chad might wet his pants. Liz seemed guilty, and then defiant. Brian just looked like Brian. He was hard to ruffle, but he had an amused look on his face.

"What?" Liz asked in an aggravated tone.

"So at least we know Chad has some sense. Not a lot, but more than you. Good job, Chad. You're leaving now."

Chad didn't need to be told twice. He gave Liz one last apologetic glance and he was out the door.

Then Liz covered up her embarrassment with anger and started to yell. "God, Mom! Why don't you trust me? It's not like we were doing anything!"

"You're going say to me 'Why don't you trust me?' and 'It's not like we were doing anything' when you are not even supposed to be here in the house? Why am I even driving you back and forth to skateboard camp when apparently you have some other ride available? I cannot believe—"

"But Mom! It's not fair! Everyone else gets—"

"I don't give a damn what everyone else gets, you are in big trouble! I am calling your father to see if he can get back here early and we are having this out." Then Cat remembered Brian was still standing in her house. She had to get him out of there.

"But Mom!"

"Liz, stop it! I have to step out again for just a minute, but when I get back you better be waiting here by yourself. You know you're not supposed to bring boys home without permission!"

Liz glared at her. "But you did."

Cat went completely still. She thought she saw Brian raise an eyebrow slightly.

205

"Go to your room!" Cat shouted.

"Make me!" challenged Liz.

Cat stood in a face-off with her daughter and Brian simply took it all in as if he had a front row seat to the hottest ticket in town. Without looking at him, Cat addressed Brian in the same deadly mom tone she was about to use on her daughter.

"Get in the car, Brian." He put Faulkner back on the shelf and looked a little scared as he headed toward the door.

"Liz," she said quietly but with a concentrated ferocity. "While you are in my home and we care for you, there are certain rules we expect you to follow. If you want to negotiate those rules you have to do so like an adult. But right now, all I see is a child, and I will strip your room of every last item and let you sleep on the floor until you are eighteen if you don't get up there right this minute. We can live together peacefully your last few years here, or you can find out the hard way just how much you have to lose. Your choice. If you are not here—and alone—when I get back, everything you think you own goes up on eBay this afternoon."

Liz was crying and gnashing her teeth a little, but she turned and ran up the stairs in the noisiest way possible and screamed, "I hate you!" as she slammed her door.

Cat met Brian on the doorstep and silently walked to the car. She was like smoldering glass. Brian let himself in on the passenger side. They drove in complete silence most of the way downtown. Cat was completely in her own head and Brian wasn't allowed access.

As she dropped him off he asked if she wanted to come by on Monday.

"I'll get back to you," she said.

"Okay."

"And Brian?"

"Yeah?"

"Don't call my phone again."

*

Cat and Nick sat their daughter down for a heated discussion. They were a firm but fair team, and Liz was unhappy, which Cat felt under the circumstances was how it should be. They contacted Chad's parents, which mortified Liz, and it was agreed that the two teens could continue to see each other if supervised, but one more unauthorized slip-up and there would be serious consequences—which in Liz's case meant an end to snowboarding and anything related to it. That got her attention. There was a lot of crying that eventually turned into serious sullen discussion. It was tumultuous, but satisfying. Cat felt she was back on track and doing what she was supposed to be doing.

It was also good to feel as if she and Nick were on the same page with something. They lay in bed together and talked until late that night in a way they hadn't in a very long time.

"How long do you think she'll hate us?" Nick wanted to know, as he lay with his arms around his wife.

"About this? A good two weeks. Then she'll hate us for something entirely new, so you won't notice a difference. You know, though, she'll forgive you faster, anyway, so it's hard to say."

"Why's that?"

"Because you're her dad and she adores you, and as far as Liz can tell you only go along with this kind of thing because I make you."

"Do you think I should make it clearer that I agree with you?"

Cat thought about it. She appreciated that he was willing to take on some of the mantle of the bad cop. "Nah. She should think someone's on her side. It's lonely where she is right now."

Nick hugged her and they just stayed like that for a while. Then Nick said, "You know, Cat, I was thinking we might sign up for some kind of dance lessons or something at that place down the street from work."

They were both bad dancers, so that could be embarrassing, but maybe fun. "What brought that idea on?"

"Nothing in particular. I've just been thinking we should find more things we can do together. It doesn't have to be dancing, but the idea of waltzing you around a room seemed nice."

Cat turned to face him better. "That's funny, because I was just thinking something very similar today! I was sitting at the park and I saw—"

"Why were you at the park?"

"Just—no reason. It was nice out today. There

were a lot of people at the park."

"Huh. So, you were saying?"

"I, um...I forgot what I was saying. You know, Nick, I think I'm going to get some sleep now."

"Sounds good." He yawned and rolled over but kept his back against hers. "Love you."

"I love you, too."

They were a good team, and she was glad he was her partner in parenting. She was glad he was her partner period. She was certain about it now. It was time to let Brian go. Nick deserved her full attention and devotion and she wanted her old life back. The same old Nick now seemed like plenty to be satisfied with. She'd experienced just enough of something different to know that predictable could be comforting and rewarding in its own way. She had risked too much.

Cat thought the rest of the weekend about how and where to handle that conversation with Brian, and most of Monday as well, which except for swimming she spent at home with Liz (much to her daughter's displeasure, but that kind of animosity was hard to maintain and was already waning).

In the end, the breakup with Brian sort of sneaked up on her in a way Cat didn't expect. Since she had missed her meeting with Tom, Cat rescheduled and headed over to the Avenue on Tuesday after swimming. She hadn't realized that other people would be there making preparations for the new season already. She ran into Brian on her way out of Tom's office.

"Hey, Cat!" he said, looking pleased to see her there. "Where were you yesterday?"

"Brian! Yeah, I was kind of caught up in something. I was going to try to find you later, actually. Um, what's your schedule like today?"

"I'm in the middle of a break now, and then I've got a couple of things to do here, but I should be able to head back to my place in maybe an hour or so. You want to meet me there? You can take my key and—"

"No, I don't think so." She looked around for a moment. "Brian, I need to talk to you, actually, but...."

"Well, I've got time now for whatever it is. Come back here...."

He glanced around to make sure they were alone, then he took her hand and led her down a hall and around a corner into a private dressing room. It made Cat a little nervous, but she decided there was no good place for this anyway, so she may as well get it over with.

Brian shut the door behind them and before she could protest he kissed her. It was a nice kiss. Still eager but familiar by now. Only Cat knew it was their last kiss and it made her sad when his lips left hers.

He smiled and held on to one of her hands and said, "So, what is it?"

Cat simply enjoyed looking at him so close for a moment. This idea had seemed a lot less hard away from Brian. She wasn't having second thoughts, exactly, but there was reluctance to see their relationship end.

"I think we should stop seeing each other."

There was a twitch in the grip on her hand and then he let it go. He looked so astonished that it would have been comical if it weren't so sad. He didn't say anything.

"It's just...there is nowhere for this to go, Brian. It has to stop sometime and I think now should be it."

He looked confused. "But, Cat...I...I want you. What am I not doing right?"

"Nothing, Brian, that's not it. I think you know that, don't you?"

"But I want you," he repeated. "I need you. How am I supposed to...?" His gaze moved down to her body and he started to reach out as if to put his hand on her waist, and Cat stepped backward slightly. He stopped, seeming to sense a new boundary had been drawn. Cat recognized it as an old boundary that never should have been moved. Brian appeared agitated and unsure.

Cat didn't like to see him upset and wanted to make it better. Maybe she was doing it wrong. She remembered the breakup she'd overheard at the coffee shop and for lack of a better idea she decided to draw on that.

"Look, you're amazing, and if anyone could make it work it would be you, Brian. It's not fair for you to have to deal with this, but the timing is bad. You deserve someone who is really available for you. We're just going to have to let this go now."

Brian's eyes widened and he started moving his mouth but nothing came out. Finally he managed, "What is happening?" And he glanced around the room as if he were waiting for some kind of gotcha hidden camera show to announce itself.

"Brian, I'm really sorry, but—"

"Cat, why? This works for us, I thought! I mean...." He leaned back against the counter in front of a makeup mirror. Cat thought it was the most unguarded posture and expression she had ever witnessed in him and he'd never struck her more as a boy. She felt uncomfortable and her heart went out to him, and she decided she should go.

She started to move toward the door while saying, "Goodbye, Brian," but he put his hand on her arm lightly and she stopped.

"But I don't want you to go, Cat, I...."

Cat looked at him and vaguely wondered if she could take it back. Of course, even if she really wanted to, she couldn't take something like that back. No, it was done and this was their new reality and it was time to start adjusting to it.

"I'm sorry. I really am. It...I thought it would be nice if we got to have everything we wanted all at once, but I'm starting to believe we weren't meant to. I don't want to be hurting the people I care about."

Brian looked dazed. He was breathing faster. "But what about...? I don't count at all? Don't you care about me?"

Cat couldn't look at him, and glanced down at his graceful hands instead. They were strong, young hands, but she realized she honestly preferred ones that did origami to make her smile and healed dogs and had held Liz as a baby. She looked into Brian's blue eyes and said again, "I'm sorry."

She left him there, his image reflected infinitely in the mirrors on either side of the dressing room, and hoped no one would notice she was crying on her way out of the Avenue.

CHAPTER TEN

Cat was sure Brian had felt them drifting toward something that wasn't working, too, and was thrown by the intensity of his reaction to the breakup. She had pictured him maybe asking if they could still talk at the coffee shop, but that he still really wanted her was a surprise. He was young, he would heal, he would find someone his own age in no time and forget this whole thing ever happened, Cat tried to convince herself. It was for the best.

She spent the next few weeks preparing for Liz's birthday and trying not to think about the fact that she herself was turning 40 so soon. Cat and Liz had birthdays only two days apart in early September, and they were used to celebrating them together on the day in between. It had been a nice tradition, but Cat was told that was ending. Liz was feeling too old and grown up to share a party, and she wanted to have a fancy dinner at a nice restaurant on her actual birthday which fell on a Saturday that year. It depressed Cat a little because she was looking forward to the liveliness that the double party provided on a year when she could use a lift. Nick didn't seem to have anything special planned for her, because he was distracted by his plans for Liz turning 15. Turning 40 was managing to look worse all the time.

Liz had been remarkably well behaved, and in a way that Cat believed for a change. She had a long talk sort of at her daughter, and Liz had listened. Cat explained the best she knew how that she was trying to keep Liz from being in danger, not attempting to keep her from having any fun. She told Liz she thought it was fine that she pushed the limits from time to time, but maybe she should start exploring more adult ways of doing it, instead of storming around like a little kid. She asked Liz to consider what the responsibility for caring for her looked like from Cat's angle. Liz was grumpy the whole time, but the speech had an impact. She was more courteous and less reluctant to share information about where she was going and with whom.

Nick and Cat agreed to surprise Liz with a new snowboard. Cat really didn't like the idea of Liz using the board with the blown edge, and a new one seemed like a good birthday present. Nick arranged for Cat to go out with Liz's closest friends from her snowboarding clique to make sure they got the right thing. It was an interesting afternoon, because unlike her daughter, Anna and Jessica thought she was a pretty cool mom. Cat paid attention to them when they talked, and she wasn't shy about any topics they wanted to discuss. She didn't talk to them like children and they appreciated it. Of course, they weren't her children, so that was easy.

When they got to the sporting goods store Cat was grateful for Nick's foresight, because choosing anything on her own would have been a disaster. Cat knew enough about what her daughter did to be able to inform a salesperson that Liz was "goofy" (which meant she rode with her right foot forward instead of her left), and that she did a lot of tricks on boxes but was at heart a freerider. That was about where her lingo ended, and the fashion element was completely beyond her. There was a huge amount of attention paid to making sure you looked as if you didn't pay any attention to fashion at all. The girls were supposed to match, but not *too* much, and Cat completely deferred to what Liz's friends decided. The board they picked out had bold neon swaths of color and skulls all over it, and the girls convinced Cat to get Liz a new hoodie to match and some new bindings and boots. She was the walking wallet, but she didn't mind. Liz's friends were funny and nice and it was reassuring to spend time with them and know that Liz was not keeping bad company.

Cat also enjoyed having a project with Nick. He wanted Liz to have a real piece of jewelry and they went to an upscale store together and admired all the pretty things there.

"What do you think she'd like?" asked Nick, who seemed overwhelmed by the choices.

"I don't know, it's not like I have any particularly good jewelry myself to go off of," said Cat, hoping the hint might land. She'd come back on her own and treat herself to something for her birthday if everyone else had really forgotten.

"I mean, does she have a favorite color?"

"Dorian Grey. All those eye rolls are making her portrait in the attic really baggy."

Nick smirked. "Aren't there, like, birthday colors?"

"Birthday colors? Like balloons?"

"No, not like—you know, each month gets a color?"

"Oh, birthstones!" said Cat.

"I guess."

Cat said, "Yes, I mean, it's not really a color, it's a gemstone, and some of those vary, color-wise. But September's is sapphire. I think she'd love a sapphire. Didn't you take a ton of geology classes in school? How did you end up thinking of birthstones as 'birthday colors'?"

"Well it's not like that's a science thing! It's a random sales tactic thing. How is there any reasonable connection between September and Sapphires? In geologic time September is irrelevant."

"Hm. I don't know who assigned what stones to what months, I'm just glad I got a good one."

"There are bad ones?"

"There aren't any that make me go 'ew' but some are definitely better than others."

"Is mine a bad one?"

"I'm sure yours is fine whatever it is."

Nick moved to a different counter where they had various jewelry made with sapphires on display. Before Cat caught up with him he was already signaling to a sales clerk to take something out of the case for him to see.

"That one. Cat, it's that one."

It was beautiful. A simple pendant of sparkling blue on a silver chain. Cat had to admit, it seemed like something Liz would pick out if she were there.

"I like it. I think she will, too," said Cat.

The salesclerk smiled at them and proceeded to package it in a velvet lined box and to wrap the whole thing in silver paper with a ribbon.

As they waited, Nick looked off at nothing in particular and said, "God, Cat, how is she almost 15? She was such a small thing when we brought her home. Remember how when she was fussy she'd fall asleep if I just put her on my chest with her head under my chin?"

"Yeah, I remember some long nights where you were stuck holding her like that for hours, though."

"I didn't mind. I used to take her down with me in the night when you needed sleep and watch games or races on TV that way. Sometimes now when I watch NASCAR I still kind of feel the weight of her there on me. The two things kind of go together now." Nick blinked as his mind returned to the present. "Where does the time go?"

"I don't know. But this year Liz will be the most elegantly bejeweled girl in the skate park."

Cat felt a bit like she was getting a chance to fall in love with Nick all over again. She knew for sure that it wasn't just a relationship she was stuck in because time had tricked her into it. Nick wasn't perfect, but she admired his talents and his sweetness. It was a relief to be with a man who was genuine, and not putting on an act. She now knew he was too trusting and she felt protective of him in a way she hadn't before. Ironic, she knew, since the only person he'd needed protection from was her, apparently.

Cat wanted to make things up to him if she could find a way to do it that wouldn't make him suspicious. Brian was behind her and her life with Nick was ahead. She'd learned she was capable of extremes that needed to be kept in check, but at least now she knew what things really mattered to her and understood more clearly who she really was.

On the evening of Liz's birthday, before going to a French restaurant, Liz insisted she wanted to put Cat's hair into a French braid to match the theme for the evening. Cat thought that sounded sweet until Liz also insisted on playing music in the room much too loud and then proceeded to botch the braid over and over. It took forever and Cat felt like she was going deaf.

When Cat finally said she would rather simply brush her hair out and not be late, Liz ran ahead of her and said she'd meet her downstairs. Cat went downstairs herself, irritatedly running a hand over her hair which was now feeling irreparably mussed after Liz's repeated attempts to essentially create knots with it. As she got to the bottom of the steps and turned to the living room she stopped. It took her a moment to comprehend it was full of people. Then they all cheered.

"How—?" she managed, her eyes filling with tears as she spotted Nick looking quite proud of himself in the crowd.

"Ha! Mom, we totally got you!" said Liz, who looked about as proud as her dad.

Her family was there, her friends Becca and Amy and their families were there, her agent, the people from Nick's clinic and a few of his siblings (although his parents hadn't been able to get away because of a church obligation). There was also a huge gaggle of Liz's friends, so it turned out the double-party was still on after all. The catering was delicious, Liz's friends took over the music, and Cat felt so loved and happy she had moments of almost feeling worthy of it all. Right when she thought it couldn't get better, there were the presents. Cat was overwhelmed.

"But the party is more than enough! This should

be my present, all of you being here. If you like what you got me just keep it and enjoy." But no one was having any of it. They'd bought her gifts and she was taking them.

Cat and Liz sat side by side and took turns opening their packages. It was hard to know what was sillier, some of the things from Liz's friends or some of the things from Cat's. But the big gifts of the night were both from Nick. Liz loved her new snowboard (which her friends hadn't been able to keep a secret after all), but she was so surprised by the silver necklace with the sapphire pendant that she actually cried.

Cat got a necklace of 40 small diamonds. She held it in her hands and was speechless. It was like holding the Milky Way.

"So 40 won't look like such a bad number to you, I hope," said Nick as he helped her clasp it around her neck.

40 wasn't looking nearly as bad. In fact, she was finally coming to believe 40 wasn't all that old. She was healthy and apparently still nice to be seen with and many years away (knock on wood) from being a grandmother, so what was her problem? She decided to wait and really freak out at 50 instead. Or maybe 60.

Cat was so happy and remorseful at the same time that she couldn't stop crying or laughing. She kissed her husband who looked pleased to see her smile. He spent much of the party with his arm around her waist as they mingled in the joyful crowd as a team, and then they split up to "divide and conquer" as they called it, in order to cover seeing more people.

And then Brian showed up.

Liz was the one who answered the door, and Cat from the dining room heard her say, "Hey, the book guy! I guess you're late. Mom's over in there with my uncle."

"I can find her, thanks," she heard Brian respond.

By the time Brian stepped into the room and spotted Cat, she had excused herself from her conversation with her brother and moved across the room to meet him before he entered too far. She hoped they were safely out of earshot of anyone else at the party. There was panic in her eyes. Brian glanced at the glass of wine in her hand and then at the diamonds around her neck and said, "Nice collar."

"What are you doing here?" she wanted to know, trying to sound normal and not suspiciously hushed.

In a low voice only she could hear he said, "Looks like a nice party. What would you do if I decided to stay and crash it, huh? Would I blend in without incident or not? Since there's space in my bed nowadays, maybe I should find someone here to bring home. Is Liz still jailbait or do I have to wait another year? Or maybe we can take this opportunity to just spill your little secret in front of everyone you know at once and kill lots of birds with one bloody stone, what do you think?"

Cat's heart was going impossibly fast. She set down her glass so her shaking hand wouldn't spill it. She whispered, "Brian, please! What the fuck is wrong with you? If you need to talk just come upstairs a minute." What was he doing? He'd had a few weeks to come to terms with the breakup, so why was he this mad? If he was trying to scare her it was working.

Brian took his time following her upstairs which made Cat more anxious. She waited for him impatiently in the bedroom and he only bothered to shut the door partially behind him.

"What the hell are you doing?" asked Cat. "I thought you cared about me more than this! Why would you come around when my whole family is here, just to torture me?"

Brian shook his head. "Everything's about you, isn't it?"

"What?"

"In bed, in your work, everything revolves around you. Who made you queen of the universe, pussycat?"

She'd have sworn he was drunk if she didn't know that was impossible. The look he'd given her when he spotted the wine in her hand when he arrived was enough to determine that nothing had changed there. "Brian, just tell me what this is about already and then you have to go!"

"The movie."

Cat stared at him blankly for a second and then

it hit her that he knew. As soon as the look of guilty understanding washed over her face, Brian looked as if he'd had his suspicions confirmed.

"You *did* keep it from me on purpose! How could you do this to me, Cat?" Brian demanded.

"Keep your voice down!" Cat hissed at him.

"No!" he said angrily, but his volume did come down considerably. "No, you don't get to decide everything. You don't get to screw me and then screw my career too! I had to find out about the movie through goddamned backstage gossip? What the fuck is that?"

"Brian, I swear, I was trying to do the right thing by you, but I don't have—"

"Some agent comes around to talk to Tom going on and on about how this whole movie deal is a definite go and they are already talking about the Zander role being the perfect setup for an Oscar nod and how Catherine Devin has added all sorts of new scenes and dialogue and holy fuck, Cat! That's how I find out, and it's been in the works for how long?"

"Brian—"

"And I was the one who told you it would make a good screenplay in the first place!'

"I know, you're right, you did, and—"

"Are you kidding me? Damn it, Cat! Just tell me, did you know before the breakup or didn't you?"

"Brian—"

"*Did you*?"

She paused, and then she said carefully, "I knew

two months ago."

He clenched and unclenched his fists and tried to get his breathing under control.

"Brian, listen to me a minute! I—"

"God, I feel so fucking used!" He gritted his teeth and for once didn't seem to know what to do with his hands. He glared at her. "I get disappointment. I've had a whole mother-fucking lifetime of that and I can deal with it, but outright betrayal? You're fucking brilliant at that so I should have expected it. All that time in my bed you think I'd know you better, beyond your stupid-ass health food quirks and those weird scars you won't talk about. I don't know why I didn't see something like this coming! Christ, you have more loyalty to a swimming pool than to any fucking human being, or any human being you're fucking for that matter."

Cat didn't know whether to try and console him or fight back. Part of her felt shattered and another part was starting to swell with resentment. "Brian, I swear to God I wanted to tell you about the movie but when I tried to ask them about casting—"

"That role is *mine*, Cat! Zander is mine and you don't get to—"

That finally pushed Cat over from fear and confusion into anger. "No! You may look like Zander and you may fuck like Zander but he belongs to *me*! You may be good, but you're not good enough to actually be Zander so stop feeling so goddamned entitled!"

Brian looked as if she'd slapped him. There was

225

genuine hurt in his eyes and she regretted what she'd said. Right then she regretted a lot of things. She wanted to explain it to him, but he was not going to be able to hear her. He didn't trust her. Because she wasn't trustworthy.

"I'm sorry, Brian, I didn't mean—" she started, and reached out to touch his arm, but he grabbed her wrist to stop her. His grip was alarming and she gasped. He simply held her there for a moment.

That was when they realized Nick was in the doorway. Cat had no idea how long he'd been there, but he looked grave, and he said simply, "Let go of my wife."

Cat didn't recognize his voice. It was lower in pitch than normal, and reminded her of dogs at the clinic when they got desperate and cornered. They sounded bigger than they were.

Brian studied Nick cautiously. Then he smiled in a way that reminded Cat of his role in *Othello* and he slowly relaxed his grip. Cat pulled her arm back and rubbed the clearly defined impressions left by his fingers. The same fingers that had brought her such pleasure not long ago, she thought to herself. It didn't seem possible.

Brian glared at Cat and then he tried to push past Nick to leave the room but Nick didn't budge. He stepped around Nick instead and on his way out he said quietly to him, "You should fuck her with her face down and her ass up, 'Jack.' That always makes her scream." And then he was gone.

Cat literally wanted to die. She'd never

understood people who committed suicide until that moment. The whole situation was too big and awful and she couldn't handle it. The look on Nick's face, the people downstairs...the humiliation was too huge. Better not to see any of it or risk having to deal with it tomorrow. She thought of the uncle she'd never met and wondered if he'd released his blood with a gun or a knife.

Nick stared at her. Neither of them moved for a long time, and then they both became aware again of the sounds of the party below.

"Is your arm okay?" Nick asked flatly.

"Nick, I—"

"Is your *arm* okay?" he asked again, this time with force.

It scared her. She nodded.

Nick glanced away from her. "I'm going to go downstairs now. I may put your mom in charge of the party because I don't feel well." But he didn't move to go yet.

"Nick?"

"What?" he asked quietly, still not looking directly at her. She thought she saw tears welling up in his eyes, but he didn't seem to notice them himself.

"Let's... Can we... Can we talk about this? Just please don't go!" said Cat.

He finally turned toward her. The look in his eyes was so detached it was as if she were a stranger in front of him. The look was devoid of recognition. "You don't want me here right now.

One of us actually cares about not doing something they might regret later, and that apparently is not you."

He started to turn away when Cat took a small step in his direction and said, "Nick?"

He paused. "What?"

"What do you want me to do?"

He looked at her again, but this time with a penetrating kind of gaze that felt as if he was seeing her too well. She didn't know which was worse. "I don't care what you do," he said. Nick left.

Cat could feel herself going into shock and she made herself sit down where she was on the floor in case she passed out. She didn't, but she wished she would. She was shaking and she was cold and she felt as if invisible hands were strangling her.

She vaguely listened to the sounds downstairs. She didn't know what everyone would think when she didn't reappear, but Cat had no intention of leaving her room, possibly ever. After about half an hour, her mom knocked lightly on her open door.

"Catherine?" she asked cautiously.

Cat glanced up from her spot on the floor and realized she should probably sit on the bed and maybe take off her heels. She started to get up but one of her legs was asleep and she stumbled a little. Her mom was concerned and rushed in to help her onto the bed.

"Sweetheart, what happened? Nick said he wasn't feeling well and he left on foot somewhere. I've been tending to the guests but wanted to come check on you. Are you okay?" she asked.

Cat was dazed but out of tears and she didn't say anything. She saw her mother eyeing the fading marks on Cat's arm that looked like they might be bruises by morning. Cat covered them with her hand and hoped her mother didn't think Nick had done something.

"Catherine?" her mother tried again.

"I'm sorry. I can't talk about it right now, but I'm really sorry. I'm so, so sorry."

Diane continued looking concerned and sat with her daughter for a while in silence. Eventually she got up, kissed Cat on the forehead, and closed the door behind her on the way back down to tend to the houseful of guests.

The adults at the party each thought that Cat and Nick were merely at some other end of the festive space, and they filtered out on the early side. Liz's guests stayed much longer and took over the television room to play video games and did a thorough (if disappointing) raid of the kitchen, but at some point Nick finally returned to the house and started easing everyone out.

At about three in the morning, a good couple of hours after the last of the guests had left, Nick came back to the bedroom. Cat got up quickly and faced him.

"I sent Liz off to Anna's house for the night. Her mom didn't mind and Liz just thought it was a birthday thing. We need to have this out, and as much as I don't like to raise my voice I feel entitled to the option."

"Okay," said Cat after a moment.

"How long?"

"What?"

"Don't make me repeat myself tonight, Cat." He was obviously mad and trying hard to stay calm. Occasionally he would rub his forehead a bit as if one of his bad headaches was back. The kind he got if he'd had to put some animals down. "How long has this been going on?"

"I stopped it over two weeks ago. I suppose it really started in mid-April, which I guess would make it about four months," said Cat quietly.

Nick's jaw dropped. He looked away from her a moment and then turned back, stunned. "How...? But we—I don't..." he stammered. He started pacing a little and then finally sat down on the end of the bed and rubbed his head again. Cat didn't know what she should be doing so she stood there silently until he addressed her once more.

"Cat, for God's sake why? If you were unhappy or, or...Why the hell didn't you talk to me?" He was starting to raise his voice.

"I don't know, Nick. I'm sorry." She started to cry again. Nick made no move to comfort her.

"Who was he?" Nick asked through gritted teeth, as if bracing for an answer that would feel like a blow.

"Does that really matter?"

"It mattered to you! Just—who the hell was he?"

"He's an actor from the Avenue."

She could see Nick's mind jump around for a second and then land on why the young, good-looking man he'd caught arguing with his wife looked familiar. "He was in that play we went to, wasn't he? The strange baby play, and the same guy who played Iago...." He stared at Cat in disbelief. "Christ, Cat! How old is he? He's just a kid! What...?" Nick sat speechless for a moment. He stood up again, but he didn't make a move to go anywhere.

Cat was feeling defensive, even thought she knew she had no right to. She also wasn't sure if this was one of the questions she was supposed to answer before Nick could repeat himself, so she said quietly, "He's 23."

Nick just stared at her.

Cat started babbling, "Nick, I'm so sorry! It's over and I never meant to hurt you and I don't know what I can do now but I'll do anything and I just.... Nick I love you! I do! You have to believe me! I—"

"*Stop it!*" He was officially yelling now. The sound of his own voice at that level seemed to add to his frustration, so he shut his eyes a moment, then continued in an emotional but more even manner. "Love is an action, Cat! How dare— You don't get to stand there saying you love me when for months, or longer for all I know, you've lied and cheated and—" He rubbed his eyes briefly. "Love is about honesty and trust and kindness. Love is a choice, Cat. And you chose to fuck some kid behind my back for months and you can stand there and say

231

you love me? What kind of twisted universe did you make up now where that's true?"

Cat didn't respond. The verbal part of her mind felt like it was in a straightjacket and being dragged down a dark corridor. Tears ran off her face and she fumbled her fingers nervously together.

Nick was balling up his fists tightly and glancing around at objects in the room as if he were looking for something to throw. He started moving toward the door. "I'm sleeping in the guest bedroom tonight."

Cat nodded. She was shaking again.

Nick paused in the doorway and without looking back at her he said, "I went online after everyone left and booked a flight and a hotel for me and Liz to stay in Colorado for a week. We leave Monday. I need to get out of here and I don't want Liz seeing any of this. I'll tell her the trip is a freerider surprise birthday present so she can try out her new board, and that you couldn't get away right now. I'd appreciate it if you and your boyfriend would refrain from using our bed, if I'm not too late in making such a request."

"Nick, I never—"

He held up a hand a bit and she stopped. "We'll figure something out when I get back. I used up all my energy convincing your mom to go back home and to give us some space for a while. I don't know. I can't look at you anymore tonight."

Nick left and slammed the door to the guest room down the hall. Cat curled up in ball in her own bed, closed her eyes and felt lost. She couldn't sleep.

*

Cat spent her birthday, and the rest of the week, alone in her large empty house. She discovered that no matter how well someone redecorated the rooms, without people you loved in them, none of them held any appeal. She cried, she swam while feeling vacant of ideas, and she poked without interest at the *County Vet* book she had a deadline on. Part of her wanted to shut the door behind her and show up at Brian's with nothing but her toothbrush and her laptop bag and not look back. But that fantasy had played itself out and was over. There was no life there for her and she knew it. This was her life and she'd taken it for granted and now she was intent on fixing it. If only she knew how.

She got one postcard from Liz saying that real freeriding out on real mountains was a dream come true and that she was having a fabulous time. She said her dad was fine and a better skier than she would have expected. Skiing was a part of Nick's life before he'd met her. Maybe that was something she should try to learn to do with him sometime, although she suspected it wasn't her thing. Sliding down steep inclines of snow quickly as a means of entertainment was something Liz inherited directly from her father.

The day her little family got back from Colorado, Cat made meatloaf, this time without the carrots. And there were garlic mashed potatoes on

233

the side the way Nick's mom made them at Thanksgiving. Liz was thrilled and actually thanked her for the meal. Nick didn't have any. He claimed to not be feeling well after the flight.

When Liz ran off to her room to call her friends and get caught up on the schoolwork she had missed, Nick and Cat argued in hushed tones in his office downstairs.

"God, Cat, I really thought a week away would give me a chance to cool down, but I think I'm angrier if that's possible! I lay awake every night in that hotel room wondering if you were with that guy!"

"Nick, I swear everything is over with Brian, I—"

"Please don't say his fucking name in front of me. When his name is in your mouth it makes me wonder what else has been in there."

Cat winced. "I don't have any good excuse, but it just kind of happened—"

"That doesn't *just happen*! It's not like tripping over a goddamned rock! I mean, I'm sure it's hard for you to imagine, but do you know how many opportunities to cheat on you have crossed *my* path over the years?"

"What are you even talking about?"

"Women with their pets who feel like flirting with 'Jack' from their favorite books! I never tell you about them because there is nothing to fucking tell! I pass them on to other vets because I would never hurt you because I love you!"

234

"I had no idea, Nick."

"What, that I love you?"

"No, Nick, it's just there are some things that… Nobody can be all the things that—"

Nick shut his eyes in what looked like an effort not to explode. "No, nobody can be all things someone else wants. I wanted a big family. A woman who doesn't repeatedly make me feel dumb might be nice. Maybe one who's not grossed out by what I do or likes car racing for that matter. Or, I don't know, doesn't act like cookies in the house are a goddamned crime. So I'm sorry I was not enough for you, but did you ever stop to think if you were enough for me?"

All Cat could do in response to that was cry again at first, but then Nick said he didn't think he should have to feel displaced from his home and his bed when he was the injured party and Cat shot back, "It's all mostly mine anyway since it's my writing that made your practice a success!"

It was a low blow and she was ashamed of herself all over again, but she was feeling desperate and scared. Nick didn't want to talk to her after that.

Cat grabbed her laptop bag and her wallet and marched out of the house. Her first instinct was to go to the coffee shop, but it wasn't worth risking a run in with Brian. She didn't want to see another psycho act of his. She ended up driving to the same park where the photo shoot had taken place. She sat on a cold bench in the dark beneath the stars with her bag on her lap and she wept.

After about an hour when she was feeling more composed she drove home again and knocked, rather than let herself in. It did seem more fair that she forfeit the privilege of the house if they couldn't be in it together yet. Nick opened the door and when he saw it was her, he averted his gaze and asked her what she wanted.

"Nick, I want to talk. I'm sorry about before. I'm done getting all defensive. Please can't we at least talk?" She reached out to put her hand on his cheek to get him to look at her, but he moved his head to avoid her touch.

Cat couldn't blame him, but it still stung.

"Please, Nick? I...I don't know what I can do but whatever it is I'll do it. I could work at your office so you could see where I am all the time, and I'll only swim if you have time to come with me. Or maybe—"

"Is that what you think I want?" he asked, finally looking her in the eye.

"I...."

"You think I want to be with someone I trust so little that I have to keep her on a leash? God, Cat, do you know me at all?"

Cat looked at him helplessly. She was trying to hold back her tears.

"I just...Nick, I don't know what to do."

"Well, when you think of something write me a novel about it." And he carefully shut the door.

"Nick!" She put a hand on the door weakly and burst into tears. "Nick just talk to me! I miss you so much and I want you back even though I know I don't deserve you! Please? Nick, please open up?"

She didn't have any reason to believe he hadn't left other than she thought she could feel him on the other side of the door. She needed to feel him on the other side.

"...Nick?"

She slumped down and sat in the cold with her back to the door. She hugged her knees close to her chest and cried so hard she had trouble breathing.

Cat didn't know where to go or what to do. Until Nick opened the door again, she was at a loss. She had a key, but it was symbolically important that he let her in. If Nick didn't open the door, she had no business being on the inside, so she waited.

But Nick didn't open the door.

Cat finally got up and brushed herself off a little. She got into her car and drove.

CHAPTER ELEVEN

Cat was driving for over half an hour before she realized she was headed toward her parents' house. There was something calming in all the automatic processes that kicked in when you got behind the wheel. She was out of tears and she'd simply been driving for the sake of driving since she didn't know what else to do. She couldn't see herself sleeping in an uncomfortable heap on the doorstep and confronting Nick again when he came out to get the paper, so she'd finally had to go. It wasn't until she'd reached the onramp to the freeway that it occurred to her that among the automatic processes that had kicked in, a homing device was among them, and she was pointed toward her home state. Seemed as good an idea as any, so she kept heading that direction.

She made a mental note of the time simply to learn how long the trip would take her. She didn't know anymore. By herself a long time ago it took six and half hours if she drove fast and the weather and traffic were in her favor. With Nick, it was closer to eight because they usually stopped once and he was not as reckless. With a small child, depending on the level of potty training, the time went as high as ten hours. Once, in blizzard conditions on a Thanksgiving weekend, it had taken them nearly thirteen hours to get home and she'd never been happier in her life to arrive inside her own front door.

It struck her suddenly like a punch to the gut that she hadn't said goodbye to Liz. Not that it would have been possible under the circumstances, but how could she fix it? What would her daughter think? And did Nick know Liz had a civics paper due that she needed to be nagged about? Or that the permission slips for both the art museum and engineering field trips were on Cat's desk? Or that Liz was running low on clean shirts and the dirty ones needed to be fished out from behind the dresser where they always fell? Cat didn't know how it would be appropriate to get in touch to relay any of that. She'd have to figure something out.

She didn't have anything in particular to listen to, just some of her warhorse CDs that had lived in her car since they bought it years ago. She turned on the radio, but there was not much there at that time of night. Cat scanned around the FM dial, then shut it off. She drove that way for another hour or so before she realized she was not enjoying being alone with her thoughts, so she switched the radio back on again.

She found an insane show on the AM band where people called in with their personal alien abduction stories, and she found herself unable to change the station. The crazy people and their testimonials that sounded much more implausible than anything she'd offered up as fiction, accompanied her the whole rest of the drive (which took a total of seven hours). Cat wondered what these people had actually experienced that believing they had been abducted and probed by aliens was a preferable memory to live with. She herself was feeling desperate, but at least her mind hadn't cracked beyond all reason. Cat accepted the big mess she'd made and didn't feel entitled to convert her pain into a fantasy that left her less responsible.

She pulled into her hometown a little after dawn. She was tired in a numb kind of way, and the sleepy state of the town seemed to match her state of being. She passed her old elementary school which now had a strange addition tacked onto the front and one side. She noticed a spot on the playground where a huge tree used to be, which was probably a casualty of the large windstorm her mother had told her about a few months ago. The tree was always base for their games of tag and provided much needed shade during hot recesses.

Now the playground looked exposed.

She pulled onto her old street and parked in front of her parents' house. It was a modest brick colonial with ivy growing up the side under her old bedroom window. She used to imagine when she was small that when the vines reached her room she would be able to climb down them by moonlight. She would explore whatever fantastic things her town had to offer after dark that all the adults were in a conspiracy to keep from their children, and she would report back at school what they'd been missing and be a hero. But the ivy never did reach that high. She'd had to be content with lying in bed and dreaming up other possibilities.

Cat sat and watched the first stirrings of her old neighborhood. There was a rabbit on one lawn taking advantage of the peaceful hour, and a jogger went by. Cat was tired and she wondered vaguely what she would do if no one let her past this doorstep either. She rubbed her eyes and finally got out of the car. All she had with her was her laptop bag. She went up to the familiar door and thought about all the different colors it had been over the years. The house being brick provided very few places to shake up the look of it with something as simple as paint, but every few years her mom had gone after the shutters and the door with some new hue. Now it was red, but was faded as if her mom had left that element of reinvention alone for a long time. Cat hadn't noticed it on her last few holiday visits.

She knocked quietly. Cat had a key, but it was too early and her arrival too unexpected to feel it was appropriate to simply let herself in as if she belonged there. She knocked again after a moment and her mom came to the door, dressed for the school day, but without socks or shoes yet.

"Catherine?"

Upon seeing her mother Cat burst into tears again. Diane looked stricken and cast a worried glance down the walk and around the yard as she took her daughter into her arms.

"Catherine, where are Liz and Nick? Are they okay? What's wrong?"

Cat continued to sob but managed, "They're not here, Mom. It's just me. Nobody's hurt, it's just..."

"Honey? Sweetheart, come all the way in here, okay? I have been worried sick about you but Nick made it sound like I needed to stay out of whatever was happening so I have been trying to respect that. Why are you here?"

"I'm sorry, Mom, I just didn't know where else to go."

"Well, of course you can come here. This is still your home, too. I was just starting breakfast for your father. Why don't you come on in the kitchen with me and sit a moment, okay? Would you like some tea?" She looked shaken, but apparently now that she knew no one was bleeding was getting down to the business of tending her family.

Cat nodded and followed her mother into the kitchen and had a seat. She grabbed a napkin and dried her face a little and blew her nose. Her mother cast her a worried look as she filled the kettle, but Cat knew she wasn't going to pry until she was ready to talk.

Cat closed her eyes a moment and it felt wonderful. She hadn't realized how worn out she was until she'd given her eyes some relief and now all she wanted was sleep.

"Catherine? Catherine, Honey?"

Cat's eyes flew open and she realized she'd been in a micro-sleep. "What?" It felt like a dream for a moment, seeing the old kitchen, and then remembering where she was.

"Catherine, your dad and I will be heading off to work soon. Why don't you go on upstairs and lie down for a while. You need rest."

Cat nodded and instinctively reached for her laptop bag. She passed the upstairs bathroom where she could hear her dad showering, and she went into her old room. It was technically a guest room now, and her mom had a lot of books and teaching supplies in there, but her bed was still her bed and there were still pieces of evidence scattered around of different stages of her young life. A small kitten poster on one wall that she had thought was the cutest thing in the entire world when it had arrived with her book order in third grade was still up in the corner. There was the only metal slinky that had survived her childhood unkinked up on a shelf. There was a ribbon from the jump rope contest she'd won in seventh grade, and a picture of her and her brother proudly holding up the fish they had caught on a camping weekend with their dad.

She laid herself down on top of the fancy bedspread that was nothing like the comforter with the colorful polka dots on it that she'd slept under for so many years. Her head hit the pillow and she was out. It was a blissfully dreamless sleep and her body got to work on repairing what it could.

Cat didn't wake up until nearly dinnertime. She could hear her mother moving around in the kitchen and her dad watching the local news. She sat up on her old bed and wondered what to do with herself. She hadn't brought a change of clothes or a toothbrush or anything. Only her laptop bag and her sorry self.

But first she needed to deal with where she was.

She decided to get up and go downstairs, because waiting wasn't going to make facing anyone any easier. On the way out she flipped off her light switch, which had been installed upside down long before the house was theirs. She marveled at how memory worked that she always reached for that switch the right way, no matter how long she'd been away.

Cat went down the stairs past the framed pictures from family vacations. She was a child in a canoe. Her brother was on a horse. Her mom and dad were smiling and sitting at a picnic table. Baxter was a puppy.

She entered the kitchen and her mom smiled at her.

"Did you get some good rest, Honey?" she asked, as she rinsed off the vegetables for the salad.

Cat nodded. She felt sore all over.

"Catherine, why don't you find out what your father would like to drink, okay? And you can help me set the table. We'll eat in the dining room since you're here tonight."

Cat appreciated not being questioned right off the bat. They were in for a big talk later, but for now food sounded good.

They had a quiet meal, the three of them. Her dad told some funny stories about a mix up at the garage, but Cat's mom didn't say much. She seemed to be deep in thought for much of the meal. Cat said enough to be polite.

After dinner her dad settled down with the television for a while, and Cat's mom suggested the two of them go for a walk. Cat agreed. They went for nearly a block before her mom finally asked her what was wrong. Cat decided there was no way other than to just say it.

"I cheated on Nick, Mom."

Her mom stopped and stared at her a moment, and then made a conscious effort to keep walking. She was speechless.

Cat didn't feel like defending herself. There were a lot of lumps she was going to have to take before she had any hope of getting her life back, so she may as well start taking them willingly and without resistance.

Her mother didn't say anything for at least a full

block.

"Well, Catherine, the most obvious question is 'why,' but you know I'm not a fan of obvious questions, so I find myself stuck. Do you have an answer for 'why'?"

Cat wasn't sure. There was no single reason "why," and she didn't know if any of them made sense alone. Outside of her own head none of them made sense, period, but in her mind they held a certain logic. Cat shook her head.

Her mom asked, "Did Nick do something?"

"No. Nick committed no crime other than being Nick for so long."

"So you were bored?" Cat could tell her mother was having a difficult time grappling with her daughter having done something so obviously wrong. Cat didn't have a simple explanation for her.

"Not bored, just...." Cat really wasn't sure what to say. Words were finally failing her. Maybe she should compose an essay and distribute it to all who needed clarification.

"Am I to assume Nick threw you out?"

"That's not really a fair way to put it. Nick doesn't want me there right now, and I don't blame him."

Cat could feel her mother flailing mentally. She tried again.

"Mom, I...I met a much younger man who was interested and I felt like I could connect with him in ways I wasn't finding anywhere else. I don't have an excuse. I was flattered and it was exciting and

I've had this sense that time is running out for me somehow and I saw it as an opportunity. I didn't want to hurt anyone, and I convinced myself that if nobody found out somehow it would be okay. I hate that I've hurt Nick so badly. I want to try and fix it but I don't know what I can do."

Her mom considered it for a long while.

"Does Liz know?"

"I'm not sure."

They walked on in silence, and before they knew it they were back in front of the house. They quietly stood there at the end of the walk for a minute or two.

Finally Cat said, "I was hoping I could stay here for a little while, if you and Dad don't mind too much. I can't really go home yet, and I'm not sure where to be."

Her mom nodded. She looked a little dazed. "Catherine, you can stay as long as you need to. Give me some time to absorb this and we'll talk again, okay?"

"Okay. I think I'm going to run out to the store before it closes. I don't have any clothes or anything with me."

"Sounds like a good idea."

Cat gave her mom a hug, and it broke her heart that her mom hesitated briefly before hugging her back. Let the proverbial stoning begin.

Cat went inside and grabbed her wallet and drove until she found a recently built discount store not too far from the neighborhood. She picked out a pair of jeans and a pair of sweats and a couple of simple shirts, some underwear, socks, and a pink hoodie that was particularly soft. She grabbed some basics like a toothbrush and deodorant and a hairbrush and some ponytail holders. She drove next to a sporting goods store that had been there since she was 15 and found a decent swimsuit and some goggles and a cap. In the morning she would join the local Y.

Her father didn't ask her anything about why she was there or about home. Cat figured her mother would fill him in as needed. Cat liked the illusion with him that everything was fine and that she was merely living there for a while as some sort of sweet throwback to an earlier time. Her dad was too kind to bring her attention to anything painful if he could help it.

Her mom, on the other hand, had other worries.

"On a practical level, you may have made a mistake by leaving the house the way you did."

Cat was surprised. "What do you mean? What else could I—"

"It could be construed as abandonment, Catherine. In court. If they have to place Liz."

Cat opened her mouth a little and couldn't speak for second. "But that's not—! I would never—"

"It sounds like there are a lot of things you're capable of that you thought you'd never do, but people will be judging you and this one concerns me most because it concerns my granddaughter."

"But Nick knows that I... he would never

248

ever—" started Cat.

"You don't know what limits you've pushed Nick to, Catherine."

She kissed her daughter on the forehead, and left her alone in her old room.

Cat lay down on her bed and thought for a long time. The legal questions had never crossed her mind before and they scared her. Somehow, impossibly, the word "divorce" had never entered her head. She had worried that what she was doing could blow up her marriage, but in an emotional abstract sense. Not in a sense that anyone would start using words like "divorce" and "custody." She wasn't ready to think about that yet.

In her dreams that night her daughter kept calling to her. Liz was somehow holding her own infant self in her arms and saying, "She needs you! Why did you leave me alone with her? Why Mom?"

Cat wanted to talk with her mom more, but it was hard because she seemed to think Cat should appear more remorseful. Cat was remorseful, but she was in a problem-solving phase at this point, and all the blubbering wasn't productive. She needed to focus on what to do, and until it hit her she needed some kind of routine. She swam in the morning, and she stared at her laptop in an attempt to work in the afternoon. She was suffering her first case of writer's block in her career, so she finally decided to call one of her friends.

Cat had always felt lucky as a girl to have two best friends. Girls usually preferred to operate in pairs and the idea of a single best friend was important, but she and Amy and Rebecca (Becca for short) had fun in any combination, so the need to exclude someone for the sake of a traditional "best friend" had been unnecessary. Of course, since Amy and Becca had stayed in town, they continued to do things together, and Cat for all intents and purposes was out of the loop, but she was always welcomed back in without hesitation. Now Cat was the one who found reasons to hesitate. She didn't want to risk losing them by telling them the truth. She called Becca, first.

"How long are you in town for?" Becca wanted to know.

"I think a while. I'm not sure yet. I was wondering if we could figure out a time when you and Amy might both be free and we could all get together for lunch or dinner or something."

"Gosh, you have great timing, Cat! If you're free tomorrow night, Amy and I already arranged for our husbands to stay home and watch the kids so we could go out. It would be great to have you along!"

So it was settled. The next night the three of them met at a small seafood restaurant in town that used to be a falafel place, and back in high school when they ate there together it was a pizza joint. It seemed appropriate to Cat for them to gather in a spot that changed phases in its history as they had.

They greeted each other excitedly and Cat pumped them for lots of information about their lives and their kids. Amy was a Spanish teacher at her old Jr. High School, and Becca had been a nurse until she had kids and now stayed at home. Cat loved them. She wondered anew every time they got together why she didn't make a better effort to stay in touch. She supposed she simply got lost in her own head so much that if people weren't in front of her they were hard to include in her plans.

"So, what about you, Cat?" asked Amy excitedly. "Are you guys here for anything in particular? I'm surprised you made the trip so soon after we all just saw you at your party."

"It's just me, this time, actually," said Cat. She was nervous.

"So how are Nick and Liz?" asked Becca. They were both looking at Cat now. They thought her life was more glamorous than theirs by virtue of her success. Cat knew being a writer who had done some work that was known was not the same as being famous. Almost no one recognized her, and few were truly interested, but her friends believed differently, and when she tried to explain it they thought she was being modest.

"To tell you the truth, I...I don't...." Cat didn't know how to do it. She could tell her mom straight out because her mom would never leave her. She wasn't so sure about her friends.

"What?" asked Amy, who now looked concerned.

"Are they okay?" asked Becca.

Cat closed her eyes and said, "I had an affair. I

had an affair and Nick found out and now I'm here trying to decide what to do and hoping he'll take me back."

She opened her eyes to see her friends gaping at her. Becca finally signaled to the waiter and said, "We're going to need some drinks here."

After a few rounds of interesting cocktails with pretty umbrellas in them, the discussion was much looser. Amy was interested but horrified. She could not understand how Cat could have done what she'd done. Becca was amused and begging for details.

"23? You got to sleep with a guy who was 23?" Becca said while twirling her third little umbrella in her fingers.

"Becca!" said Amy, who was still on her first drink.

"I'm just saying! That's, like.... Geez, 23! Wow, Cat, and you said he was cute, too?"

"No, he was beyond cute. He was like some sort of Greek god in marble in a museum that as you're staring at it you wish would come to life and ravish you right there," said Cat, who was also twirling her third umbrella. She couldn't help but think how far Brian would have run from her at that moment with all that alcohol in her system.

"But that doesn't matter!" said Amy. "You took vows, Cat! I mean, it shouldn't matter if he was Bradley Cooper or Brad Pitt! You made a promise, and you have a kid, and—"

"Oh you and the Brads!" said Becca. "Like you wouldn't jump at that if any of your movie star crushes showed up at the most opportune moment!"

"No, I wouldn't!" said Amy.

"See, now, you can say that because you know it's not going to happen, but if it really did I don't know if you would be so sure!"

"Well, would *you*?" Amy asked Becca.

"What, with Bradley Cooper or Cat's guy?"

"He's not my guy," said Cat.

"Whatever. Look, Amy, I'm just saying that you can't judge because you don't know. I love my husband and I like my life, but if some hot guy seriously showed up wanting me in a way like Cat was just describing, I don't know.... That's hard to imagine passing up. Tell us the part again about where he pulled you through the secret door during *Othello*. That is like the sexiest fucking thing I've ever heard."

"No! Don't make Cat tell that again. You'll make her think it's okay," complained Amy.

"But, I'm not so sure it isn't!" argued Becca. "I mean, if no one had found out, what would it have really hurt? Cat got an itch scratched and is now more sure she wants her marriage than ever! How is that bad?"

"You have been reading too much Dan Savage," said Amy.

"Well, you read too little."

Cat interrupted, "I don't think it matters at this point because I *did* get caught and the hypotheticals don't help me."

"I'm just saying in the situation you described—

and that I'm hoping you'll describe again before we go—that it's not a crazy idea to cheat," said Becca.

"But, then, there are like, no limits! What if Cat came around your house and wanted Bill or something?" asked Amy.

Becca finished the last bit of drink in her glass. "Now, we all know no one wants Bill!"

Cat laughed. It felt good to laugh.

Even Amy had to laugh. Then she looked seriously at Cat for a moment. "I guess I just don't get it because your life seemed perfect, unless there's something you're not telling us."

"Well," said Cat, "Nobody's life is perfect, and the things in your life can all be fine, but that doesn't always make who you are inside fine, or mean that there aren't still things you want. It just came out of nowhere, this chance, and it seemed to offer something I felt I was missing and it felt as bad to pass it up as it did to take it and...."

Becca was trying to get her little umbrella to stand alone on the table without success. "Well, I get it," she said. "And I'm not going to pretend that I'd be strong enough to pass that up, but I get to be declared virtuous merely because temptation of that caliber does not cross my path. Geez, 23! They can just keep going at that age, can't they?"

"Well, my sample size is pretty small," said Cat, which made Becca snicker. "No, not that Brian was! Trust me, no! I'm just saying, you know, before this I'd only been with Nick. So, I mean, I'm not much of an authority of what 23-year-old guys are like as a rule."

"So that was really true that you and Nick were both virgins when you got married?" asked Amy. "Because I always figured you were just saying that in case your mom ever asked us and you wanted to have all your tracks covered or something."

"I can't believe you didn't believe me!" said Cat.

"Well seriously, you have always been so pretty and there were lots of guys who liked you in high school," replied Amy.

"Like who?" Cat wanted to know leaning forward with interest.

"Oh my God you wouldn't go with us to any of the parties and *now* you want to know which boys liked you?" said Becca. "As the former reigning queen of the sluts in our little group I can tell you when I used to do it with Ricky behind the bleachers—or was it Mike? No, definitely Ricky. Or Steve. Anyway, whichever sweaty dude that was, he used to say that you were the one all the guys thought was—"

"Wait, hold up—why are you the *former* queen of the sluts?" asked Cat.

"Well, Cat, you're married," explained Amy. "I mean, that kind of, you know… "

"It's just super slutty," said Becca. "Which I have no problem with. You're my hero."

Cat felt like protesting but didn't really have a non-slutty leg to stand on.

"But that's why I get it," continued Becca. "I mean, I got to test drive lots of guys, and there's a lot of variety out there, and I feel like I get the gist. That's why I'm good with Bill. I don't wonder a whole lot about what I'm missing, because, you know, I enjoyed my sample size or whatever you called it."

"No, Becca, you super sized your sample size, especially back in college," said Amy getting toward the bottom of her glass and able to laugh a little more.

"So are you really telling me that Becca, with a number she can't narrow down, is farther down on the slut scale than I am with my two guys? And one of them I've been married to forever? And the other one I only slept with for a matter of months?" asked Cat.

"I know, but that last guy counts as, like, ten guys it sounds like. Plus, you know, married."

"That doesn't seem fair," said Cat.

"Life isn't fair! Now tell me about theater guy's sample size again," said Becca, laughing.

Amy shook her head, but she had finished her drink finally and was signaling for another as she said, "Becca! That's terrible! You guys are depraved. Want to get together next week, too?"

The night out with her friends helped Cat a lot. Things were still tense with her mom about the situation, but it meant a great deal to have some outlet where she could discuss her fall from grace openly without feeling as if it was the end of the world or that she deserved the death penalty. It was a bright spot in the darkness.

As Cat's visit dragged into its second week, her mom became increasingly concerned. Diane came to sit by her daughter one evening where Cat had been reading on her bed in her old room.

"Catherine, that was Nick just now on the phone."

Cat's throat tightened. "How is Liz?"

"Liz is confused, but fine it sounds like. I took the liberty of talking to Nick about the legal concerns I had and he assured me he wasn't looking at those sorts of options yet. You've put yourself into a dangerous position, but if I believed anyone about not using their child as a pawn in this kind of game, I would believe Nick. He's deeply hurt, but he's being quite rational under the circumstances."

"Well, that's Nick," said Cat softly. Even when she didn't deserve it she could count on him.

"He was mostly calling because you missed your deadline. Your publisher is apparently very upset and he's been fielding all the calls and thought you should know."

Oh, the deadline. Yeah, they were not going to like where that was going. All Cat could think to say was, "I wish Nick didn't have to deal with that, too."

Her mother sighed. "Catherine, Honey, tell me again how you decided cheating was what you wanted to do. I don't understand how you could disregard Nick the way you did."

Cat gave her mom a tired look. "I know it doesn't make any sense to you, but it did to me at the time. I felt like I could love Nick and still have something else, too. I felt like I was denying myself something that made me a whole person and it had nothing to do with Nick. Being with Brian was really a way of exploring myself and it didn't seem hard to rationalize after a while. I should be allowed to learn about myself. I just let that override my desire not to hurt others, I guess, but I didn't think anyone really would get hurt which made it easier to do."

"You don't sound like you regret it."

Cat was silent.

Her mom looked concerned and asked, "Did you love this much younger man? How did you just refer to him—Brian? Did you love Brian?"

Cat had never thought about it. "I don't think so. Not like you're thinking. If I did, it was the most innocent part of the whole thing."

Her mom shook her head. "Catherine, I won't pretend to understand any of this because, honestly, I don't. Nick is a good man and he tries hard. You have a nice life and a nice home and a nice family and a nice career, so why you weren't content with that is beyond me. It hurts me not to be more sympathetic on this for you, but it's difficult."

Cat nodded and just listened.

"I've given it a lot of thought, Honey. You said you wanted my advice and I take that as a great responsibility. If you are serious about making it work with your husband, I think there is a good chance. Nick is a forgiving man and he loves you.

258

But you have to have more true regret than I'm seeing. I'm seeing regret over getting caught, and that's not going to be good enough. You have to accept that it was wrong, Catherine. Nick is going to have to know you believe that if he's ever going to trust you again. I wouldn't blame him if your insincerity caused him to leave the marriage."

Cat sat very still. "I see," she said. "Thanks, Mom."

Diane offered her daughter a combination of a worried look and a weak smile from the doorway as she left. Cat noticed the smile didn't quite reach her eyes.

Cat lay back on her bed and looked at the crack on the ceiling above it that she'd been studying from that same vantage point since she was small. It could be a smile or a frown depending on which direction you laid you head.

The first question of the moment she had to answer for herself was did she regret the affair? On the surface that was an easy "yes" because the result was so bad. But did she have to regret all of it in order to have true remorse? That didn't work for her. From the perspective that she hurt the people she loved and her life, then yes, she had great regret.

But she had learned she could abandon herself to passion in a way she didn't know she was capable of. She had learned to appreciate certain elements of age over youth. She had learned how easy it was to betray your values given the right temptation, and that she shouldn't be so quick to judge others who had committed what looked like bad choices. She had learned how easy it was to take love for granted when you were spoiled by it. She had learned which things in life actually mattered to her, and it was impossible for her to disregard all of that information as useless. It was part of who she was now. She could feel bad about causing pain and still see value in other elements of what had happened.

Was she supposed to pretend the sex was bad? Not possible. Had it been worth it? Probably not. The funny thing about the sex itself was that, as amazing as the reality of it had been, for it to exist for her at all now, she had to dredge her memory and recreate it all in her mind. From her current perspective, there was no difference between a fantasy and her memory of the actual event. The experiences felt identical, so what had been the point? She was left with phantoms either way, so maybe the sex hadn't mattered on any lasting level with Brian.

What *had* mattered with Brian? Beyond the sex part—which was the only part everyone else seemed to care about—her affection for him had been real. She missed talking with him. She missed his attention and his insight. She supposed she had to deny all of that now, too. It was a good puzzle if it weren't so depressing. There were many parts of the affair she looked back on fondly, even as she also beat herself up over it.

How much could you keep from an experience

you were supposed to have remorse about and not still be bad? Apparently none of it if you wanted forgiveness. And she did want forgiveness, even as she believed it might be wrong to ever choose to forgive herself.

Cat realized the true penance she was going to have to pay was to live with one secret for the rest of her life. Nick would never understand, her mom would never understand, and the world would never understand, if she did anything short of condemn everything about the whole affair. The fact that on some level she was glad it had happened was unacceptable and unforgivable and she would have to choke on that silently until she died. She was prepared to do that.

Now came the business of making it up to Nick. Something had actually occurred to her that morning while swimming. The last thing Nick had said to her that night on the doorstep was that when she figured out what to do, she should write him a novel about it. Not a bad idea. She'd had a glimmer of a concept earlier, and she planned to get a good night's sleep and attack the problem first thing after going to the Y.

Cat didn't sleep well but got up early anyway, put in a good two hours of swimming while she hashed out details in her mind. She came straight home and opened up her laptop. She pulled up the latest *County Vet* book which was almost finished. She transferred most of what was there into a new file and put it aside to use another time, possibly. If there was another time.

She left the opening mostly the way it was, with Jack doing his famous Jack thing, taking on a sad cat case. But then the story shifted. Susan, normally in the background lending an apple pie smell to the whole thing, stepped forward. She had her own chapter and her own voice for a change. Susan was troubled.

Cat typed all afternoon and into the evening. She didn't come down to dinner. Her mother checked in on her and Cat simply said she was on a roll, so her mother brought her up a plate. Cat typed into the night. She slept for a while, and she didn't swim in the morning. She woke up and she started typing first thing. Cat got up to use the bathroom and to relieve leg cramps from time to time, but she continued to work. At some point her hands hurt, so she took a break and asked her mom to go on a walk with her.

Cat told her mother that she was attempting to make things right. She regretted the affair completely and she loved her husband. She had terrible remorse and would take it all back if she could. It would never happen again, because why would she repeat such a large mistake? Such an obvious wrong would haunt her for the rest of her life. She was bad but would try to do better. She was sorry.

Her mother seemed relieved. People believed what they wanted to believe. Cat wanted to believe people would still love her if she were only mostly sorry, but she knew better.

Cat wrote essentially nonstop for three straight weeks. The new *County Vet* book was finished.

The next part of her plan she needed help with.

"Mom?"

Her mother looked up from the book she was reading. "Yes, Honey?"

"You know how to format things for self-publishing, right? Didn't you help somebody from your garden club do that last year?"

"Two years ago, actually, but I can't imagine it's changed much. Why?"

"I need you to proofread and maybe edit my latest book, but I want to get it out as fast as possible and I think self-publishing is the quickest option."

"Oh my, are you allowed to do that in that way?"

"I don't care."

"Well, maybe you should before you get sued for everything you've got and Liz can't go to college. Just a minute," she said, getting up and going into the den where she kept her files. After some brief searching she ushered Cat over to the dining table where she laid out Cat's latest contract.

"Where did you get that?" said Cat, astonished.

"Nick sent me a copy."

"Nick? Why?"

"He always reviews your contracts and business dealings with me. He knows I like to stay in the loop since I was the one who started you off.

Although I think he regretted it after this last go round where I asked about the digital rights clause. Technology is changing everything nowadays you know. I wanted to give you more options. Did you know all of your contracts have a line about how not only do they own everything you do, but they own it on technology that hasn't even been invented yet? It's a bit much. Most authors have to put up with signing their lives away because they are just so grateful to get published, but you have clout. The millions you bring in for them is worth more than all the other people they have contracts with combined. So I figured you were in a position to ask for something that was a bit of an exception."

"Wait, whatever that new clause is, that was you?" Cat had no idea what to do with this information, but was glad something might finally be working in her favor.

"Yes, now let's look. Here. They jury-rigged a sort of compromise about self-publishing because I felt like you should have an outlet for your work if you wanted to get something out there that they didn't like enough to publish the regular way. I just had a feeling that some of those darker things and stories that don't sell as well are in danger of getting declined the way things are going, and then you'll feel you can't do them."

"So can I self-publish without breaking my contract?" asked Cat.

"You can do it, but there are strings attached. If it makes more than a certain amount of money, they get the rights again and all the old rules apply about their having control over it."

Cat thought about it a moment. "What if I make it free?"

"Well, then I guess you would forever retain control over the content because you'd never trip the money amount they are interested in."

"Even for a new *County Vet* book?"

Diane looked briefly shocked as she considered it. "I don't know, Honey, that's a huge deal for your publisher to just give that away. I think—"

"But legally, Mom. Legally, if I self-publish a *County Vet* book, am I okay?"

Her mother pored over the contract for a long time.

"Well, Catherine, I'm no lawyer, but it looks to me like they didn't think to specify in that way, so I think you're all right."

"Good. Put on your proofreading hat and help me upload this book."

CHAPTER TWELVE

"Are you crazy?" asked Michelle. "Are you trying to kill me?"

"No," said Cat. "This is just something I have to do."

She and her mother were almost finished editing and formatting her new novel and within a week they would be hitting "publish" on the self-publishing platform they were planning to use. Cat felt an obligation to warn her agent before all hell broke loose, so she had forwarded her a copy with a note about what they were planning to do. Michelle had called before she even got through the first few chapters of Cat's new book.

"You don't seriously expect me to support this, do you?" said Michelle incredulously. "It's some kind of joke, right? Where people pop out with cameras or something hoping it will go viral, isn't it? Some weird new publicity stunt you didn't clue me in on?"

"Michelle, I will send you a check for what your cut would have been. I don't want you to get hurt, but I have to do it like this. I need it out now. Besides, they aren't going to like this one anyway."

"No, they really aren't. They'd force you to gut it and start over and still have a new one ready to print before Christmas. But I just want you to be aware of what you're doing. You understand this could kill the series?"

"I don't care about that, Michelle. If it's the last thing I write that ever gets published I'm fine with that, but I want it out there."

There was silence on the other end of the line. Eventually Michelle said, "Okay, Cat. I won't promise you anything, but I'll do the best I can from my end to defend you."

"Thanks."

Now all there was for Cat to do was wait, which she wasn't good at. It gave her too much time to worry about Liz and how she missed her. It physically hurt sometimes to know one more day was going to go by that she wasn't there to be a witness to the person her daughter was growing into. There had been many times in the past when Cat was feeling bogged down as a mother—overwhelmed to the point of exhaustion or bored with the tedium—that if someone had offered to let

267

her drop everything for weeks at a time to do as she pleased she would have thought that sounded like paradise. But not if it was involuntary and not when the endpoint was uncertain. She missed her baby. That was the sacrifice in all of this that blindsided her. She'd worried so much about Nick she'd somehow forgotten to truly factor in Liz, and now she was paying for it.

But something the distance from her daughter had provided became an unexpected blessing. Cat discovered texting. And along with it, a way to connect with Liz more deeply than she could have guessed she would experience during her daughter's teen years.

Of all the modern technology habits Cat had most eschewed, texting—with it's grotesque abbreviations and lack of proper punctuation—had most rankled her. But a few days into her stay at her parents' house she had sat on her bed, gripping her cell phone, and realized it was a way back to Liz.

She had started by texting Nick that first day back in her old house let him know where she was, even though he had probably figured out where Cat was headed before she did. She also told him she missed him. Nick didn't respond.

Liz, however, did.

Cat texted notes to her daughter saying she hoped to be home soon, that she was deep into an important project, and to please eat some vegetables other than french fries while she was gone. She told Liz she loved her and that all her grandparents said,

"Hi."

Communicating with her daughter in Liz's preferred medium inspired a cascade of information that normally Cat was not privy to. The texts were simple at first, mostly basic updates about the dog and school assignments. She was running low on shampoo. Her dad was buying her new clothes, but she thought it was because he couldn't find her laundry.

Then the texts got more personal. Maybe from so far away Liz found her mom was easier to confide in, Cat wasn't sure, but Liz was telling her things Cat used to have to infer herself from bits of evidence. There was a boy Liz liked who didn't like her back and it hurt. One of her friends seemed to be spending more time with their third friend than with her and what did that mean? She was starting to feel as if she should know what she wanted to do in life because her counselor wanted her to narrow down her college major before she decided where to apply in a couple of years and she was freaked out.

Cat addressed each concern with care and tried not to be preachy. She told her daughter the only secret to adolescence she knew of now that she thought was important to pass on, was that no one was looking at her as hard as they were looking at themselves. It feels like everyone's staring, but they're all worried about their own zits and their own crushes and their own freak outs. Don't interpret everything as being about yourself, or more precisely, against yourself. Relax. And eat some vegetables.

Texting with Liz was Cat's lifeline, and the one truly positive part of her self-inflicted exile. Maybe the phone wasn't so bad. Maybe she shouldn't be so stingy with her number. Maybe Cat should be texting her friends and her mom and her husband. If he still was her husband.

Her mom was working on the edit and formatting on her own computer, so Cat didn't need hers for a while. She packed her laptop up in its bag and set it in the corner of her room. When she got back to where she belonged she would write again. She hoped it would be in her own office at home where her family was. If it had to be in her own apartment somewhere in town so she could still see her daughter, so be it. But while she was a resident again of the town where she grew up, there were other things she needed to do.

She called Nick's mom. Cat could tell by the uncomfortable silences on the phone that her son had already talked to her. Cat asked if she could come over. Judy Ryan said of course.

The meeting was not as upsetting as Cat expected it to be. She pulled up in front of Nick's childhood home which now seemed hollow with Judy and David as its sole occupants. She knew the last of their six children had moved out a long time ago, but Cat had only visited the house during holidays and big family events when it was brimming with people and grandchildren and noise. Seeing it in its true regular state was unusual. She wondered if Nick had ever seen it like this.

Judy answered the door and calmly looked at Cat a moment. Then she invited her in where she had tea and homemade cookies waiting in the living room.

"Judy," Cat started. "I don't know how much Nick's told you, but I want you to hear from me how sorry I am. I never meant to hurt your son or you or...."

"Thank you for thinking about me, but this is all about Nick and Liz as far as I am concerned. I've already prayed about it and forgiven you. Nick is still struggling, and Liz just wants you to come home."

"She does?"

"Of course she does. You're her mom. You're the standard by which she measures herself as a growing young woman, and in your absence she doesn't know where to look. What Nick and I have talked most about is what that means for her when you go home, to have her look at the person you are now. We teach best by example, and my son doesn't want Liz presented with this particular example. I don't blame him, but I've told him your absence has influence, too. He can't erase you from Liz's life just like you can't erase what you did."

Cat thought about that and took a sip of her tea. There were no fewer than five different displays of the ten commandments in the living room alone. The word adultery popped out at her in gothic script and plain type, and even one done in crayon.

Cat said, "I'm just not sure what to do now. I've given Nick space, and I'll wait to go home until he tells me he's ready, but you're right. I can't erase it. I want him to know that I'm willing to do what it takes to earn back his trust, but it's hard at a distance."

"I think volunteering to come here is a good start, Cat. This must be very difficult for you. But you need to repair your soul whether Nick ever sees you again or not. You can't do it for *him*. I pray that you will find the right path and Nick will be by your side on it."

Cat drank some more tea. She took in all the crosses and Jesus figurines and thought how sad Judy must have been when Nick left the church. It would be as if Liz grew up to be an organizer of book burning campaigns. Would she still love her then? Of course, but it would be painful.

"So, you would still accept me back into the family if Nick did?"

"You're Liz's mom, and therefore a part of this family no matter what Nick decides." She studied Cat for a moment and then added, "I'm not in judgment of you. I can be disappointed by what you did and still not condemn you. We're all sinners, Cat. You, me, Nick, all of us. I'm not naive enough to think that if you went to church you would have been protected from temptation, but it might have helped remind you of what's important. I go to be reminded to be humble and to love my enemies, no matter how hard that seems."

Cat finished her tea and got up to leave. She felt she understood Nick better, having had such a conversation with his mom. She missed him and hoped they could come back there together sometime, when the house was quiet and they could really talk with his parents like adults.

On her way out, Cat remembered to warn Judy about the new book. She wanted her to be prepared in case.... Well, she didn't know what, she just didn't want Judy blindsided if it got more attention than usual.

"Sounds like a throwback to *Bending Chance* and the short stories from around that time," said Judy.

Cat was surprised. "You've read my other work?"

"I've read everything you've ever written. I even have both copies of that first one, with the extra chapter in the end of one of them."

Cat just stood there a moment. "But Nick said you—"

"Nick doesn't always give me enough credit."

Cat thought to herself, "Neither do I." There were tears in her eyes, then, and she gave her mother-in-law a hug that was warmly returned. It was relief from an unexpected source and Cat was grateful.

Cat volunteered at her mom's school, and even gave a talk in each of the English classes about writing, and what it was like in town while she was growing up there. She was welcomed at the local humane society where she did a book signing to help raise money, and she put in some time walking dogs and petting unwanted cats. She spent time with her dad handing him tools at his garage while he worked under different people's cars. She only swam occasionally.

She hung out with her friends when they were available, and started texting them when they weren't, which they were thrilled about. Cat realized she needed to not only stay in touch with them better, but also try to make real friends at home finally.

Although she was starting to worry that was going to be hard. Her secret wasn't officially out, but hints of the shunning to come had arisen. Becca was fine, but Amy was really having trouble looking at Cat the way she used to. And then there were her mom's neighbors.

"Mom, did you tell Mrs. Applewhite what happened with me?" Cat asked her mother one afternoon.

Diane looked a bit pained. "Why, Catherine? Did she say something? She promised she wouldn't say anything."

"Mom!"

"I'm sorry, Dear, but this has really been bothering me and your father doesn't want to hear anything that sounds like I'm criticizing his little girl so I ended up confiding in Lucy. She tells me all the time about what's going on with her kids and grandkids and I just thought she'd be a good ear to bend. But she feels like she knows Nick through the *County Vet* series and she's very upset for him."

"Mom, you were the one who taught me that gossip was wrong, remember? She glares at me now every time she sees me coming up the walk. And so do the Pickets. Did you tell them, too?"

"No, but I think Lucy may have spread it around once she knew."

"God, Mom, Mrs. Picket actually crossed the street rather than pass me on the sidewalk yesterday and I couldn't figure out what about me looked so scary. Now I know it's that big scarlet A I'm wearing. This is ridiculous."

"Is it?"

"What do you mean?"

"It's just… Catherine, you know I love you and will always support you and be there for you, but this was wrong. Maybe you should start accepting that people aren't going to give you a pass on something like this. If you're going to do something socially unacceptable, then it stands to reason that a consequence of that would be to seen as unacceptable socially."

"Oh, I get there are consequences, but crossing the street? Adultery is not contagious. It's not cooties," said Cat.

Diane frowned at her daughter. "Do you think this isn't a big deal? Because I happen to think it is. It says a lot about one's character."

"One's character? You mean *my* character."

"Fine, Catherine. *Your* character. But I'm just

275

not understanding this. I'm trying, but I'm having trouble seeing what was so wrong with your life that you were inclined to ruin it for something so unseemly."

Cat just looked at her mom. "Nothing was wrong with it. I messed up. I— I don't know what else to tell you about my unseemly inclinations."

"Catherine, I'm sorry, this is just the first time I've found myself truly disappointed in you and it's hard on me, too."

Cat sighed. This conversation with her mother was never going to end. It was going to cycle around forever until it made sense to her, which it never would. That was Cat's new reality, and one that wouldn't have crossed her mind as a possible consequence to eventually result from a kiss in the shadows of a theater.

Cat looked sadly at her mom and said, "I'm sure it is. I think I'm going to bed early tonight and we can pick up on the edits tomorrow."

"Catherine..."

"It's okay, Mom. Just... Don't think I don't understand what a big deal this is. I'm here instead of my own home which is killing me. I love you. Goodnight."

*

Then the day came just after Thanksgiving when her mom was done with all the edits and formatting and Cat was ready to release the new *County Vet* book. She hit "publish" at 8:30a.m. which seemed anticlimactic while simply sitting there in her parents' house. But by 8:34 the feedback was already starting to come in.

First came the shock that the newest likely bestseller by Catherine Devin was apparently available for free. Many were speculating that there had been a mistake and the book had been leaked by a competitor. The publisher was desperately trying to figure out what had happened and there were several different attempts at PR spin as they grappled with changing stories and everyone's competing theories.

After people actually had time to read it, there was a different kind of shock to deal with. The *County Vet* stories were usually such wholesome, family books. You could give them to your kids or your grandmother and they made good, safe holidays gifts.

Not this time. There was such an outcry from her fan base she was glad she was living at a different address.

Normally Cat didn't read her reviews. The smaller works she was interested in didn't sell enough to grab anyone's attention, and the *County Vet* books usually got panned in the publications she respected and lauded in the ones she didn't. This time it was reversed. She kept a representative sample from each camp.

From the family magazine that usually promised dieting miracles on the same cover as a picture of their latest cake recipe, she usually received glowing praise.

No longer.

"With a disgraceful disregard for her readers, Catherine Devin has plunged the once-beloved story of a county vet and his family into the same sewer of immorality and depravity that we are subjected to on a daily basis in the rest of our culture. Instead of providing a refuge from our sordid world with her uplifting tales of animals and their owners finding help and hope in the presence of Jack the heroic vet, we are instead led down a disturbing path of adultery and dark thoughts. *The Strove Guy Accident* (a confusing title, but maybe the lack of the words 'County Vet' in this one were a clue that this book was already off track) begins deceptively enough like the others in the series: A man comes in with his injured cat in need of a miracle, and Jack takes the case. Unfortunately, in the second chapter the book departs from the expected pattern, and Susan, the (until now) charming vet's wife and mother of their two children, takes center stage for the first time. She is lonely, she is feeling old, and seems to have found this enough of an excuse to have an affair. (Which the title implies is somehow an accident?) When Jack finds out that his wife has not only committed adultery, but with the owner of the cat from the first chapter, we are made to endure the implausible debates of Jack with himself over whether or not to heal the cat! From everything we know about Jack from past books this is preposterous, and of course in the end he does save the cat, but why waste any time pretending he might not? This is merely a cruel manner in which to torture cat lovers and has no place in this book. There is an equally ridiculous story line about Susan believing she is somehow deserving of forgiveness, and this leads to her shaving her head for some reason. In addition to the story itself being disturbing, it is told in a confusing manner where time is presented strangely and makes the whole thing difficult to follow. Waste no time or money on this book. Catherine Devin can be safely removed from our list of family friendly authors."

From the book review magazine that she subscribed to that usually included a cursory mention of her most famous works on their list of books most undeserving of notice, she found this:

"At first glance, Catherine Devin's latest installment in her *County Vet* series appears the same as all the others. A lightweight, trite collection of work about people and their pets and the ever-perfect vet, Jack, who heals the animals, and by extension the lives of their owners. But this is the truest case of 'not judging a book by its cover' ever presented to this magazine for review, beginning with the fact that *The Strove Guy Accident* lacks the familiar words 'County Vet' in its title, until you check it for anagrams. This is a completely different novel. Instead of focusing on the vet and the saccharine coated animals he heals, this is the story of his wife, Susan. Susan has, until now, been at best an accessory to the veterinary practice. She is beautiful with flowing blond hair, and no life worth mentioning aside from her perfect tending of the children and her unwavering support of her husband. Apparently there have been disquieting undercurrents beneath Susan's Stepford Wife role to which we were not privy until now. She struggles with mortality and missed opportunity and the panic of losing her youth. She finds herself drawn to a much younger man, a poet named Ryan Strove, who is able to captivate her with the perfect words. The book is laid out in a non-chronological manner that takes the reader by surprise the first time through (and, yes, I am implying the book is worth reading more than once). We are led through Susan's affair only after being introduced to her lover at the beginning of the book, when he is forced by necessity to take his cat to Jack to be healed. Jack is faced with a difficult choice, because he knows the right thing is to help the innocent cat, but his instinct is to let the cat die in order to hurt the man who hurt him. He does indeed save the cat, but then must replay similar arguments in his mind about whether or not to do the same for his marriage. Although few people know of the affair, he is humiliated and hurt, and confronts his wife with the fact that in his new cuckolded status they cannot walk down the street together without feeling people are staring at him. Susan, who ends the affair (technically before the book begins) and realizes what a terrible mistake she has made, suffers in isolation for a while, then returns home having shaved off all of her golden locks. She explains to her husband that now if he chooses to walk with her again, people will stare at her instead. She has sacrificed her one feature that, until then, warded off her insecurities about still being attractive. She has literally and figuratively bared herself in an attempt to prove the sincerity of her repentance. The story remains open-ended and we are not privileged to Jack's final decision about his marriage. One can only hope there is another book one day that answers that question while introducing us to others of such thought provoking intensity. I will be first in line for it if there is."

Cat had officially shot, beheaded, and trampled the golden goose and wondered if she had any kind of career left or not. She would always write, but she might not be able to make a living at it anymore. She didn't care. She just wanted Nick to read the book.

One evening, about two weeks after the release of the most critically acclaimed and most reviled *County Vet* book ever, Cat's cell phone rang. It was her husband.

"Nick?"

"Hi," came the familiar voice.

"Hi."

"How are you?"

"Okay. Not great. How about you?" asked Cat.

"Okay."

They were both quiet for a moment.

"How is Liz?" asked Cat.

"Good. She wants you to come home."

"I would like to come home."

After a pause, Nick said, "I think I want you to come home, too."

"I can get in my car right now."

"If you want to wait until morning that might be safer, you wouldn't be too tired."

"I won't be able to sleep tonight anyway. I want to be there with you," said Cat.

"Okay. I'll leave the light on for you."

"Thanks. I'll be there as soon as I can, Nick."

"Cat?"

"Yes?"

"You don't have to shave your head."

Cat smiled to herself. "Thanks."

Cat threw the book she'd been reading into her laptop bag and told her parents she was heading home.

CHAPTER THIRTEEN

On the drive Cat thought about how hard it had been spending Thanksgiving away from Nick and Liz. She knew the two of them had gone to the home of one of the other vets in the practice for the big meal, but she wasn't sure how Nick explained her absence. She hoped things worked out so that they could enjoy a quiet Christmas together in a couple of weeks. Cat hoped a lot of things in her car on the dark roads home.

It was a six-and-a-half-hour drive, and she arrived at three in the morning. Nick was still up. He'd heard her car in the driveway and turned the knob right as Cat was putting her key into the lock.

They stood and looked at each other a moment, then Cat walked into Nick's arms and pressed herself into him as hard as she could. She started to cry a little and he squeezed her tightly. He shut and locked the door and they went silently to bed. Cat thought it felt like heaven to be putting on her familiar pajamas and climbing under her own covers again. After their initial hug Nick seemed to want distance again. He climbed in on the far side of the bed after Cat fell asleep.

Cat was gratified that Liz was excited to have her home when she came into her parents' room to say hello before going to school. The thrill wore off by dinner when Liz realized the family meals with tofu in them were back, and the fast food meals her dad let her do with her friends were history. Cat texted her, "I love you. Get over it."

Nick stayed home from work that first day Cat was back. There was a lot to discuss.

"How have things been here with Liz?" was the first thing Cat wanted to know.

"Odd. At first, I'll admit, she was glad you were gone. But when she realized that I expected certain things of her, too, that it was not just you who had been coming up with stuff she didn't like, she kind of turned on me."

Cat nodded. "Welcome to the club."

"Yeah, well, it's a pretty crappy club. Suddenly everything was all about how you did things and I just wouldn't understand and when were you coming home," said Nick, looking tired.

"Hey, she's alive and in one piece, so your solo parenting job was a success."

"Great. A couple of the plants are dead, so I'm not batting a thousand by any means."

Cat smiled.

"So, you know," Cat said, "your mom is pretty amazing."

"I know. She sent me your book and told me to read it. Not that I didn't know it was out—the hate mail is piled up in your office."

"Hm."

"I read your book and I wasn't sure I got all of it, at first. My mom talked me through a bunch of it on the phone one night. I couldn't figure out why I might not help the cat, but she said it was just a symbol for our marriage."

"Your mom does a pretty good literary analysis. Plus the word 'cat' should have been a clue, don't you think?"

"Yeah yeah yeah, don't get on me about all that now, okay?" Nick looked a little annoyed, but he actually smiled a little despite himself. Cat felt poking fun at him again might be a small step toward normal. It felt like them, but maybe it was too soon.

"I'm sorry. What else did she say?"

"She said the thing about Susan cutting off all of her hair was really you and the book. That since everyone thinks she's you, it was like announcing to everyone what you did so you would take a lot of scorn. So everyone would look at you, instead of me."

"Your mom's good."

"Well, she wouldn't tell me how the book should end. She said it was my story to finish and she would love me either way."

Cat studied him more closely. He seemed thinner. She wondered how he'd been eating. She wanted to kiss his sweet mouth. "How do you want it to end?" she finally asked.

Nick rubbed the back of his neck with his hand as he thought. "Cat, I want us to be together, but...do you have any idea how difficult this is for me? I mean, it's beyond humiliating. And it makes me angry that you felt like you could go do whatever you wanted but could have this life too, as if it doesn't take effort and sacrifice. That's just outrageously unfair, Cat. And I'm stuck every time I touch you, every time I... I have to feel like I'm being compared..." Nick took a deep breath. "And now it's just, I've wracked my brain and I didn't notice anything out of the ordinary the whole time that you...." he grimaced briefly. "Either I'm a complete idiot or blind, or you are so good at hiding things I don't have a chance. How am I supposed to trust you again?"

"I don't know. I was willing to humiliate myself symbolically in front of the world, so I'd be surprised if anyone trusts me. You've got legions on your side now, so I shouldn't be in a position to get away with anything. I'm sure I couldn't cheat at cards at this point without some dog lover reporting back to you. Beyond that, all I can do is promise not to go behind your back and mean it. I'm open to

286

suggestions."

Nick nodded. "I'll think about it some more."

Cat wished he would smile again. He had the sincerest smile she'd ever known and she'd missed that most of all while she was away. But Nick was not up to smiling more just yet.

"So, Nick?"

"Yes?"

Cat hesitated. "Did you tell Liz?"

"No. I decided if you want to you can, but I don't want to. Though, don't be surprised if she already knows something. That's just Liz."

"But what have you told her about my being away? That's been tearing me up. I can't ever do that again. I won't. I'm not sure how we could have handled it differently but my not being with her... Whatever happens can we make a pact? To put her first?"

Nick looked somber. "Of course we put her first. I *was* putting her first. And I kept things vague. Because frankly they were, and still are, kind of vague. I said you were at grandma and grandpa Devin's and you needed to be there for some family stuff and to get some work done. She kept asking why you weren't doing work here. I just kept saying there was adult stuff that didn't concern her and you needed to be where you were until it got sorted out. I didn't lie, but I let her think it was stuff you had to help your parents with. I really didn't want her to worry about us. Remember how freaked out she got when my sister got divorced?"

"Yeah, she didn't understand why her uncle wasn't her uncle after that."

"Probably times a million with her own parents so I didn't want to scare her. I mean, if we did have to, I would think, maybe... but I'm not ready to think about that."

"I'm glad," said Cat.

"So, I know Liz was confused and I felt bad I didn't know how to fix it, and she seemed to blame me for your being gone. Which was so weird because, like, as much as she took advantage of maybe eating more like she wanted, on everything else it was like she was being you in your absence. I had to hear about how I was folding laundry wrong and wasn't buying the right soap—I mean it's soap. Who cares? But everything was supposed to be the way you do it and it was all my fault if anything was different, and I was really frustrated at first until I figured out it was her way of trying to get me to get you back here. She talks a big game of being annoyed by you, but she needs you."

"Do you think it does any good to tell her why right now?"

"Honestly, no. Would you want a detail like that about your mom?"

That was an unsettling thought. "No, I don't think so," said Cat. "What about the book?"

"She kind of tunes out most stuff with your work, doesn't she? She knows there is a controversy but I think she thinks it's about the money and how you screwed over your publisher. I think anyone who wants to speculate to her about what her parents are like based on a book you wrote she's going to ignore. You write a lot of disturbing stuff, and she knows she wasn't a baby switched at birth or that either of us were locked in a closet for a year when we were kids and any number of messed up things, so no. I think she'd ignore what anyone wanted to say they thought they knew about us based on a book."

"You don't think this will be different?" asked Cat.

Nick shrugged. "There's no way to know. How about we cross that bridge when we come to it? If she asks we'll deal with it somehow. Right now I'm hoping she won't."

Cat nodded. She'd given a lot of thought to whether or when to tell Liz. Her daughter was probably smarter than she and Nick put together and she was only 15. Maybe if Cat waited long enough Liz could explain it all to her instead. But telling her now, although it would explain Cat's confusing absence for the past two months, didn't provide anything positive for Liz that she could see. Cat still needed to have some credibility in her daughter's eyes over the next few years. Unless Liz figured it out on her own and came to her, she didn't need to be burdened with her parents' problems. When her daughter was older and in a position where any of the lessons Cat had learned might apply, maybe she could share them with a purpose. But even then, most people only took their own mistakes to heart.

Other people's experiences were only stories.

They ate a late breakfast of waffles with syrup that Cat found in the fridge, instead of the yogurt and fruit she usually served with such things. She didn't complain. They ate in silence and then Cat cleaned up and made a shopping list. There were lots of frozen dinners taking up room in the freezer she didn't know what to do with, and old takeout boxes that had been in the fridge too long. She started straightening up the house, which was looking a bit like someone had grabbed it by the foundation and given it a small shake.

Nick kind of hovered in whatever room she was cleaning. While Cat went on a scavenger hunt for dishes she asked him how his work had been going.

"It's been really strange since the book, Cat. Though the new clients are balancing out the ones who left, I guess. Some people feel like they need to punish you by avoiding us, and others feel like they need to rally behind me by bringing us their business. I can't believe people are going to let their feelings about a book get in the way of health decisions for their pets. It's just weird. The first day, when nobody could believe the new book was free, there were a lot of news people calling about that part. But after people read it? Damn, Cat. I'm sure it will blow over, but I don't think you should come around the clinic for a while." And then, with a sheepish look he added, "And the flirting situation has gotten worse. I guess because a lot of people figure 'Jack' will be on the market soon." He shook his head a little. "As if there's a 'Jack'," he said.

"Maybe I can kill them off in the next book," said Cat as she fished a cup with six spoons in it for some reason from under an endtable.

"Who, the flirts? That seems excessive," said Nick, although he didn't look like he disapproved.

"I can kill them off, too, but no, Jack and Susan. I think they should be done."

Nick appeared thoughtful. "Will there even be a next book?"

"Probably not one that makes money, but I can put whatever I want out into the world for free if I feel like, thanks to that weird thing you got put into my contract."

"That was your mom."

"I know."

"And that was only possible because you were your publisher's cash cow and they bent the rules to keep you happy. They are decidedly *not* happy. They kept calling and pressuring me to give them your cell phone number, but I wouldn't. So maybe you got spared some of that wrath."

"I did, thank you."

Nick helped Cat carry the plethora of dishes back to the kitchen, and as they loaded the dishwasher together Cat said, "Maybe Jack and Susan can go off and live in Maui."

"And pick mangoes?"

"Do they grow mangoes in Maui?"

"It's your book. You can have them pick Mangoes on the moon if you want."

291

They continued to do a careful imitation of normal life for about a week before Cat wanted to contact Tom Olsen and see about the play project which had been on hold all this time. She talked to Nick about it one night after dinner when Liz was safely ensconced upstairs.

"I was thinking I could invite Tom out here," Cat offered.

Nick was wary of anything associated with the Avenue. "But, I just don't see why you have to have any contact with anybody from there."

"Because it's a project I'm interested in, and it doesn't in any way have to mean I'll cross paths with...with anyone you don't want me to."

Nick agreed to have Tom come work at the house, and the ensuing collaboration was a good experience for Cat. It wasn't easy writing with someone else, but it wasn't as difficult as she would have thought, either. They each deferred to the other's areas of expertise, and it was nice to have someone else appreciate her efforts all along the process rather than only at the end. Tom was the strangest combination of smart and oblivious Cat had ever met. He congratulated her on taking the latest *County Vet* book to a level of such pure fiction.

Before going over the final draft of the script with Tom while getting ready to send it off to the publisher, Cat needed to see the stage to visualize certain elements better. Nick wanted to go with her to the Avenue for the meeting, but Cat promised she

292

wouldn't be there long. It was a step toward restoring trust that he agreed to her going alone.

She and Tom walked on the empty stage so she could get a better sense of how the timing would work between certain lines when combined with actual motion in a physical space. At one point they sat together backstage on a daybed while making changes to their work. There was something familiar about the way it held her weight, but she didn't register that in her conscious mind enough to dwell on it.

When they were finished, he asked her back to his office for a moment.

She stepped gingerly inside the messy space as Tom started busily looking all through his desk.

"I know I just had it somewhere," he said cheerfully. "Give me one more minute, I promise you it will be worth it, Catherine!"

But she didn't hear him speak or notice the sounds of the drawers opening and closing. All she noticed was the framed poster leaning on his wall.

"Um...." she started.

"Oh! Finally. Right where I left it, of course. I just wanted to find some way to thank you for giving me such a rare and wonderful opportunity to work with someone of your talent. I've really enjoyed our little exercise in teamwork, and I hope you'll consider doing it again sometime. Between novels, of course—wouldn't want to disrupt your real life, now would I?"

Cat was still staring at the poster.

"Catherine?"

She looked up and noticed him handing something to her from across the hodgepodge of a desk.

"What?" she said. He smiled and she reached out and took a beautiful silver pen from his hands. He'd had it engraved with the words *Catherine Devin, Playwright*.

"Oh, Tom, that's wonderful! What a kind thing to do. All I have for you is a box of raisins in my purse if you're interested."

He laughed. "No, no! Keep your raisins. I'm just looking forward to doing a world premiere here next season. I'll make sure you know when rehearsals start so you can be here."

"Um, Tom?"

"Yes?"

"May I ask, is that poster over there from Brian's apartment?"

"You may ask, and it is indeed. Alhough, I believe it's only his apartment for another few hours and then we'll have to find a new name for it."

Cat tried not to stare at him and mustered everything she'd learned about acting in the past several months to appear nonchalant.

"Huh. Well, is he moving into bigger quarters on the fabulous salary I'm sure you pay him?" she asked.

"Oh my, no, I'm sure he'll end up in a shoe box. New York is not known for its capacious abodes."

"New York?" She hoped she didn't sound

294

alarmed.

"Yes, I'm surprised you didn't know. The two of you always had the liveliest conversations. I quite envied your rapport. I just assumed he'd have told you he was leaving town. He came and cleared out his things a few days ago and he left some furniture for the props department and I paid him for the poster and rug. I don't really need them, but he's going to need all the change he can scrape together for his first few months in that city and I wanted to help in some way."

Cat didn't know exactly what she was feeling, but whatever it was, it was rapidly overwhelming her.

"Well, that's interesting. I hope he does well there."

"Brian's a splendid actor. He'll either take the town by storm or get eaten alive, but I suspect the former rather than the latter. He certainly has a way about him, so I think he'll get noticed," said Tom.

"I'm sure he will." Cat looked at the poster again. It had been on Brian's wall over his dresser. She had admired it from his bed many times. It was the only decent reproduction she'd ever seen of Gustav Klimt's famous painting *The Kiss*. She'd actually seen that painting as a child in a show traveling from Vienna, and in real life one of the most startling elements of it was the electric quality of the violets at the lovers' feet. Most reproductions were so poor that you didn't notice the flowers at all, but this one was closer to what she remembered.

Close, but still not real.

"Are you planning to steal *The Kiss*?" asked Tom playfully.

"What? Oh, no." She forced a small laugh at the small joke. "It's just...it's a lovely painting. I saw the original once, a long time ago."

"Ah, well there is nothing like the real thing, is there?"

"No, no there isn't. So...." she said looking at Tom as blandly as she could to appear less interested in the words she was about to say than she really was. "So, Brian Smith is leaving today. I wonder what time? That can be a full flight depending on the time of day. Lots of people always seem to be heading to New York."

"I think he told me his flight was at four. That shouldn't be too bad, I wouldn't think."

"You're probably right. Well, I should really get moving, Tom! I'm sure my husband will start to miss me if I'm away much longer."

"I can't imagine he isn't pining away! Let me walk you out."

*

Cat drove home trying to sort out everything that was rushing around her head. Why should it matter that Brian was leaving? It shouldn't. She had no plans to meet with him again, ever. Or was that true? Cat realized part of her was bothered that the last thing between them had been the ugly exchange in her bedroom. That didn't sit well with her.

She was a bit ashamed of herself that this was

296

what she was focusing on. She deserved to be left feeling unhappy and disturbed by all of it. What difference did it make if the end was disturbing, too? But it did make a difference. Cat felt there were things left unsaid and it gnawed at her. She wanted a chance to have one last conversation. One that made sense of things. She wanted to say goodbye.

Liz was still out with her friends when Cat came back from the theater. She went to her office. Cat was restless and she felt time and opportunity slipping away from her. She fretted and considered her options and then she finally went to talk to her husband. He was at his desk.

"Nick?"

"Hm?" He glanced up from the paperwork he was sorting through from the clinic.

She lingered there in the doorway. Could she really ask this? How much was one decent guy supposed to get hurt in a lifetime? She knew she was pushing the limit, but—

"What is it, Cat?"

"I...I found out today that, um...." She swallowed. "That he's moving out of town."

Nick simply looked at her. His face was devoid of expression. He waited.

"Um...." Cat didn't know if she could say it.

Nick was looking understandably irritated by then, but he still didn't say anything.

Cat straightened herself up a little and said, "I would like to say goodbye and clear up a couple of things. His plane leaves in about two hours, and if I leave now I can just catch him. It would really help me to get a couple of things off my chest, and if I'm lucky a couple of answers."

Nick stared at her, mouth slightly agape. "Are you seriously asking me if you can go see him again?"

"But it's not like that! It's just like tying up loose ends. Nothing could happen! We'd be in public and it's not like.... It's just *over*, so nothing...."

"Are you in*sane*?"

"But, I'm coming to you about it! I'm not doing something behind your back or, or...."

"So that makes it okay? So if you tell me you're going to rip my heart out before you do it, I'm supposed to applaud you or something?"

"But...."

"If I announce I'm going to beat you before I do, you'd find that acceptable?"

Cat bit her lip. He was right, of course, but she.... She didn't even know exactly what she was looking for, but it felt wrong for Brian to leave with no resolution between them. No final words. That wasn't the way the story was supposed to go.

Nick rubbed his eyes with the heels of his palms a moment and then put his face in his hands. Cat waited. He spread his hands on the desk in front of him and looked at her for a long time.

"I'm willing to try to make this work again, Cat. I still love you, and I thought you loved me."

"I do love you."

"Then you can't go. If you love me, you can't go. I don't even know how you can ask and that worries me. I have gone about as far as I am willing to go for you, but this is it."

Cat nodded and kept her gaze on her feet.

Nick waited for a moment until she looked up again. "I swear to God, Cat, if you leave this house any time within the next hour I will change the locks and you will never step foot in here again."

She looked into her husband's eyes and wished so much she could erase all the hurt she saw there. She wanted to hug him, but didn't sense he would be receptive to that at all, so instead she said, "I'm sorry. I don't know what I was thinking. I really wasn't trying to hurt you, I was just...."

"...thinking of yourself," he finished. "You'll excuse me if I'm not impressed by the direction that seems to take you."

"You're right. I'm sorry. I'm really sorry, Nick."

Cat left the room and closed the door quietly behind her. She stood there a moment with her hand still on the knob when she heard noises from behind the door that sounded like things being knocked off the desk and something hitting the wall. Something heavy like a book. She flinched and felt even worse if that were possible, and then she went to her office and grabbed her laptop. She carried it with her to her bedroom and crawled under the covers. Cat propped the trusty computer against her lap and stared at it a moment. She was a writer with a problem, so she was going to address it with a writer's solution. She opened the computer and began to type.

Cat started with the conversation she had just had.

"Nick," she had herself say on the page. "Nick, I need to go talk to Brian before he leaves town." She decided she was wearing the purple shirt with the v-neck that made her neck look longer, but on the page she made it blue. Blue was associated with the Virgin Mary and with change and baptism and purity. Her true intentions would seem clearer in blue.

She had Nick look at her and consider the request, and although he still looked hurt, she had him say, "Okay, Cat. I know you need to tie up loose ends in your work, so I'm sure it applies to your life, too. I'm not happy about it, but I trust you and I love you, and I know you would never hurt me again."

She had herself smile appreciatively enough that he would know his trust was not misplaced. She put her arms around him and he held her for a moment the way he used to. She kissed him in a way that reassured him that his insecurities were unfounded. That it didn't matter what she had experienced with anyone else because what they had between them involved so much time and love that no one could ever match that.

She had herself say with great meaning, "Thank

you."

And as she turned to leave she had Nick say, "I love you, Cat and I always will."

She had herself return his love, then hop in her car and head to the air— no. Since none of it was real, the train station was a better location. Airports were not romantic. *Casablanca* came about as close as you could come to a perfect airplane departure farewell, but she couldn't think of another one. Besides, it would be too hard for her not to include details like the endless 'don't leave your baggage unattended' announcements, so scrap that. She arrived at the train station, and fate was smiling on her because she found parking right out front.

She rushed into the terminal in a graceful way, and she searched around for Brian. Cat included a brief moment of suspense where he couldn't be seen, but then she spotted him. He was sitting out by the tracks on a bench (his baggage already checked so there was no visual clutter around), legs stretched out in front of him and he was leaning back and reading a novel. Something by Conrad, or maybe Salinger. He was in jeans and a t-shirt and a crisper looking version of his jacket, but she made it brown instead of blue. She didn't want the two of them to match—that was too cute—and brown was earthy and stable and grounded and she wanted him to be okay.

She stood and looked at him a moment and remembered everything they'd had between them. As wrong as it was and as much as it shouldn't have been, there was still something. The thing only he knew. She was about to say goodbye to the only other person to whom she could acknowledge that truth. The truth that she would undo it if she could, but part of her was glad it had happened. This truth probably proved for certain that she was bad, but at least she could know that part of herself and take proper precautions in the future.

Eventually she had Brian look up. He was surprised and not surprised to see her there. "Cat?" he asked, as if it might be too good to be true. She had him hope briefly that she was there to go with him, but then had him realize he knew better. It was not to be.

She had him slide down the bench to make room for her and motion that she should come sit with him one last time. She did. Her hair looked good and she didn't smell like chlorine.

"Brian, I'm sorry."

He gazed at her tenderly and squeezed her hand. He was more handsome than ever, but not in a way that pulled her toward him now. Just in a way that she knew would make him successful on Broadway soon. "No, I'm sorry. I should never have tried to seduce you, Cat. We could have had something that lasted a lifetime if I hadn't wanted to know every part of you. We could have been friends."

"I don't know if we were ever meant to be just friends. Am I bad for still seeing something that felt right in the midst of something so obviously wrong?"

"You're not bad, Cat. You may be the first person I ever truly loved, and I can't see that person as bad."

"Then what am I, Brian?" she wanted to know.

He touched her cheek lightly and closed his beautiful blue eyes briefly as he enjoyed the feel of her skin again. Then he said softly, "You're human, Cat."

And she felt absolved. She was not Mother Theresa, but she was not Hitler either. Like most of the human race she was somewhere in the middle of that continuum, and she'd learned new things to help keep her pointed the right direction. She would do better.

The train made hissing sorts of train sounds and they realized it was time for Brian to go. Everyone else boarded first as the two of them stood facing each other and holding each other's hands. Wait, back up. Where was his book? Maybe his back pocket—that had a jaunty look, and it freed his hands. She was crying a little, but it didn't make her blotchy or cause her face to contort in unattractive ways. Brian looked down at her sweetly, and when it was time for him to board the train he kissed her forehead and said, "Goodbye, Cat," with a hint of regret.

And she said, "Goodbye," back without bursting into a crying fit or anything so unappealing. She stood looking beautiful and impossibly young for a woman of 40—oh hell, *39* still. And she waved as the train pulled away and continued to stand there long after it was out of sight.

She went home where her husband was waiting for her. She had Nick ask her, "Did you get what you needed?"

"I think I did."

"You're okay now to really commit to us?"

"I am, Nick. With all my heart. I love you and will spend the rest of my life making sure you know that to be true."

"Just be yourself, Cat. That's who I love. I know this whole episode is really over and we can put it behind us. We have the rest of our lives together and I think there are wonderful things to come."

"I think you're right. Thank you for understanding and loving me. I don't deserve you, but I will try. I love you and I will try."

Nick took her hand and led her to bed where she was fine with making love to Nick who was the same old Nick—but who maybe worked out a little and had remembered to shave and who didn't smell like whatever weird chemicals sometimes got under his skin while doing surgery. Nick was human, too. They would work together, because he might someday come across something that could cause him to stumble off the path, and she would be there to help and to forgive and to love him. She would always love him.

Cat read it three times straight through. From a writing standpoint it was a mess, but for what she needed it to do it was good enough. Way more schmaltzy than her normal writing and the dialogue not believable. She almost wished she had one of her original Zander fantasies to compare it to, because that was what it most reminded her of.

She did a spell check, and corrected her grammar and punctuation where necessary. She was irritated that she had made Brian say her name every time he spoke, but she would let it go. It worked, and it was dialogue that no one else would see. It was an ending she could reflect on that didn't leave her feeling left in the lurch.

She selected everything and paused with her fingers over the keyboard. She hit delete.

Cat was tired. The light was fading outside. She wondered briefly what she should make her family for dinner, but she needed to close her eyes for a moment first. Cat started to fall asleep in her clothes under the covers with her laptop in her arms. Her eyes were closed, so she didn't see her husband standing in the doorway, but she knew he was there.

"Nick?" she said, her eyes still closed.

She could hear him shifting his weight. Finally he said, "You stayed."

"I did," she answered softly.

Cat heard him make his way over to the bed where he hesitated, and then she felt the weight of him settle on top of the covers on his side of the bed.

The last bit of light was slipping from the room.

"You don't regret it, do you," said Nick evenly. It wasn't a question.

"You know I never wanted to hurt you," said

Cat.

"That's not the same thing."

Cat didn't reply.

"You don't regret it because you never really regret anything. You think you do, but you don't really. That's just who you are."

The room was completely dark now. Even though she wouldn't be able to see him if she opened her eyes and rolled over to face him, she knew Nick was lying on his back, his hands laced behind his head, his ankles crossed. After so many years of marriage it was as if their proprioception overlapped, and she knew how his limbs would come to rest in certain situations.

After a moment Cat said, "I bartered it."

"Bartered what?"

"The beautiful necklace you gave me. I didn't deserve it. We now have a lifetime's worth of dance lessons lined up at that place you wanted to go to. If you still want to."

"I'll think about it."

They lay in silence for a minute, listening to each other breathe.

Then Nick continued, "I know you think I don't get things but—"

"No, Nick, it's not that I—" started Cat.

"No, just let me finish. You want to know what I really got out of *The Play About the Baby*?"

Still hugging her computer Cat rolled herself onto her other side so she was facing Nick in the dark.

Nick went on, "Because I read it. You've had it on your desk for a long time, and I just made my way through it bit by bit, and without the distractions of the actors I found a lot there. I don't know if it's a proper analysis the way you would do, but what I got out of it is that it's all about contrasts. That without pain you don't know who you are. Without bad you don't appreciate good. Without hurt you won't recognize happiness."

Cat wondered if in the dark he knew there were tears running down her face.

"So, what I'm hoping, Cat? Is that maybe after all this there is a whole lot of happiness we're due someday, and we'll know it when we see it."

"I hope so, too," said Cat quietly, the weight of sleep starting to press on her fully. "And Nick?"

"Yes?"

"I like your analysis just fine."

As Cat drifted off, her grip on her laptop loosened. Nick pulled it gently from her arms. He reached over her to set it on her nightstand where it would be safe.

ACKNOWLEDGEMENTS

When writing is not what pays your bills it is a difficult thing to justify making time for. I write in the cracks and crevices of my days, between bow rehairs and violin cleanings. I need to practice, I need to feed my kids, and I need to do any number of never-ending chores before I ever feel like I'm entitled to take time to write. But the truth is, I also need to write, and I am grateful to the people in my life who have helped make that happen.

First, I need to thank my husband, who has never once implied that writing isn't the best use of my time, even when it takes time away from him on occasion. When I needed a mini-writing-retreat to finally buckle down and finish this novel, he made it happen by handling everything at home and with our business while I was away and unplugged. He's the best.

Next, I need to thank Fernanda Moore, who accompanied me on the aforementioned mini-writing-retreat where we shared soup and crackers and brownies while we wrote and read and wrote and talked and wrote and it was wonderful. Without her guidance and encouragement this book would not have gotten finished. I can't thank her enough for helping make my writing so much better.

My mom, Karen Klein, drew the beautiful cover,

even though she had no spare time in which to do it. My mom is amazing.

My brother, Barrett Klein, helped with all the formatting and technical things that gave the book its final appearance, and I can't thank him enough. (My brother, Arno, I'll just thank here for being my brother because he's good at it.)

I want to thank Alit Amit for coming all the way out to Milwaukee to see *The Play About the Baby* with me so many years ago, and for thinking this book inspired by our discussion of it was a good idea.

I wrote the first draft of this book over a decade ago, and I'm struggling to remember who my original test readers were, so I'm reluctant to name them in case I leave someone out. But I'm going to take a stab at it and thank Gabriella Hanna, Linda Binder, Tammy O'Connell, Nancy Weisser, Mary Eufinger, Julie Snyder, and my parents. (Did I forget you? I'm sorry and I love you!)

A huge thank you goes out to Julie Gardner. Her input with the final edit was invaluable. I've never had the pleasure of meeting Julie in real life, but I hope to someday. She is the grammar expert I trust now that I no longer have my dad to ask about my lie/lay/laid/lain confusion. I feel better about the world in general knowing someone as generous as Julie exists.

Thank you to Gretchen Leanna for assuaging my worries that the book was any good by reading it all in one night and then wanting to read it again.

I'm sorry my grandma didn't get to read this book. I'm sorry my dad didn't get to read the final version, although I do get to live with the uncomfortable memory of his proofreading the sex scene. (He was not fazed.)

I want to thank my children for not reading this book now.

Thank you to Joe Robson for wanting to wait to buy a copy of this book rather than read it for free as a draft. (Ironic, since he's one of the few people I'd want to just give one to.)

A quick shout out to the Pleasant Ridge Book Club who promised to put this novel on their list, and that makes me happy.

Thank you for reading. I can't wait to write more.

ABOUT THE AUTHOR

Korinthia Klein was born in Detroit, Michigan, studied music at The Ohio State University, went on to graduate from The New World School of Violin Making, and currently lives in Milwaukee, Wisconsin with her husband, Ian, and three children: Aden, Mona, and Quinn. She and her husband run a store called Korinthian Violins. More of her writing can be found at her blog, Korinthia's Quiet Corner (the-quiet-corner.blogspot.com). Her first novel, *Almost There*, is available on Amazon.com

Made in the USA
Middletown, DE
10 May 2019